PRAISE FOR MORE THAN CHEMICAL

"A charming tale…entertaining, light, and overall a heartening story. Adriana and Dallas offer plenty for readers to root for, but the supporting cast—particularly the hilarious Priya…and the more cautious, protective Emma—[are] equally engaging."—*Publisher Weekly's The BookLife Prize*

"A cute New Adult Romance. Entertaining…with just enough drama and emotion."—*Readers' Favorite, 4 Stars*

"Thoughtful, sexy, and genuinely moving—a perfect choice for readers who like their campus love stories with brains, heart, and a touch of risk."—*Reedsy Discovery*

"Ade and Dallas are instantly likable characters who are easy to root for, with a believable and engaging connection set against a crisp, icy Minnesota backdrop."—*BookSirens*

more than CHEMICAL

a novel

LEANNE FARELLA

TWINKLING STARS
PUBLISHING

MORE THAN CHEMICAL

Published by Twinkling Stars Publishing
Minneapolis, Minnesota

Print ISBN: 979-8-9994092-1-8
E-ISBN: 979-8-9994092-0-1
Library of Congress Control Number: 2025913986

To Mom and Grandma (1927-2022), I finally did it

ONE
GIRL MEETS BOY

I wondered if anyone in the dining hall would notice if I passed out, face down, on top of my breakfast, right in my half-eaten pancakes sitting in a pool of syrup. It could happen. It almost had. Even the smell of fried bacon wasn't keeping my head from bobbing.

"Ade." My dorm friend Emma squeezed my shoulder. "It's time to go."

I blinked, the insides of my lids like sandpaper scraping my corneas. "But I'm so tired."

"No problem." Her cheeks turned from a pale pink to a warm blush, camouflaging the spray of freckles across her uptilted nose. "We're about to take the polar plunge. It'll be the perfect way to wake you up."

Across the table, my roommate, Priya, slurped orange juice through a reusable straw. Her dark eyes sparkled against her amber-brown skin.

I hunched over. Insomnia. It wasn't funny. It was a curse. A terrible, horrible curse. And frigid water was never going to fix me. Usually, when a person got tired, they slept. Not me. I was constantly fatigued, twenty-four seven, but I couldn't fall asleep and stay that way. My control-alt-delete command had stopped working.

Emma swept away my tray.

I nabbed my energy drink just in time and finished it off. Caffeine and glucose. The only things that gave me a boost in the mornings.

"At least we won't have to go all the way underwater." Priya folded the silicone straw into a carrying case. "Only up to our chests."

"Wonderful." My body was already shivering, my teeth chattering.

Emma returned from disposing our trays, *#MinnesotaUPride* typed across the front of her shirt.

This was probably bad timing, but I think it was finally the moment I should let her know how I really felt about jumping in a frozen lake.

"Emma," I said.

"Yeah."

"I know that you and the dorm advisory board worked really hard at organizing this charity plunge, but the thing is…"

I paused. It was hard to form the words. Mostly because she was so enthusiastic about everything related to dorm life.

"Is what?" she asked.

"I don't think I can go through with it."

She frowned.

For a moment she did nothing. Didn't move. Didn't speak. But then she grabbed my black Adidas duffel bag off the floor. "You have to. There is no choice. You've raised the money. Now you have to follow through with your end of the deal and jump."

I glanced away. Guilt. It got me every time.

So I dragged myself up, pulled on my green winter jacket, and followed them through the lobby to the front doors. I should never have signed up. Never have taken a day off from my Saturday shifts at the Minnesota University Bookstore for this.

We tried to squeeze past a group of residents with bulky shoulder bags, but we got stuck.

"Four years of probation, postseason bans, and scholarship reductions," said one of the guys. "That asshole Coach Bianchini ensured the hockey program will never recover."

My ears turned hot. My breath shortened. We needed to keep moving, and quick, before I was forced to listen to strangers speak ill of my dad. Or worse, find myself trapped in a discussion with Emma and Priya about the scandal once again.

I thrust the girls toward the windows on the far wall.

Emma glared back at me. "Jeez, Ade. No need to push our way through."

She didn't understand. Neither did Priya. Because they didn't know the truth about me. They had no idea I was the daughter of the once well-loved former head coach of Minnesota University's prestigious NCAA Division I men's hockey program.

Last summer had been a terrible scramble for me. First, I'd tried to find an alternate school with an engineering program to attend other than the same one from which Dad had been terminated. Somewhere far away, in some corner of the country where no one had heard of him. But the cost of out-of-state tuition was too much. And then it turned out only a few of my classmates from my suburban high school would be going here, a university with a student population of thirty thousand. So, instead, I changed my name from Bianchini to Blankin. That way I could start anew, incognito, as a college freshman. No past to burden me. No scandalous father to ruin my chances for success.

Of course, my mom had been upset at the name change, but I'd told her that Blankin was the English form of our Italian last name. I was sure Ellis Island immigrants had done the same thing over a century ago.

We made it to a spot out of earshot of the gossip. I closed my eyes and waited for my heartbeat to slow. That was close. Too close.

Priya peered out the window, which was layered in January frost. "Wow, look at all the buses. Three of them, I think."

"We had to reserve that many because one-third of the dorm is going," Emma said. "About two hundred people signed up."

Unbelievable. We were ridiculous, all of us. I mean, we were kind, of course, for raising money for the Special Olympics, but foolish for participating in a challenge that could give us hypothermia.

We were ushered outside, and I winced as freezing air burned my face and the hairs inside my nose turned into icicles. I tugged my fake-fur-lined hood over my head and snapped it under my chin. There must be a way to get out of this without hurting Emma's feelings. I was not jumping into thirty-two-degree-Fahrenheit water. Only absurd people did that.

Our bus was nearly full, so we sat in the last open spots, next to a vent blowing hot air onto our legs. Emma and I were on a bench seat together with Priya in front of us. The buzz of conversation filled every inch of space around us.

Then silence spread like a shock wave all the way to the back. I looked up from under my hood. Everyone's attention was on a guy in a fleece beanie moving down the aisle.

The tips of my fingers tingled. Not from the cold, because they'd warmed up. But because I was so glad I wasn't him. If I'd walked onto the bus and everyone had stopped what they were doing and stared at me, I'd have died. Seriously died. I hated attention of any kind. The anonymity I'd established on campus this year needed to be kept that way.

He passed us.

"I didn't know *he* signed up to take the plunge," Emma whispered.

Priya leaned over the seat back. "Who is *he*?"

"He's the guy in our dorm rumored to have slept with thirty girls since the beginning of the school year," Emma said.

I perked up. I wasn't sure if the energy drink had finally

kicked in or if Emma's words had done it. My grogginess lifted as if it were smog, and I could finally breathe again.

"Did you say thirty?" I asked.

Emma nodded. "Gross, isn't it?"

If the rumor was true and this guy had slept with that many women, that would be more than two girls—two *different* girls—per week. That seemed ridiculous, insane, untrue.

But even if a small part of the story were accurate, all that sex was making me think of the scientific study I'd shown Priya and Emma the other day. The one about how the release of hormones during sex, like oxytocin and prolactin, improves sleep.

For weeks now, I'd been trying to find a drug-free remedy. Eye masks, deep breathing exercises, chamomile tea, tryptophan supplements. Nothing had worked. But this "just have sex" theory sounded promising.

"Definitely gross," I agreed with Emma. "But I'm a still jealous. I bet he's the Yoda of falling asleep."

"Oh right. Your sex-cures-insomnia idea." Priya craned her neck to follow his progress down the narrow aisle. "Maybe he'd be a good candidate for you."

"Priya." Emma frowned. "Don't give her any ideas."

I kept my eyes straight ahead. The neurons in my brain pulled on my shoulders, begging me to watch him, but I gripped the seat back in front of me and resisted the urge. The last thing I wanted was to shower more attention on the dorm's Playboy of the Year.

The noise in the bus picked up again.

Priya fell back in her seat. "Well, he is hot. I'll give him that. What's his name?"

"Dallas," Emma said.

Priya lowered her chin. "As in Dallas, Texas?"

"That's right."

My stomach shook. I sputtered a laugh.

Priya's brows knitted together. "What's so funny?"

"His name is perfect." I sat back in the seat. "What comes to mind when you think of Texas?"

"Football," Emma said.

"Cowboys," Priya suggested.

"Good guesses." I nodded. "But I was thinking more along the lines of 'Everything's bigger in Texas,' if you know what I mean…"

We all giggled together.

"Um." Priya's voice hummed like the radiator in our dorm room. "Here he comes again."

He brushed by, heading for the door. Probably to find a different bus with open seats. This time, I checked him out as best I could. Weird that we'd lived in the same dorm for an entire semester and he didn't look familiar to me. Just for fun, I scrolled down my list of requirements for the kind of guy I'd even consider having sex.

Number one: appearance. Texas had a good shoulder width, a trim waistline, and a strong profile. But he'd moved so fast, it was hard to get a complete assessment. I might not have enough information to determine whether he actually fulfills the appearance section of my list.

Number two: attraction. I didn't feel any butterflies fluttering, so there was no instant pull, but again, I didn't have enough data.

However, I knew for certain he'd never pass the rest of my requirements.

Number three: personality. If Texas's reputation was any indicator, he'd be one of those self-absorbed guys. The kind I had no time for.

Number four: social skills. He'd been alone on the bus with no friends, which might mean he had no sense of humor either.

Number five: intelligence. This one was the most difficult to satisfy. This and number two—attraction—were rarely, if ever, packaged together. I should know. I had many male engineering classmates, and all of them were smart. But could I find one I was attracted to in the bunch?

No.

I raised my chin. Priya was wrong. Texas was not even close to being a good candidate for Operation: Get Laid.

———

Campus was located in the heart of Minneapolis–St. Paul, and it took the bus only fifteen minutes to drive to the plunge site in an urban neighborhood. Lake Nokomis was surrounded by pedestrian and bike paths that had been converted into cross-country ski trails for the winter. When we pulled to a stop, my stomach tangled like a ball of string. I still didn't want to do this, not at all.

Maybe with so many people, no one would know whether I plunged or not.

Emma found us a spot in a warming tent and peeled off her jacket. "When we get up there, the three of us should hold hands and go in together. It'll be awesome."

A pang shot through my chest. Forget about getting lost in the crowd. Emma wasn't going to let me out of her sight.

Soon we were on the wooden boardwalk leading out over the ice to the hole. A thermometer showed a balmy six degrees. There was nowhere to go, nowhere to hide. The only things between the ice-cold water and me were my fleece joggers, tennis shoes, and shirt.

My stomach churned. While others around us shouted and cheered, I focused on me. The thought of what we were about to do was making me sick.

"When this is over," I said, "I'm going to cocoon myself in bed for the rest of the weekend."

"Don't forget about tonight." Emma hooked her arm through mine.

"What's tonight?" I asked.

"Our floor is going to that house party," Priya said.

Great. The first party night of the semester. I'd stress about how much alcohol I should or shouldn't consume, and then, when we got back home, my anxiety would mushroom. When everyone else passed out, I'd still be wide awake.

Suddenly, we were there—on the platform. Below us, an EMT in a wet suit stood chest-high in black water. Behind us, people waited for their turn. I could still make a run for it, straight across the ice and into the tents.

Emma grabbed my hand and smiled.

She and Priya jumped, and I was forced to follow.

I hit the water and froze solid. My heart seized. My lungs squeezed so tight I couldn't even scream.

The soft lake bottom made me stumble. Water rose past my shoulders and numbed the lobes of my ears.

The EMT pushed me to the ladder. Another person hauled me out of the water, my clothes plastered to my body. I started shaking so hard it was like I was standing next to someone jackhammering a sidewalk.

My legs wouldn't move. They were made of one-hundred-pound ice cubes.

I looked up...and there was Texas, standing in line and looking straight at me. His chocolate-colored eyes made direct contact with mine and fused. I couldn't glance away. Couldn't stop staring. As much as I tried, my gaze remained frozen to his. As if a Fudgsicle held us together.

Priya was right. He was good-looking.

He flashed me a young Heath Ledger smile. The kind from *10 Things I Hate About You*, where the muscles tug up at the corners of his mouth and form half-moon creases.

Ugh. It was official. Texas passed my appearance requirements.

TWO
THE KISS

closed the bathroom door behind me, and the loud volume from the house party's speakers muted. But that didn't stop the bass from rattling the empty beer can on the sink.

On the knee of my favorite party jeans, I noticed a splash of bright pink. Vodka mixed with fruit-punch-flavored Crystal Light. Not my favorite. I hated the aftertaste, and artificial sweetener tasted sweeter to me than one of my energy drinks.

Playing a drinking game with the girls from my floor had been fun, but I'd topped it off with my second—maybe third—Coors Light. Mixing hard alcohol with beer was never a good idea.

Standing, I peeked into the toilet. Just as I thought. Clear.

Like Cinderella hearing the clock toll midnight, clear pee meant only one thing. It was time to leave. I'd drunk enough to be able to fall asleep without problem when we got home, but not so much that I'd get a bad hangover.

I finished and stumbled out the bathroom door, bumping into the girl at the front of the line. "Sorry," I muttered.

She gave me a blank stare. Must have had some cannabis gummies.

I walked into the main area, where multicolored lights flashed in the dark, and the music thumped. I scanned the room, but my vision was failing. Or maybe the circling white lights from the disco ball were making me dizzy.

Now to find Priya and Emma. They wouldn't have left without me.

I studied the room again, and my wobbly gaze landed on Texas. He wore a baseball cap pulled down low. He was standing on the dance floor with another guy, and together they were chatting up a girl with long, wavy hair.

From the tip of my nose to the ends of my toes, my body quaked. Right there, in the flesh, I was witnessing Texas on the prowl.

How did he do it? What was his trick?

Fueled by a little alcohol and my continued euphoria from the plunge, I needed to know the answers to those questions. I needed to know them *right now*.

I marched across the floor, tripping on a few treacherous spots and smacking into a couple of partygoers before I pulled up alongside him. I didn't give the girl a second look. She was unimportant. I wanted to know how he practiced his lecherous ways.

"Excuse me." I tapped him on the shoulder.

He turned. Save for the continuous blobs of light whizzing past, his visor shadowed his face. But I could tell he had an angular jaw and a strong nose that didn't overwhelm his chin.

"Hey." His bottom lip was full, but not too full. "I know you."

"No, you don't."

He took a sip of his beer. "You live in my dorm. You were at the polar plunge today."

"Right, but that doesn't mean you know me." Because he didn't. No one really did.

"True." He took another sip, wetting his mouth even more than before. "What I meant to say is that I've noticed you, and I'd like to learn more about you."

A lump lodged in my throat. I hadn't expected him to say... well...something honest.

I'd crossed the room determined to ask him questions, but

now those questions were superficial, ridiculous. He'd risen to a level of flirting outside of my abilities. Outside of my comfort zone.

So, without another word and before I could embarrass myself, I turned and walked away.

He grabbed my elbow and pulled me back. "Don't leave." His hand slid down my forearm and cupped my fingers. "My name is Dallas. What's yours?"

His touch was silky smooth and sent a shiver down my spine.

I couldn't move. I didn't want to. His eyes held mine.

He rubbed the flesh between my thumb and my index finger. Jesus Holy Mary. The guy didn't have to talk. His touch alone could hypnotize a girl straight into bed.

"Your name?" he asked again.

When I was a child, there were times I'd been too shy to answer an adult's question. But right now, right here, it wasn't shyness that was my problem. I was dumbfounded. I wasn't sure I had a name.

Then it registered. I didn't even have to ask him how he did it. All he had to do was ask a girl her name, caress her hand, and, *poof*, he'd performed his magic. It didn't hurt if his conquest had a little alcohol in her either.

His brows drew together.

"Dallas isn't a person's name." I'd finally found my voice. "It's a city."

He smiled with one corner of his delightful mouth. "Lots of people are named after cities. Boston, Paris—"

I tried to pull away, but he hooked a finger with one of mine, sending a bolt of energy straight up my arm. What was wrong with me?

"Please, stay," he said. "Just give me one minute."

I was no easy target. I had brains, and brains could outsmart a flood of attraction.

Oh no. He'd just satisfied number two on my list. I hated to admit it, but I was attracted to him. Most definitely.

Well, he might have satisfied the first two points. But he'd never meet the others. Never. And number five—savant-like intelligence—impossible.

Was he still holding my hand?

I yanked it out of his grasp and back to my side where it belonged.

He studied me.

"You know," he said, "I've been wanting to talk to you all year."

"What?" I glanced around for the girl he'd been talking to, but she was nowhere to be found.

"To talk to you."

The music seemed to be getting louder. His mouth kept moving, but I didn't catch what he said next. "I can't hear you."

He leaned in, but still the ringing in my ears blocked out sound. I shook my head.

Enough. I needed to find my friends.

He turned his hat backward and came closer. So close that his breath brushed my earlobe. His chin grazed my cheek. He smelled good. Not like when a guy splashes on the latest Calvin Klein cologne. His scent was of freshly cut cucumbers. So subtle that it was probably from the shaving cream he'd used earlier that day.

"You remember, before winter break, when the fire alarm went off in the middle of the night?" he asked into my ear.

I nodded. Who could forget? It had been freezing. The entire dorm had been stuck outside for what had seemed like eternity.

"That's the first time I saw you. You had the periodic table wrapped around you."

I sucked in a breath.

He'd noticed my quilt. The one I'd found on Etsy.

"You are beautiful." He exhaled against my face.

My heart fluttered. My legs went weak. Seriously. He couldn't be real.

His forehead touched mine. "Dance with me."

My mind screamed to break free. He was nothing but bad news.

But I couldn't help myself. My arms slid around his neck. My breasts pressed against his solid chest. They felt *right* there. Like they belonged.

We moved together. Barely, but it felt much better being in his stable arms than having to keep myself upright among the spinning lights.

The next thing I knew, we were kissing. It was the wettest, hottest kiss I'd ever had. And when I said wet, I meant not just from saliva. My panties had turned slick. I wanted him to use those masterful fingers of his and explore parts of me.

"Ade." I heard a voice. Distant. As if far off in an echoing cave. "Adriana." Someone pulled on my belt loop, and it wasn't Texas. "We have to go."

The kissing stopped. His eyes sparkled. The blue hat was still turned around.

I looked around. We were in the center of the room, and the lights were on.

That gossipy girl who worked at the front desk in our dorm pointed at me and whispered to another girl.

Emma was next to me, pleading. Lines creased her forehead. "We have to go now."

I looked back at Texas. Oh God. What was I doing?

He flashed me a grin. "Nice to meet you, Adriana."

Emma dragged me to the front door and out onto the stoop.

Priya stood at the base of the stairs looking tipsy. To her side, a guy was puking into a snowdrift.

Emma marched us to the street and down the shoveled sidewalk to the stop sign. "Do you have any idea who you were just making out with, Ade?"

I bit my lip, but I could hardly feel it. I wasn't that drunk, was I? Priya might be, but not me.

"You kissssed someone?" Priya spent much too long pronouncing the esses.

"Am I the only one who's sober here?" Emma's tone had grown harsh. She pulled us along.

"Thank you," I said to Emma as I concentrated on placing one foot in front of the other. "I owe you big-time."

"Who did you kissss, Ade?" Priya asked again.

My face turned hot. I didn't want to say his name. It was too humiliating.

"Ade?" Priya stopped and swayed.

"Oh, for God's sake." Emma glanced at Priya. "It was that guy we were talking about this morning. Dallas."

I put a hand to my head. I couldn't believe it. It wasn't like I hadn't known who he was.

Then Priya started to giggle. Loud and uncontrolled. "Texas." She belly laughed. "You kissed Texas."

We made it to the dorm. Thankfully, the lobby was empty.

Emma brought us to our room, and I foraged for snacks and fluids.

Priya lay down on her bed and moaned.

Emma sat in our saucer chair. "Are you going to tell us what happened?"

I crawled into my bed, closed my eyes, and rested my head on my pillow. Even though I thought I'd had the perfect amount of alcohol to doze off, I was never going to be able to fall asleep now. Never. All I could think about was that kiss. His touch. This was terrible. Because with the amount of alcohol in my body, it wouldn't be safe to take an Ambien to shut off my brain either.

Outside the door, squealing and shouting echoed in the hall. Other girls from our floor must be back.

I glanced at my periodic table blanket, folded at the foot of my bed. He'd known what it was. He'd remembered it. I reached for it and pulled it over me. It was our shared secret.

"Well?" Emma asked.

I cringed. "He might be what you say he is, but I'm not going to lie. He's a great kisser."

Emma sat back and folded her arms. "I knew it. The bad ones are always so good at it."

"Ade and Texas sitting in a tree," Priya bellowed in a singsong voice.

"Please," I said, "not now."

"K-I-S-S-S-S-I-N-G," she continued.

"Stop it."

More laughing outside in the hall. Rustling. Footfalls scampering away.

Emma retrieved a piece of paper from the floor.

"Where did that come from?" I asked.

"Under the door." Emma twirled a finger through her dark-blonde hair. "Oh, this is funny."

"What?" Priya asked.

Emma's shoulders shook. Her face crinkled, and she laughed. So hard that she could hardly breathe. She passed the sheet to Priya.

Priya, even in her stupor, had no reaction. "I don't get it."

"Give that to me," I said.

She handed it over. Surrounded by colorful squiggle marks were words drawn in large bubble writing. It read *Debbie Does Dallas.*

What?

I tossed the paper, and it floated to the ground. I dropped my head back on the pillow. "Who's Debbie?"

This sent Emma rolling. She couldn't talk. She just kept laughing.

"Oh, Ade." Emma finally found her breath. "It's a classic 1970s porn film, and, I guess, you're Debbie."

My face turned hot. How embarrassing. Not only could I not sleep, but now I didn't want to leave this room. And next time I saw Texas, I was going to have to walk...no, *run*...the other way.

THREE
BOY HAS BRAINS

"Excuse me." I crawled over legs in the four-hundred-seat lecture auditorium. "Sorry." I plopped down in a red-cushioned chair next to Jay and pulled out the folding table.

"You're late." He raised an eyebrow. Being of Afro–Puerto Rican descent, his skin was golden brown, his hair black and cut short to coil against his scalp.

We'd known of each other since ninth grade, and last fall when I moved into the dorm, I discovered that not only did we live in the same building, but we were both in the College of Science and Engineering and had classes together. After I'd made him promise not to tell anyone who my family was, we'd become instant buddies.

"I know." With my hands shaky and my head like mush, I dug in my backpack, retrieved my notebook, and placed it on the tiny table. Maybe the three ibuprofen I'd popped to get rid of a pounding headache and the two Red Bulls I'd drunk to fight exhaustion had been excessive.

"Why weren't you at breakfast this morning?" Jay asked.

I shrugged and opened to the last page I'd made notes on. "Have I missed anything?"

He peered over my shoulder. "The professor's reviewing titration."

The skin on my arms prickled. That was the subject of our last lab, and it hadn't gone well. Not yet having finished my write-up, I needed to pay attention.

Like some students in this class, I was on the chemical engineering degree path. Since touring a test kitchen and full-scale plant facility when I was a kid, I'd only ever wanted to be one thing—a chemical engineer in the food industry. But lately I'd been having serious doubts about whether I'd make it. Especially after my fall semester grades.

Besides everything else, insomnia was killing my GPA.

"Didn't you get my texts?" He tapped a finger on his thigh, which stretched so far that his knobby knee bumped against the seat back in front of him.

"I've had my phone on silent."

"So how was Saturday?" Jay had gone home over the weekend for his mom's birthday. He'd been lucky enough to miss not only the party, but also the plunge.

"Shh," I said. "Not now. I need to listen."

He stayed quiet for exactly three minutes, until the professor turned to write on the whiteboard. Then Jay whispered, "Emma said I should ask you for details. Something about a boy."

I jabbed him with my elbow. "Seriously. I mean it. Stop talking."

"Come on," he said. "Tell me what happened."

I sighed. He wasn't going to give up. I knew him too well. "I kissed a guy. That's it. No big deal."

"What guy?"

"A guy from our dorm."

"I didn't see you at dinner last night or at breakfast this morning. You're avoiding the dining hall, aren't you?"

For the past thirty-six hours, I'd kept away from the lobby and gone to the dining hall just as it was about to close. I didn't want to see Texas or anyone else who would remind me of what had happened.

To think I'd fallen for his act in front of everyone. How embarrassing. But another part of the problem was sleep. I hadn't gotten more than a couple of hours the entire weekend. Since I'd taken Saturday off work for the plunge, I picked up a substitute shift at the bookstore on Sunday, and it had almost broken me. Hence the headache.

I stared him down. "Are you done interrogating me now?"

A glint of evil passed through his eyes. "What's his name?"

"Omigod," I muttered under my breath. I could just not answer, but Emma and Priya would eventually tell him anyway. "His name is Dallas. It was a mistake. I'm not talking about it anymore."

I focused back on the instructor.

"Well." Jay cleared his throat. "You won't be able to avoid him for long."

"Try me."

"For starters, he's sitting ten rows in front of us."

My heart jumped into my throat. "What?"

"Right there." He pointed.

I sat up and looked over the dozens of heads before me. There, sitting below us, was a blue baseball cap. Nice shoulders.

Oh eff.

Jay's smile glowed as bright as a cell phone screen. I sat back in my chair and slouched. It couldn't be. How could Texas be in my chemistry class?

The memory of his mouth moving on mine sent goose bumps down my arms.

"How do you know him?" I mumbled.

Jay shrugged. "He was in my freshman orientation group. A standoffish dude."

Heaviness filled my stomach, and I flashed Jay a glance. "He's in engineering?"

He nodded. "Interested in mechanical, I think."

"Just because someone says they're going to major in a certain engineering discipline doesn't mean they'll have the GPA to get into the program they want."

"I'm pretty sure he will. I saw his name on the dean's list last semester."

I put my face in the palms of my hands. Not only had Texas satisfied my appearance and attraction requirements, but he had just satisfied number five on my list—the most impossible requirement to meet—intelligence.

———

The lecture was over, and I was hiding under my jacket. "Is he gone?"

"He's talking to the professor," Jay said.

Seriously? Only extreme nerds spoke with the teacher after class. Who was this guy? How could he be sexy, smarmy, and academic all at the same time?

"Where is he now?"

"Just a minute." Jay exhaled. "One more second. Okay. He's gone."

I peered out. "Did he look up here?"

"Ade, you're absurd." All six feet two of Jay's runner's body towered over me. "You don't want him to see you, but you want him to look for you. I don't get it."

I zipped up my coat and gathered my things. "Remember last week when I told you I read online that sex can cure insomnia?"

He frowned but nodded.

"Well, that guy, Dallas, he might be the one who could do it for me. Especially now that I know he satisfies some of my requirements for the right candidate."

"WTF, Ade." Jay walked out of the row and down the stairs.

I followed. He was wearing his university jacket with the cross-country logo on the back.

At the bottom, he waited. "Did he message you after the party?"

"No." I stopped a couple steps before the landing, so I was the same height as Jay. "He doesn't know my number."

"If he was really into you, he would have figured out a way to get it."

I remained still. Jay was right. I was losing it. Reliving the encounter moment by moment and trying to process how I felt about it was destroying me. Meanwhile, Texas had shrugged it off.

My heart cinched tight, as if a beanstalk had grown around and around it, cutting off the circulation.

"I'll see you in calc." I brushed past Jay. "I need to go to the bathroom."

"I'll wait for you," he called from behind me.

I went straight into the restroom, set my backpack on the sink, and stared at my reflection in the mirror. My brown hair was matted down from my hat. My hazel-green eyes were bloodshot.

Adriana Bianchini. Ugh. I mean Blankin. Adriana Blankin, you look terrible.

My mascara had smudged. Not from crying, even though I wanted to. Probably from my eyes watering during the freezing-cold trek to class. I waved my hand under the paper towel holder and tore off a piece. Using hot water, I tried my best to get the black off.

According to Jay, Texas—the guy rumored to do multiple girls every week—had decided I wasn't interesting after all. That hurt. That hurt like hell.

"He isn't worth it," I said to my reflection.

One of the stall doors creaked open, and a girl walked out. "I'm sorry," she said. "Did you say something?"

I shook my head and went to use a toilet. Scrawls of graffiti decorated the light-blue door.

Now I was talking to myself. *Enough.* I needed to focus on what was critical—my classes. I should be on the dean's list too.

And that was exactly what I would do. No matter what happened, no matter how little sleep I got, in May, I would make certain I was on that list.

I finished up and headed back into the hall. Jay was leaning against the radiator in the vestibule. He shouldn't have waited. I opened the door, stood by him, and bundled myself up.

He looked odd, a blank stare fixed on his face. His posture was all wrong.

"What's the matter?" I asked.

His eyes narrowed and focused on me. "Guess who I just spoke with?"

"Who?"

"Him." The side of his mouth scrunched.

A current of heat zapped through me. "You mean…"

He nodded.

"But you said he left."

"He left the lecture hall but apparently not the building."

My heart sped up like I'd just taken a five-hour energy shot. "What did he say?"

"I…" He shifted his weight around and gazed at the floor. "Well…"

"Please," I pleaded. "You have to tell me."

"He asked me if you were my girlfriend."

Blood rushed into my head. "Girlfriend?"

Jay nodded.

The skin on my neck tingled. Texas thought I was with Jay.

The idea almost sent me flat on my butt. It had never occurred to me. But I supposed it made sense. We were with each other quite a bit. We ate together. Sometimes it was just the two of us, but most of the time we were with Emma, Priya, and other girls from my floor or guys from his cross-country team.

Suddenly, I felt empowered. Maybe I was wrong. Maybe Texas was interested in me, and he hadn't talked to me yet because he needed to find out if I was taken.

"What did you say?" I asked.

He rubbed the back of his neck but said nothing.

"You didn't tell him about my sex cures insomnia theory, did you?" The muscles in my jaw quivered.

"Of course not." He ran a hand through his hair. "The whole idea of you having sex with someone for that purpose alone is… well…off-putting."

I flinched. There was nothing appealing or unappealing about casual sex. It just was.

"I told him he wasn't your type," Jay said.

My lungs deflated, the air replaced by a burning, scorching pain. I wrapped my scarf around my neck and tightened it. I pushed open the door, only to get hit by a fierce wind blowing against my side. I had criteria, yes, but not a specific type.

"Ade, wait." Jay grabbed my arm. "I said it because I was doing you a favor. You're too good for him."

I snorted. Too good? Ha!

I pulled away and stomped through the accumulating snow.

No, I wasn't. I'd known that for a long time. I wasn't too good for anyone. Including Texas. Which meant I had some figuring out to do about him, irrespective of Jay's assumptions and meddling.

FOUR
GIRLFRIENDS WEIGH IN

P asta night.

I took the top tray from the stack and asked for spaghetti with Alfredo sauce. I carried the tray to the salad bar and added greens and veggies to the plate. No dressing. There was already enough of my allotted fat intake in the white sauce. Not to mention the fact that it was congealing into globs.

There must be some kind of ingredient that would prevent that from happening. When I finished with dinner, I'd do a search on it.

Scanning the dining hall, I saw Priya and Emma sitting at our usual table, already half done with their meal. I sat next to them.

"You're here." Priya chewed and swallowed. "What are you going to do if you-know-who shows up?"

"At this point, it's inevitable." I placed my napkin on my lap.

Priya's eyebrows shot up. "It is?"

"I saw him today. He's in my chemistry lecture."

She gasped.

"That's unfortunate." Emma turned her fork face down on her plate and stared at me.

"Maybe." I stabbed a piece of romaine. "Maybe not. I now

know he's good-looking, attractive, *and* intelligent. There's a good chance he might be the one."

"The one?" Emma asked.

"The one to cure my insomnia."

Her eyes widened, and she grimaced. "You can't be serious."

The hairs on my arms stood up. "Why not?"

"Because he's a sleazeball."

"You do realize, Emma, that you're basing your opinion of him on a rumor."

"Well, have you talked to him since you mauled each other?" she asked.

"No." I shook my head.

"Ade, listen to yourself. A guy makes out with a girl, and two days later he's still made no contact." Emma's face was turning red. Her voice was getting louder. "I don't care how smart he is, I don't like him."

I stared down at my dinner and lost my appetite. My brain was telling me that she was probably right. But my body was telling me something different. This attraction was like a covalent bond. I'd shared my electrons with him, and now I couldn't figure out how or if I wanted them back.

"Where's Jay?" Priya took a sip of water.

My stomach dipped. All I'd wanted was to have a quiet dinner at a quiet hour and chat about anything but Texas. But even the subject of Jay led straight to him.

Her eyes narrowed. "Did something happen?"

"I'm sure he's fine." I twirled my fork through the noodles. I should have skipped dinner and gone straight to my room. I had plenty of mac-and-cheese containers to microwave. "We had a disagreement this morning. That's all."

"About what?" Priya asked.

"After chemistry, Jay waited for me outside of the bathroom. While I was inside, Texas came by and asked him if he was my boyfriend."

Priya's face lit up. "Well, there you go, Emma. Maybe Texas isn't so awful. He's merely taking his time, doing his research."

Emma's jaw stiffened. "I hope Jay said yes."

My heart froze. What was her problem?

"He said no." I glowered at her. "But he did tell him that he wasn't my type. That should make you happy."

Priya covered my hand with hers, and I looked at her. A sad smile spread between the corners of her mouth. "Don't let Emma get under your skin. She's having a rough day. She saw Thad on campus."

I glanced back at Emma. Thad was a guy who'd ghosted her last fall.

"What happened?" I asked her.

"Nothing." She frowned. "He ignored me."

My arms went slack. "I'm sorry, Emma."

She shrugged, maintaining her unhappy look. "It sucks, but it's not unexpected."

"So I guess that means that among the three of us," I said, "Priya appears to be our expert on boys." She had a serious boyfriend, Luke. They'd been together since the eleventh grade.

Priya sealed her lips shut then opened them again. "I'm not sure if I'm as great of an authority as you think. Luke and I—we... well, we might not last."

"C'mon, you and Luke are perfect together, and you know it."

Her mouth twisted. "My mom and dad make things with him very difficult."

Her parents were never going to like anyone she dated. Anyone who wasn't in medical school, law school, or getting a master's in engineering. Poor Luke wanted to become a social studies teacher.

I nodded. "The thing with Texas is that, even though he has this reputation, I can't stop thinking about him. I can't stop wondering what it would be like to kiss him again. I'm not sure what to do."

Priya leaned back and folded her hands together. "If I were

you, I'd give it time and not worry about it. The last thing you need is something else to lose sleep over."

Easy for her to say.

Emma leaned in close and lowered her voice to a harsh whisper. "I wasn't going to say anything, but I don't think I have a choice. You need to know this, Ade. After you made out with Dallas Friday night, he took a different girl home and fucked her."

I didn't move. I couldn't. It was like I was adhered to the seat. "Who told you that?"

"Sandra."

My pulse drummed in my ears. A wave seemed to crash over me and suck the breath right out of me. "Isn't Sandra that girl who works at the front desk?"

"Right."

"I saw her that night at the party gawking at us."

"He's an asshole." Emma pushed her chair back. "My advice is not to spend one more second thinking about him."

She grabbed her tray and walked away.

I sat there, dumbfounded. I wasn't sure if I should thank gossipy Sandra or hate her. Regardless, I needed to put Texas out of my mind and move on.

FIVE
BOY TO THE RESCUE

n January, the best place to do homework was next to the clothes dryers whirring away in the dorm basement. They provided an endless amount of white noise and constant heat.

Despite the perfect conditions, I was still struggling with my chemistry lab write-up. It was due by the end of the week, and I wasn't close to finishing it.

A Minnesota University hockey sticker stuck to the desktop I was at kept bothering me. I picked at it with my fingernail, but it wouldn't scrape off. A bottle of Goo Gone would really come in handy for this job.

I stopped, staring back at my lab results, and the numbers swam together. I opened my textbook. I needed to stay focused, needed to figure out how to do the analysis.

A thud echoed from the washers, and two voices sounded over the machines.

The door to the laundry room shut, and I peered around the corner to make sure I was alone again. But I wasn't. A head of brown hair bobbed over the appliances. I went back to my work.

I stared at the numbers again. Okay. I had this. All I needed to do was dive in and finish it up. *C'mon. Concentrate.*

"Hey," said a male voice.

I jumped in my seat and turned.

It was Texas, without his baseball cap.

"How are you?" he asked.

But my throat had swelled shut. Like when my dander allergy flared up in a house filled with cats.

I swallowed hard and tried to breathe. "F-F-Fine."

He set his arm on a machine. "You want to get some coffee?"

My skin tingled. "Right now?"

He nodded.

My heart raced. *I think Texas is asking me out. On a date.*

I stared down at my lab book and then up again, straight into those chocolate-candy-colored eyes of his.

In a businesslike voice, I said, "I can't. I'm busy right now. Maybe some other time."

Some other time? I didn't even know what I was saying.

Because he was supposed to be an asshole who hadn't said one word to me since he'd stuck his tongue down my throat then banged a different girl. I couldn't stop Emma's disapproving words from playing on repeat in my brain.

The reality was I shouldn't go with him anywhere, ever. Dorm people would see us together and wonder who I was, what kind of girl Texas had chosen to chew up and spit out. Never again would I be able to handle being the subject of mass ridicule, heckling, and gossip. Last year and the stuff with my dad had been enough.

He peered over my shoulder. "Are you working on your chem lab?"

I nodded, but I needed him to go away. Or stay. Or...

He hooked his foot around the chair next to mine, pulled it over, and sat down.

My heart was pounding so loud, I wasn't sure I'd be able to hear him.

He grabbed my notebook and slouched back to look at it. "You're using the wrong equation, that's all."

"I am?"

He sat up, scooted forward, and paged through my textbook.

I smelled cucumbers again, this time with a hint of mint ice cream, and I imagined myself melting in my chair. One big puddle of sweet desire.

Flipping to a page, he pointed. "You need this one. Calculate the concentration of your analyte for each stage of the titration and chart the curve so you can see both of your equivalences. Then you'll have it."

I felt like a marble statue in an art museum. I couldn't move. I'd heard him. I'd understood him. I was grateful for his direction and the fact that I hadn't been too far off. I just couldn't figure out what to say.

Ding. My cell phone sounded on the desk.

I grabbed it.

PRIYA
Where are you?

Studying

I pressed send and set it back down.

He folded his arms and examined me. I wanted to crawl under the tabletop.

"Are you afraid of me?" he asked.

I shot him a laser look. "Of course not."

"It sure seems like it." He stood and pushed the chair back where he'd found it.

I wanted to grab his arm. Tell him to stay. To let me explain. Even though I'd never be able to put words to any sort of explanation that would make sense.

He picked up my phone. The screen still on and unlocked.

A flood of heat raced through me.

"Wait..." I reached out to stop him. "What are you doing?"

He stepped back out of my reach, and my fingertips grazed his arm.

"I'm putting my number in here." He started typing. "When you're ready, you can text me and we can get that coffee."

He set my phone back on the desk, and my heart dropped like it had decided to jump off a bridge and I hadn't been able to stop it.

"See ya." He walked away.

"Thank you for the chemistry…" And for some embarrassing reason, my words stopped. *Help. I meant to say chemistry help.* I hadn't finished the sentence, and now it was too late. Too awkward. My face heated to the temperature of a Bunsen burner.

He swung around and smiled, creases sinking into each side of his mouth. He lifted his hand and waved. "No problem."

And then he was gone. The pulse in my throat fluttered to a frenzy. I snatched up my phone and scrolled through my contacts to *D*. There it was. No last name. Just Dallas.

My thumb hovered over the entry, but I didn't tap on it, afraid I'd accidentally call him. I turned off my screen and put my hand over my heart. *What had just happened?*

SIX
ONE PERSPECTIVE

'd arrived early to chemistry lab, uploaded the write-up I'd finally finished, and was now sitting on a stool next to my workstation, staring at Dallas's name in my phone. It had been three days since he'd put it in there. I still hadn't touched it.

Emma had been disgusted, told me to delete it right away.

Priya remained neutral.

I still hadn't decided what to do.

True to Dallas's style, he hadn't pursued me. In fact, I'd barely seen him since the laundry room. So it was up to me. If I wanted to connect with him, I would have to do the connecting.

I turned off the screen and slid the phone into my backpack. I'd checked the dean's list. Jay was right. Dallas had been on it last semester. Finding his name had also solved a mystery.

His last name was Reynolds. Like the tin-foil. It was a bit disappointing. I was expecting something magical, not kitchen supplies.

As soon as I had his full name, I did what any girl would do—I looked him up on all my social media platforms. Strangely, I came up with nothing.

Everyone was on social media. Even I had accounts, under my new name, of course. I'd deactivated all my others.

I chewed on my bottom lip. Maybe we were more alike than I thought. We were both hiding from something.

Out of the corner of my eye, I saw a long, lean body enter through the doorway.

Jay.

I hopped off my stool and cornered him at his lab station. "Hi, stranger."

"Hi." He unzipped his backpack and got out his work, all while he avoided eye contact with me.

"I'm sorry." My stomach was in knots.

"For what?" He put his lab notebook on the table, still not looking at me.

"For being mad after class the other day."

"No big deal." He glanced at me. "I've already forgotten about it."

"You have?"

"Yeah." He looked away from me again to fish through the lab drawer.

"Then why haven't you answered my texts?"

"I've been busy getting in some long runs."

"So we're cool?"

"Sure."

For three days I'd missed talking to him. I'd wanted to tell him what had happened with Dallas. I needed his opinion. A guy's perspective.

"So Dallas asked me to get coffee with him."

Jay paused and finally stared at me without blinking. "You don't like coffee."

"I haven't completely ruled it out."

"I've never seen you have a cup in my life."

I shrugged. "You've seen me have a shot of espresso."

"Sure." His brows melded together. "And if I remember right, you said it tasted like dirt."

He was right. I hated coffee. That was why energy drinks were my go-to for caffeine. "Well, you can get other things at a coffee shop."

"Jesus Christ, Ade." He started rummaging through his backpack. "You don't see it, do you?"

"I told him no." My voice grew louder, and I tried to bite it back. "He asked me out, and I said no. Does that make you feel better?"

"Not really."

"Then I suppose you don't want to know that he also gave me his number and I'm trying to figure out what to do with it."

He buried his head in his hands and then dragged his fingers down his face. "Emma told me all about his reputation. He's not worth it."

My body tensed.

At that moment, the TA came into the room and whistled for our attention.

I started back to my workstation. At least we were back to talking, Jay and I. Better, but not perfect. Things were still off, because I didn't get it. I didn't understand why he thought Dallas wasn't worth the time.

"Ade," Jay called out.

I spun around.

"The guy's going to cause you stress, and you already have too much to manage as it is."

A burn traveled up my throat and into my nose. Nothing could be more horrible than being told you were an anxiety freak show and at risk of making things worse.

I swung back around.

Jay's observations couldn't be ignored. He was the only person at school who'd known me last year when the FBI arrested my dad on federal corruption charges and he was immediately terminated, thrusting our family into the spotlight.

Eric, my older brother, who'd played for my dad during all four of his college eligibility years, had no knowledge of or involvement in the scheme, but no matter—his future, like mine, had been wrecked. First, his name was scratched from a short list of Hobey Baker Award nominees, and then, though he'd been drafted years before, his NHL team refused to give him a contract.

As if that wasn't bad enough, this past fall, the NCAA came down with sanctions. The worst ones being scholarship reductions and banning the school's team from Frozen Four tournament appearances for four years even if the team had a good enough record to make it.

Back at my lab station, I went through my things, contemplating Jay's advice. I didn't need to be around a person who'd add to my anxiety. I'd listen to Jay and delete Dallas's number. I'd put it in the trash and not think about it again.

SEVEN
ANOTHER PERSPECTIVE

S aying I was going to do something didn't mean I'd done it. When I arrived at the dorm Friday night, I still had Dallas's number in my cell. I promised myself I'd get rid of it by the end of the night, but my heart needed time—alone time—to catch up and accept what my brain had decided.

In my room, Emma, Priya, and Luke—Priya's boyfriend—were finishing up soft-serve ice cream cones and wearing their Minnesota University hockey jerseys. It was game night. The hockey team—what was left of my dad's former team—was at home for a two game series, and the three of them had season tickets together.

Not me, of course.

"Ade, get your school colors on." Priya was jumping up and down. "We snagged you a ticket to the game!"

I swallowed hard. This was the main reason I couldn't tell them who I was. They were super fans. They'd never understand. And I was afraid they'd hate me forever.

"Wow," I said. "I wasn't expecting that."

"The team sucks this year," Priya said. "All because of the despicable Coach Bianchini. But the seats are sold out. So much support out there for them this year."

"I'm sorry," I said, ignoring the comment about my dad, "but I really can't go."

Silence dropped over the room. You didn't have to be the daughter of a hockey legend to know that, whether you were born here or were a transplant, this state lived and breathed hockey. Saying no to a chance to go to a game was unheard of.

"You *have* to go," Emma pleaded. "Afterward we're going to the Station, and I need you for encouragement."

The muscles in my neck corded. The Station was a sports bar and nightclub where the hockey team went after their games. Recently, Emma had become obsessed with one of them. Thankfully, it wasn't anyone I knew, but still. I couldn't chance it. Being near anyone who might know my dad was a very bad idea.

I cleared my throat. "I could use a quiet night to catch up on some studying, so I'll pass."

"It's Friday." Luke tipped his head. "No one studies on Fridays."

Well, I needed to. Especially if I wanted to make the dean's list.

"Luke." I squared my shoulders. "Haven't seen you in a couple of weeks. How are you?"

Every home-game hockey weekend, Luke made the four-hour drive from his college to ours. His presence meant I'd be vacating my room and staying with Emma for the next two nights. Priya had said I could sleep in my own bed while he was here. But really, I didn't need to listen to them humping on the other side of the room. No thanks.

"I'm good," he grumbled. "I was just saying…"

I shrugged as if it were no big deal that he'd called me out. But the thing was, I always worried that someone was on to me.

Priya sat up straight and rested her hand on Luke's arm. "Ade, I think you should go. You need to get out and do something."

"I'm not in the mood." I went to my closet and hung up my jacket.

"But tonight's a big game. They're playing Duluth."

I looked at Priya. "I'll be fine."

"We'll call you one of those campus security escorts to walk you back here so you don't have to go out with us afterward."

I frowned. She wasn't listening to me.

She leaned in and opened her eyes wide. "You'll still have time to get some studying in later tonight."

It was hard for me to resist Priya. She had a way of making me feel like if I didn't do what she asked, I would disappoint her. Disappoint my friends. Disappoint the world. I took a deep breath and sighed. I supposed I could wear my winter hat and jacket the whole time so I would be unrecognizable.

"And if you end up going to the Station with us, we won't mind." Emma's smile was as shiny as the jumbotron that hung from the ceiling of the arena.

"Fine, I'll go to the game," I said to Priya, but then glared at Emma. "But not to the Station."

So, we went—all of us.

Between periods, I realized that Priya had been right. I was having fun. At first, I'd scanned the stands looking for Dallas, but eventually I stopped when our team scored a big goal and the entire student section rose to their feet, pointed to the goalie on the opposing team, and chanted, "Sieve, sieve, sieve!"

I'd really missed this. I'd grown up going to these games.

But after the second period buzzer sounded and I'd finished singing my favorite school song, I remembered Dallas again. I came close to taking out my phone and staring at his number just to make sure I hadn't deleted it. Instead, I gathered my willpower and stayed my hand. I didn't want Priya or Emma to see me.

Luke and Emma left to use the bathroom, and Priya and I watched the Zamboni driver wave to the crowd before he exited the ice. I loved the Zamboni. It was satisfying to watch it going back and forth in rows, covering the ice in strips of water until there was nothing but a glossy finish.

"So have you figured out what to do with Texas's number yet?" Priya asked.

"Delete it," I mumbled.

"That's probably for the best, isn't it?"

"Yeah, probably."

"I mean, he sounds like the kind of guy who would play you, and—"

"Priya," I interrupted her, "I really don't want to talk about him."

"Sorry." A flush crept across her cheeks. "I promise I won't say another word."

I crossed my arms over my stomach, wishing I hadn't stopped her so abruptly. "I'm sorry. I didn't mean to sound rude about it."

"It's okay. I understand."

"So, how are things with Luke?" I asked.

"Fine. I guess. You know...I've forgotten what it was about him that attracted me to him in the first place."

"If I took a guess, I'd say it's his kindness and thoughtfulness."

"Sure, but I don't remember being so excited that I couldn't stop thinking about him. Like you are with Texas." She glanced at me. "Oops, I didn't mean to bring him up again."

"It's okay." I smiled. "No worries. It'll come to you. You've been dating Luke so long that you just can't remember right this moment."

"Maybe."

At the end of the third period, our team scored the winning goal during a power play. It was a thrilling victory. My throat felt scratchy from screaming the rouser. My cheeks hurt from smiling. Definitely worth coming for.

As we climbed the stairs out of the stands to get to the concourse, I noticed all the upbeat fans who'd stayed to the end. This meant crowds of people would be swarming the sidewalks to return to their parked cars.

I insisted I could walk safely home by myself.

My friends disagreed.

So here I stood, resting my hands on the iced-over metal ledge of an exterior window in the north entrance. As promised, Priya,

Luke, and Emma were still with me, waiting for a campus security guard to come and escort me home.

"Are you sure you don't want to come with us?" Emma asked again.

She'd been working on me. The more she talked, the more I couldn't wait to get back to the dorm. If I went with them, the risk of running into someone I might know related to my dad's hockey scene was too high.

A small guy in a dark-blue security uniform entered the vestibule. His eyeglasses fogged up instantly. He removed them, wiped them on his jacket, and squinted. "Adriana?"

I raised my hand. "Right here."

Priya gave me a hug. "See you later."

"Have fun." I flashed her a glad-I'm-not-you smile.

The three of them left in the opposite direction. I took a longer look at my knight in shining armor and had to suppress a laugh. Shiny and knightly didn't describe him. Businesslike and speedy were better.

As we walked to the dorm, I had to double-time my pace to keep up with him and the bike he was pushing. One of those fat-tired bikes, the kind I couldn't imagine having enough strength to pedal through the snow for more than a couple of blocks.

I should have been concentrating on keeping up, but I pulled out my phone, opened my contacts, and stared at Dallas's phone number.

It was still there. Relieved, I turned off the screen and looked up. My escort had stopped and was waiting for me.

"Sorry," I said.

"It's okay."

He started off again, but slower this time so we could walk side by side. I glanced at him and had a thought. He might be somewhat of an awkward type, but he was male. He might have perspective.

"Can I ask you a hypothetical question?" I asked.

"Sure."

"Let's say you put your number in a girl's phone. Why would you do that?"

"Is she my sister?" His tone had changed.

"No. Just a girl. Maybe she's in class with you. You might have met her at a party. Why would you put your number in her phone?"

"It seems pretty obvious to me. I'd want her to text me."

"So, you're probably into her?"

"Probably."

I rubbed my brow. "Do you think she should do it?"

"Do what?"

"Should she text you?"

He shrugged. "If she's interested in me, why not?"

And there were the words I'd been in search of for days. The campus security guard had confirmed exactly what I'd been thinking. There was no harm. Nothing could possibly be wrong with having coffee with Dallas.

He dropped me off at the front door of my building.

"Thanks for the advice," I said. "It's greatly appreciated."

"Sure." A dopey grin spread across his face. "No problem."

With renewed giddiness, I opened a new text message on my phone, inserted Dallas's number, and began to type while I walked the darkened hall past the closed dining room.

Hey, how about that coffee?

I pressed send before I could think about it. Before I hesitated and deleted the message. My heart soared higher than all four stories of the building.

At the bottom of the stairwell, I stopped and glanced at my phone. It said my message had been read. No going back now. So I waited for his answer.

But nothing happened. One minute went by. My phone went dark. I woke it up. Two minutes. It did it again. I shut my eyes and groaned. What had I done?

I took the stairs two at a time. My heart was no longer flying, it was racing.

I fumbled with my key. I shouldn't have done it. I shouldn't have texted him. He might never respond. It was a moment of weakness. I'd stuck myself out there, and I couldn't take it back.

Stupid security guard.

Inside, I swung my jacket around the back of my desk chair, changed into my pajamas, and crawled into my bed. I pulled the periodic table blanket over my head.

My heart was still pounding. I breathed in and out, trying to make it stop. I loathed myself. For being unable to stop thinking about Dallas. For wanting to have sex at all. I curled onto my side and burrowed deeper into my bedding.

A *ding* came from my jacket.

My heart stopped, and I almost choked.

I flung off the quilt, but it was wrapped around my legs. I moved like an inch-worm, trying to free myself. My legs went over the edge, and I landed on the ground, the quilt coming with me. I shook it off and ran. My fingers trembled as I grabbed my phone.

> **EMMA**
> No hockey players tonight
>
> We're on our way home

My stomach cramped, twisting into dozens of knots. I tossed my phone on my desk. I was a failure. A complete failure.

EIGHT
BOY TEXTS GIRL BACK

As soon as my friends arrived home, I brought an Ambien with me to Emma's room and took it before going to sleep. The next morning Emma's alarm went off full blast.

Thanks to the sleeping pill, I'd gotten at least eight hours of uninterrupted sleep. My back, however, screamed at me. Her cushioned chair that flipped out into a bed was the most uncomfortable thing to sleep on.

I rolled over and rested my gaze on my phone, laying on the floor next to me. Chills ran down my legs. I'd texted Dallas.

My arm shot out like a frog's tongue. I grabbed the phone. But there wasn't a single new message on it.

I should throw this damn phone out the window. Or maybe take a hammer to it, break it into millions of pieces, ensure that no one could recover the data that proved how much of a loser I'd become.

"Good morning," Emma mumbled, so softly it was like she'd put a towel over her head.

"Morning," I said. My own voice wasn't any better. It was deep and nasally.

I set my phone back on the carpet. I didn't want to touch it. I wished I didn't even own it. I wished…I wished cell phones didn't exist.

Maybe that was what I should do. Give up my phone. No need to worry about guys or what they were thinking, or know what my friends were doing every minute of the day. Perfect.

"Are you okay, Ade? You look awful."

"Thanks." I glared at her. I didn't really need her brutal honesty this early. "I'm going to the bathroom."

I stood, slipped on my flip-flops, and trudged out of the room to the shared toilets. After taking care of business, I stood at one of the sinks, washing my hands and looking at myself in the mirror. I did look pretty horrible. The whites surrounding my eyes were red, my eyelids were puffy, and my cowlicks were making my hair stick out in all the wrong places. I was a disaster.

In the hall on the way back to Emma's room, I decided I needed to pull it together. Maybe I should come clean to Emma. Admitting to her that I'd texted Dallas and hadn't gotten a response might be the first step in freeing myself. If I could do that, it might be like nothing had ever happened.

I stepped into her room, and she was already dressed.

"I'm starving," she said, putting on some mascara. "Let's get Priya and Luke and go down to breakfast."

The room turned on its side and spun like I'd just experienced g-force on an amusement park ride. I might be trying to forget about Dallas, but my embarrassment over him continued. I was *not* going to the dining hall. After that unanswered text, if I saw him there, I would die. Absolutely die.

"They're probably not up yet," I said.

"They are." She switched to the other eye. "Priya just messaged."

I walked over to my phone. "Since Luke's here, maybe we should get breakfast somewhere else."

"Like?"

"How about the diner on Stadium Street?" I opened my phone. There was a message from Priya saying they were awake.

A new text appeared.

Omigod…Dallas.

My arms went numb. My hands limp. A sickening feeling overcame me. Nausea, but at the same time, an electrical current running from my heart down to my toes.

DALLAS
How about today @ 3PM?

My body started to tremble uncontrollably. *Get it together, Ade. Don't let Emma see you like this. Think. Think.* I managed to text back. It was clumsy, and my autocorrect had to do the bulk of the work.

I have to work. 5:30PM is better, where?

"Ade?" Emma said. "Did you hear me?"

She'd been talking, and I hadn't been paying attention.

"What?" I asked her.

"I said let's go ask them."

Ding went my phone again. I glanced down at the screen.

DALLAS
Starbucks on Fifth

K

"Who are you texting?" Emma approached me.

My heart raced as I turned off the screen and slid it into the pocket of my pajama pants. "Jay."

"Do you think he'd want to go?"

"Go where?"

She sighed and rolled her eyes. "To the diner for breakfast."

"Oh." I'd totally forgotten what we'd even been talking about. "I doubt it."

"Is he busy?"

Shit. Shit. "He's out for a run."

"He's texting you and running at the same time?"

"Yes. No." *Sheesh*. Being a liar was hard when the person I was lying to wouldn't stop with the third degree. "He's *going* for a run."

"Oh," she said.

Together, we went back to my room so I could change and we could get Priya and Luke.

Because of Dallas, my hands were a sweaty, shaking mess. My whole body was sticky. I could hardly get my pajamas off and my jeans on. *Five thirty*. That was in eight hours. Eight *long* hours.

The four of us went downstairs to walk to the restaurant. As we were exiting the dorm, Jay and one of his teammates entered in their running pants, Saucony running shoes, and wicking layers, smelling of frozen sweat. *Crap*. I should have said he was done with his run, not starting it.

Emma stared hard at me, her brows dipping into a tight frown.

Clueless Priya yammered away. "We're headed out for breakfast. You want to come with us?"

Jay politely refused. Something about showering and a group project. He left and so did we.

Emma came up beside me. "Strange that Jay was coming in from a run when you said he was going for one."

"I must have mixed it up." I kept on, not missing a step.

"Humph." She didn't say another word—all the way to the diner.

Thank God, because the lying had to stop. I'd meet Dallas for coffee and figure out that I really didn't like him, that he didn't meet all five requirements on my list, that he was not a good candidate to cure my insomnia. Then it would be over. No harm done. After that, I'd tell my friends the truth. And we'd all have a good laugh about it. I hoped.

NINE
GIRL MEETS BOY FOR COFFEE

After breakfast, I showered off the smell of eggs, bacon, and hash browns and changed into something casual but nice. I had my shift at the bookstore, and right after, I'd meet Dallas at the coffee shop.

I wore my dark-blue jeans that hugged me in all the right places and a green wool sweater to match my eyes. I made sure to wear the only sexy bra and matching panties I owned. The ones I'd bought with a gift card from Christmas and still hadn't removed the tags. They were black and lacy, and the underwear was a T-back-style thong.

"Where are you going?" Priya was on her computer as I was about to leave.

"Work." I zipped up my jacket and could feel the string of the thong in the crack of my butt. I sure hoped I'd get used to it.

"Oh, that's right." She stopped typing. "We didn't get an extra ticket to tonight's game. Do you want to meet us after?"

I paused. Until this moment, I hadn't thought past the coffee shop. If Dallas and I hit it off, maybe he'd want to keep hanging out. "I'm not sure. Text me after the game?"

"Okay." She nodded as I left.

Now the challenge would be keeping myself in job mode for

the next few hours. I was already dizzy, and my chest was growing tighter with each minute that passed.

Somehow I powered through and remained calm despite the constant flood of sorority girls demanding a form-fitting hockey shirt we'd gotten in and already sold out of in a few days. But when I showed up at the coffee shop after work, I could barely breathe. My insides were a pulpy mass. As if spring had hit, the snow melting and turning the ground into a soggy sponge.

I walked in and glanced around. I didn't know why I looked. Dallas wasn't there. I could feel it.

In line, I scanned the menu on the wall behind the counter. It was past four o'clock—my self-imposed cutoff time—so I couldn't have caffeine. I decided on decaffeinated herbal tea. Citrus blend.

I ordered, grabbed the paper cup, and settled at a small table for two in the back. I didn't want to be near the front windows where Dallas could see me eagerly waiting when he arrived.

From my jacket pocket, I took my phone out and woke it up. Five twenty-eight. I checked my inbox. Nothing but spam and an email from Mom. She'd gotten into the habit of communicating with me this way.

Hi Honey,

I was going through boxes in the basement and found one with your figure skating awards. I think you should go through it, keep what you want and throw out the rest. I can come pick you up from school and drive you back anytime.

Love, Mom

It was her passive way of asking when I'd be coming home again. I wanted to answer her with *never*. I couldn't go home, not with Dad there. I'd cut him off, deleted him from my new college life. I couldn't have him around when I was trying to be someone completely different.

Quickly, I typed back a response, telling her that I was busy at school, didn't have time, and wondered if she wanted to come here and get dinner together the following day. I pressed send.

"Hi," a familiar voice said above me.

I glanced up, and the sensation of rising waters filled me. "You're here."

The moment I said those words was the same moment I wanted to take them back. I sounded uncertain, desperate.

"Of course." He stripped off his jacket and put it over the chair across from me. "I'm going to get some coffee. Want anything?"

I shook my head and pointed to my cup. He'd just proved me wrong on another item on my list. Number three. I thought he'd be self-absorbed, but he'd just offered to buy me a coffee. Selfish people didn't do that.

He turned away, and I pressed a hand to my stomach, suddenly overly aware of the rhythm of my breath, my heart, even the rush of air in my ears.

If I'd been standing, I was sure my knees would have been weak.

Clearly, I was still as attracted to him as I'd been the night of the party. Maybe more so, because I knew what it felt like when he touched me.

He was at the counter now. I couldn't hear him, but the order taker called out to the barista, "Venti Americano with room."

It was confirmed. Not only did I hate coffee, but I was also coffee ignorant. What in the world was an Americano?

He sat in his chair. "Did you come here right from your job?"

"Yeah." *Oh, great response, Ade. Way to be a conversationalist.*

"Where at?"

"The bookstore. Just on Saturdays."

"Cool." He took a sip of his coffee. "You get a discount?"

"Not on course materials, but on other merch."

"Sounds like a good gig."

"It's okay." My gaze shifted to the table. He was so dang

gorgeous. I couldn't look at him without thinking about all the feels I'd had last weekend. "The people I work with are decent."

He spun his cup in a perfect circle. "I'm glad you texted me."

My heart did a little leap. "You didn't think I would?"

"I wasn't sure." He smiled, and I noticed that his teeth weren't perfect. They had a bit of a gap in the front, which was cute.

After this confession, I knew exactly what I had to do. I had to be honest too. This wasn't a game of hide-and-seek. It was real life, and I needed to find my footing.

"You're right though. It took me a bit to decide." I took a sip of my drink but this time didn't take my eyes off him.

"You are afraid of me, aren't you?"

"No, not exactly." My hands were clammy. "I think I'm afraid of your reputation."

"My reputation?" His brows folded inward. "I didn't know I had one."

"Well, there are the thirty girls."

His eyes narrowed, and he tilted his head. "What thirty girls?"

"The rumor is you've had sex with thirty girls since school started."

It took a moment for him to digest this. Then from somewhere deep inside him, he laughed loudly. "Wow. I had no idea. That is some kind of reputation."

"Crazy, isn't it?" The notion of it made me want to giggle too, but I didn't, because he stopped laughing and his expression sobered.

"Interesting gossip, but rather impossible, wouldn't you say?" He lifted his cup and drank.

I swallowed. He had a point. He was in school, on the dean's list, maybe had a part-time job like I did. Finding the time would be difficult. But I hadn't completely changed my mind about him. A rumor might be just a rumor, but it had to start somewhere— there had to be *some* validity to it.

"Thirty does sound a bit ridiculous."

"Is that why your boyfriend told me I wasn't your type?" He smiled with a corner of his mouth.

My jaw stiffened. "Jay is not my boyfriend."

"I know. I know." He made a tear in his napkin. "I'm just guessing your type is not someone who has thirty one-night stands in less than five months."

"My type has less to do with whether a person sleeps around and more to do with me not wanting to be with someone who everyone gossips about."

He tapped the lid on his coffee. "So what you're saying is you don't like to be the center of attention."

If he only knew what last year had been like for me, then he'd understand. First, it had just been school—dealing with the stares, the ridicule, the whispering behind my back. Then it had been the reporters showing up at our front door wanting to hold interviews, the evil glares at our local grocery store, my dad's pictures and mug shots plastered across the evening news. And the hatred. Hatred from an entire metropolitan area. No, worse than that— hatred from an entire society.

"You got it," I said.

He took a drink and leaned back in his chair. "I think I might know where that rumor started."

"You do?"

"There's a girl in our dorm—"

"A girl you've slept with?" I lifted an eyebrow.

He smiled again but didn't answer my question. "I did something she didn't like, and we had a falling out. It doesn't surprise me that she'd make up a story to get back at me."

"What did you do?"

"Do you really want to know?"

I sighed. That was a good question. Did I, or didn't I?

If I didn't want people to know the embarrassing details about myself, I shouldn't want to know his.

"No." I shook my head.

He took another swig of coffee. "So what are you doing tonight?"

"Nothing definite."

"I'm meeting some high school friends down at Sporty's. Do you want to come with me?"

He had friends. This was number four on my list. And he was asking me to meet them.

I shrugged. "I don't have a fake ID."

"I know the bouncer. I can get you in."

I rested my chin on my hand. I thought if I met Dallas here and talked with him, I'd know what to do about him. But I didn't. I was still confused.

"I'm not sure if it's such a great idea."

"Come on. It'll be fun. There's a pool table, and we can get something to eat."

I wanted to go. I did. But I'd told myself I was done with lying to my friends, and going with him would mean doing more of it.

His gaze searched mine.

I supposed I could just wait until tomorrow to start telling the truth. Today was still my day. I deserved this.

"Okay," I said. "I'll go for a bit."

TEN
FROM HOT TO NOT

texted Priya to tell her I wasn't going to meet up with them after the game. I could tell she was upset, but there wasn't much she could do when she had no idea where I was or who I was with.

Dallas and I walked to Sporty's, and as we were approaching the door, he pulled me to a stop facing him. It was cold enough that I could see the intermingling of our breath.

"I need to make something clear before we go in there," he said.

Great. What now?

He reached out and touched my face. *Those hands.* I remembered how they'd felt when he held me at the party. He moved closer and cupped the back of my neck.

His lips touched mine. Warm, soft, wet. It was like stepping into a time machine. I was brought back instantly to the party. I'd been yearning for this feeling for a week now, and I didn't want it to stop.

The kiss started slow but intensified fast. I couldn't get enough of his heat, his mouth.

He broke it off far quicker than I wanted. I wasn't sure how he did it, but he made me feel like I was the most wanted girl in the entire world just by kissing me.

I caught my breath. "What was that for?"

"We're going into a bar. I need you to know that I don't want to kiss you only when I'm drinking."

My thudding heart swelled into my throat. I couldn't talk. Even if I could, it wouldn't matter. I was speechless.

He opened the door for me, and we ascended a flight of stairs. At the top, sitting on a stool, was the bouncer.

"Hey, man." He gave Dallas a high five. "How's it going?"

"Good," he said. "I brought a friend with me, is that cool?"

He waved us through. "No problem."

And without showing our IDs, we were in.

Dallas made a beeline for the bar, and I followed him.

"What do you want?" he asked.

Behind the counter was an array of taps. The only kind of beer I'd ever had was the inexpensive stuff.

"Um." I started reading the labels, but I had no idea. I frowned.

"Why don't you try a Blue Moon?" He gestured to the light-blue label. "I think you'll like it."

I nodded. I actually didn't think it mattered. I wasn't that picky.

The next thing I knew, I had a glass filled with an orange slice floating in cloudy beer in my hand. And it tasted good—really good. Like nothing I'd ever had. Piss-warm party beer out of a plastic glass was awful. This was like an icy heaven.

Dallas introduced me to a group of his high school classmates. I found out most of the guys were people he'd played hockey with as a teenager. They seemed ordinary—well, as ordinary as your average hockey player could be.

"I didn't know that you played," I said to Dallas with a changed pitch in my tone.

"Yeah." He shrugged. But he offered nothing more. Which was fine by me. Hockey and I didn't go well together.

Feeling a bit awkward while Dallas was on the other side of the room, I struck up a conversation with a quieter guy. He sat a little away from rest. A former goalie named Charlie. He was nice but, like most goalies, quiet and a bit quirky. He kept rearranging the condiment basket in the center of the table.

I tried to find things to chat about, but the only thing Charlie and I had in common was our shared knowledge of hockey. A dangerous subject for me, and a couple times I almost messed up and said something damning about my father. Somehow I got through the conversation without giving myself away.

There were girls too. Some were part of the crowd, and some were girlfriends.

One of them, Penny, sat down next to me at a high table. "You look sort of familiar to me."

I smiled politely even though my stomach did a nosedive. The media didn't have many videos or photos of me. The only ones were from a while ago, when I was younger. I was sure I'd never seen her before.

"What's up with you and Reynolds?" she asked.

I straightened. "You mean Dallas," I said.

"Right, what's up with you and Dallas?"

I'd figured someone would ask, and I was prepared. "We live in the same dorm and have chemistry together."

"So you're in those nerdy classes too?"

Dallas was playing pool with Charlie and some of his other buddies. With a cue in hand, the butt resting on the ground, he lifted his gaze from the table and looked at me. He smiled, and I smiled back.

"Yeah, I'll admit it." I looked back at Penny. "I'm a nerd too."

She was watching Dallas now as he lined up the tip of his pool stick with the cue ball and the eight ball. "It's so bizarre. I would have never imagined Dallas hooking up with someone like you, but then again I never imagined he'd be going to school here either, taking engineering classes and going to a campus bar while the hockey team plays on television either."

I slid down a little in my chair.

Wait a second. I wasn't with him like that. I mean, we'd come here together, but he'd introduced me as his friend. And at the moment, that was it. "Just to be clear, we're not hooking up."

"Not yet." Penny shrugged.

Which was what I wanted. I wanted Dallas to be a foregone conclusion. But she had a way of making it sound cheap.

"And I'm confused," I said. "Why are you surprised he's taking engineering classes and watching a hockey game at a bar?"

Dallas slid up next to me. "You hungry?"

I nodded, and before I could mull over what I wanted, he'd waved over a waitress and ordered us both new beers and appetizers. Normally, I'd be offended by not being asked to make my own choices, but in this situation, it was nice of him to relieve me of decisions when it was hard enough for me to navigate his friends.

Penny folded her hands together on the table. "Adriana just asked me a really good question. Dallas, do you know why I'm surprised you're watching the Minnesota University hockey team play on TV?"

"No." He pursed his lips.

Penny tipped her head and flashed him a smile. "I think you do."

Maybe me hanging out with his friends had been a bad idea.

What followed next was an awkward bout of silence. Dallas made no attempt to divulge anything more, and Penny seemed to think she'd proven something.

I was completely lost.

"Do you want to play pool?" Dallas asked me.

I nodded and got up from my chair. Anything to get away from NFP. No-fun Penny.

And then the night got better. Way better. The hockey game started playing on the screens, which distracted most of Dallas's friends, while Dallas and I stepped into our own little world.

He wasn't paying attention to the game. Only me. Finally,

someone who might not obsessively follow the school hockey team.

Together, we loosened up. It might have been the beer, but who cared?

We played pool against each other, and as the game went on, things got...well, touchy-feely. His hands always seemed to be on me. My arms, my back, my waist. I didn't mind. There was something appealing in the heat of it. The possessiveness in it.

"Why are you taking engineering classes?" I asked him as he pondered his next move.

"Huh?" He looked up.

Contrary to Penny's thoughts, there had to be a perfectly logical reason. "What do you want to be when you grow up?"

"Oh," he said, smiling. "I'm interested in refrigeration, so I'm thinking of getting a degree in mechanical engineering."

"An obsession with ice rinks maybe?"

"Possibly. Or just HVAC in general. What about you?"

"Chemical engineering. I'd like to work with food scientists in the food industry."

"Cool."

"It always seems like ideas about food are changing," I said. "What's good for you, what's bad for you. I'd like to be part of that."

"It's not because you want to study their aphrodisiac properties?"

My ears perked up. "Aphrodisiac?"

"I'm kidding." He gave me a wide, mischievous grin. "I think what you want to do is really interesting."

"No, I want to know. What properties?"

"You know, phenylethylamine, serotonin, B vitamins."

"And those chemicals do what?"

"I think they relax blood vessels, improve blood flow, and increase the production of testosterone."

"Like Viagra?"

He started to line up his shot. "Kind of, but naturally."

He took the shot. Eight ball in the center pocket. He beat me.

I put my cue back into the rack and brushed my front side up against his back to get around him.

He turned and raised an eyebrow.

"I'm going to go to the bathroom," I said. "I'll be right back."

When I came out, there he was, standing in the hallway, waiting for me. He wanted to kiss me. I could tell.

"'Do or do not,'" I said with my best serious tone. "'There is no try.'"

His eyes sparkled. "Is that a Star Wars quote?"

"Yoda, to be exact." I couldn't help but smile back.

"I love Yoda."

"Me too."

"So." He paused. "You're saying commit or don't commit, right?"

"Yeah, but if I were you"—I tipped my head slightly—"I'd definitely commit."

He pulled me into an alcove where a door led to the kitchen. He pressed me against the wall, pinning me with his body. His mouth consumed me, sending me soaring into the sky. His tongue probed and smoothed, but it was his lips that were as soft and gentle as I'd remembered. His fingers slipped under my sweater and trailed across my abdomen, sending waves of heat through me.

But then the kitchen door swung open and hit Dallas in the side. He grunted.

My face was hot, and I was sure my cheeks were as red as a billiard ball. Dallas didn't seem to mind. We walked back to the bar area, his hand on the small of my back. Before we separated, he trailed his fingers over the small of my back, and I turned gooey.

I held up my hands to the light, and I'd swear there were parti-cles in Brownian motion inside them, buzzing and colliding. I was breathless, weightless, and the happiest I'd been in a long time. I didn't want the night to end. I wanted it to last forever—or maybe

I just wanted there to be more nights like this. More time being with Dallas.

We finished another pool game, and finally I glanced up at the TV. There was a basketball game on. Professional basketball. *What?* I shifted my gaze to the tables where his friends had been sitting, and they were almost empty.

"What time is it?" I asked Dallas.

He pulled his phone out of his pocket and showed me. Half past midnight.

Shoot. I'd wanted to be back at the dorm before the others got home, so I wouldn't have to make up more lies. But the game must have ended over two hours ago. Now what was I going to do?

I hung up the pool stick and scurried to my purse to check my phone. It was filled with new text messages from Priya. Where was I? When was I coming home? Did she and Luke need to come get me wherever I was?

"Do you have to go?" Dallas came up behind me.

"Yeah." I pulled on my coat. "It's my roommate. She's worried about me."

"Does she do that a lot?"

"Sometimes."

"Okay," he said. "Let's go."

"No, you can stay. It isn't a big deal."

He was already putting on his jacket. "I've got no reason to stay. I'll walk you home."

Outside, snow was coming down in big, wet flakes and building up on the sidewalk. A continuous blanket silencing the streets. As we waited at a corner for the light, he brushed the top of my hair, sending a clump of snow to the ground. Then he pulled my hood up before he stuffed his hands back into his pockets.

"Charlie said you know a lot about hockey." He kept close to me but not touching. "Do you play?"

My toes curled, but I forced them to relax, to stretch out in my boots. I wasn't going to be able to avoid the topic of hockey for long, especially if it was something we had in common.

The light turned green, and we set out.

"I did when I was younger," I said, "but it didn't last."

"What happened?"

I hesitated to answer, but then I remembered I was trying to be honest with him. "My dad."

"What do you mean your dad?"

"Hockey was his life, and I was never good enough at it for him."

"Hmm." He clasped his hands together to push his gloves on better. "I'm sure he was just disappointed when you quit."

"I doubt it, but he was definitely angry when I switched to figure skating."

"You figure skate?"

"Yes. I've passed all my skating skill tests and many of my singles tests, but I haven't done much of it this year."

"Are you good enough to be one of those hockey cheerleaders? Do the jumps and spins on the ice between periods?"

An image of my dad flashed in my brain. Early last spring, before the scandal broke, he'd written an email to the hockey cheer coach, trying to throw his influence around to get me on the cheer team. I hadn't even wanted to try out. I might love figure skating, but that didn't mean I wanted to be a cheerleader. Yet somehow he'd gotten it in his mind that I wanted to do it and wasn't good enough to make it without his help. How embarrassing. How irritating.

"Do I look like one of those perky girls who have all that rah-rah-rah going on?" I asked Dallas.

"No..." His voice wavered. "No, you don't. I didn't mean to imply..."

Ugh. I sounded horribly self-righteous. "Sorry. I shouldn't have said that. Hockey cheerleaders need plenty of skill, athleticism, artistry, and determination. It's just...sometimes when I'm thinking about my dad and the things he's done or said to me, I get upset."

"It's okay." He looked at me intently. "Your dad sounds like he has high expectations. Was he a hockey coach or something?"

Even though the temperature was cold, a flood of heat filled every crevice inside my body. I didn't know what to say. The only thing I knew was I'd promised myself to try and be honest. As honest as I could be. "Yeah, he was."

My answer hadn't revealed much of anything, but an alarm started going off in my head and my heart sped up. Maybe I should tell him. We'd had such a great night together. He'd been kind and understanding. I really liked being with him, and if things kept going as they were, I might not be able to keep it secret.

No. No, I shouldn't. It would be too much of a risk. No one at the dorm knew outside of Jay.

"What level?" he asked.

"College." I held my breath. I shouldn't have said that.

"Seriously? Maybe I know him. What's his name?"

I put a hand to my forehead. This wasn't a question I wanted to answer. But it was right there. The truth begged to come out. I wasn't sure why, but I thought I wanted to set it free. Get it off my shoulders and tell someone who wasn't an intense Minnesota University hockey fan and could maybe understand my position.

"David Bianchini."

Dallas stopped dead in his tracks. So did I. He stared long and hard at me. "Coach Bianchini is your dad." His voice cracked.

I tried to read his face, but his expression was empty, maybe a bit dazed. "I know. He's in a slew of trouble, but if you can, it would be most appreciated if you didn't say anything to anyone. Especially here at school."

"And…and Eric Bianchini is your brother?"

"Yes."

"But I thought your last name was Blankin."

"It is. I changed it. I mean, not officially. My driver's license says Bianchini, but I was allowed to submit a preferred name request when I registered for school."

He nodded, and that was it. He said nothing more.

We set out down the sidewalk again. All I heard was the crunch of snow under our shoes.

Crap. I'd read him all wrong. He must like the Minnesota University's hockey team more than I thought. He did think my dad was despicable. The questions were, after he had the chance to fully digest my revelation, what was he going to do or say? Had I ruined everything?

With each step we took, we got closer to our dorm. To base camp. Where the answers would become apparent. Where I would know if the bond we'd been forming all night remained intact or if it was disintegrating. Like salt melting ice.

We reached the front entrance, and I rewrapped my scarf to cover more of my face. It was late, and the lobby might be empty, but that didn't mean gossipy Sandra wasn't working or lurking by the front desk. I didn't want to chance it.

Dallas took out his wallet and flashed it against the panel. Inside, there was a guy working, and he was busy texting on his phone. We walked by and went down the deserted hallway to the stairwell. I undid my disguise.

On the second floor, he stopped, and I did too.

"This is me." He brushed the floor with the sole of his shoe.

I looked past him. "I'm on four."

"So." He gave me a glassy look. "I guess I'll see you around?"

"Yeah," I said, moving closer to him, hoping we might kiss again.

"I had a good time tonight," he said, but made no move.

"Me too." I forced a smile. "Thanks for the food and the beer."

"No problem." He turned and left.

A knife went straight through my heart.

What.

The.

Hell.

It was all I could think as he walked away. Although I knew my night with him couldn't continue, he'd left me with nothing. Not even a good-night kiss. What misery.

I finished going up the stairs and pulled out my phone to text Priya. I didn't want to walk in on her and Luke.

I'm home. Can I come in?

PRIYA
Yes

The handle was unlocked, and I stepped inside. There sat Jay, Emma, Priya, and Luke, staring straight at me.

Seriously? All of them? I sighed and shut the door behind me.

ELEVEN
CAUGHT

"Hey," I said casually, even though walking into the room was like stepping into a plasma lamp and I was the high-voltage electrode in the center.

Jay lounged in the saucer chair. Priya and Luke were on the edge of her bed. Emma sat in my desk chair, legs crossed.

Priya spoke first. "We've been worried sick, Ade. Why didn't you answer your texts?"

I moseyed over to my closet and hung up my jacket. "Sorry. I didn't know you'd been pinging me."

"We were just about to call the campus police." Emma's voice was low.

I turned back. None of them had taken their eyes off me. "I told Priya I'd see her later. Now is later, and here I am. I'm not sure why you're making such a big deal about this."

"Where were you?" Jay asked.

I stared at him hard. If it were just Priya, Luke, and Emma in the room, I could lie, no problem. Maybe I took a late shift at the bookstore to stock shelves and make some extra pay. Or I could have been meeting with a study group for a project. But with Jay here, I couldn't lie. The second I started to spin my tale, he'd know. He was perceptive like that. He'd also known me longer than the rest of them.

"I was at Sporty's." *See*, I wanted to say to him. *Not a lie.*

"How did you get in?" Priya leaned forward.

I still had my gaze pinned on Jay. Because what I was about to say next would tell me everything I needed to know about who was and wasn't on my side. "I went with Dallas. He knows the bouncer."

Jay's eyebrows rose.

"I *knew* it." Emma shot to her feet and balled her fists. "I told you guys she wouldn't delete his number." She started circling the room. "Gross, Ade. Really gross."

"What the hell?" I'd been dying to say that out loud since it had come to mind on the stairs. "You don't even know him! How can you hate him?"

"We don't hate him." Priya shifted her weight on the bed. "We care about you."

"Care about *me*?" Now my body temperature was rising.

"We just want the best for you." Priya's forehead tightened. "That's all."

Emma wouldn't sit still. "Just so you know, my bet is you're going to get hurt over this—big-time."

Ha. If she only knew. If she only knew that going to a bar with Dallas would never—could never—devastate me. My dad had already accomplished that last year. Dallas might be a mistake, but I didn't care, because I had nothing left to lose.

I put my hands on my hips. "You're being hypocritical. No way you'll get hurt going after a college hockey player, now is there?"

"That's different." Emma pressed her lips together.

"It *is* the same, and it doesn't seem like anyone's stopping you."

"It's different because it's a fantasy. Nothing will ever happen, because I'm too shy to speak with one. You though... You'll actually end up having your first time with a total douchebag."

The words *first time* hit me so hard I lost my breath. I dropped my head and stared at the tight-looped gray carpeted floor. I couldn't believe she'd said it out loud. One night, not long ago, I'd told Emma and Priya that I hadn't had sex yet. They'd said they'd never tell anyone. But now Emma had spilled it in front of Luke and Jay.

"Emma." Priya stood and sharpened her tone. "That's quite enough."

My body started to shake.

"I think you should leave," Priya said to her.

"Fine with me," Emma announced. "I'm going to bed."

Without even an apology, she stomped out of the room.

"I think I will too," Jay said quietly.

I looked at him, and he didn't even glance at me. Shoulders slouched, he followed Emma out the door.

Great. The virgin was now stuck with the humpers.

"Are you okay?" Luke finally spoke up.

"Yes." I positioned my closet door so I could change into my tank and yoga pants in private. But I balled up my clothes, wound up, and threw them into the back.

Priya's bedside light switched off, and the two of them sifted through the bedding, getting situated.

"Emma was really worried about you," Priya said. "I'm sure she'll be back to normal tomorrow."

I grunted a response. Normal? What was normal?

In fact, I wasn't sure life could ever be normal for me.

I grabbed my toiletry bag and my cell phone and went to the bathroom in my flip-flops. Standing under the fluorescent lighting, I flossed and brushed my teeth.

Just as I was spitting into the sink, it came to me. My quest to have sex had changed into something bigger without me even realizing it.

Screw my list of requirements for the kind of guy I'd have sex with. What I wanted was to be with someone who lusted after me as much as I lusted after him. Who understood how to tap into the chemicals stored inside me. Then it would be worth it.

I hated normal, because normal meant being disappointed and sad. I wanted novelty. I wanted excitement. And that was what I was going to go get.

TWELVE
THE SINGLE

nstead of going back to my room, I set my jaw, tightened my
shoulders, and went down the stairwell to the second floor.
Finding Dallas shouldn't be hard.

The hallways of our dorm were H-shaped—two vertical legs
connected at their midpoints by a center horizontal hallway. From
the stairwell, I stepped onto his men's-only floor at one end of the
first leg.

The off-white walls were bare, and except for a few hockey
pennants, the doors stood blank. On my floor, the girls knew how
to dress them up and make it homey. There were silk flowers,
beads, and excessive amounts of bling. Here, it was like walking
down the wing of a hospital.

As my terrible luck would have it, only half of the rooms had
names on them, and none of them said *Dallas*.

I turned into the center hallway to access the second leg. A guy
with shaggy blonde hair passed by, sliding a glance at me. I could
have asked him where Dallas's room was, but I was embarrassed.
I knew what kind of girl went in search of a guy like Dallas at one
o'clock in the morning.

I made it to the end of the center hallway, by the bathrooms, and turned back to look down the long passages. I pulled my phone from my pocket. I could text him.

But that might be too weird. I mean, I had this concrete intention now. I wanted him, but if he responded with his room number and I knocked on his door, I wasn't sure what I would do next.

Come on, Ade. You're such a wimp. Just text him.

I started typing.

Behind me, a door creaked open. I moved to the side to avoid whoever was coming out.

"Adriana?"

When I heard his voice, I jumped and spun around.

Dallas wore a white T-shirt pulled tight at his shoulders, a pair of loose plaid pajama pants with the drawstrings hanging and wool clogs.

I swallowed hard. He looked even better comfortable and rumpled with his hair mussed and his eyes glassy.

"Hi," I said in a bit more of a high-pitched squeak than I'd intended.

He glanced down the hallway. "What are you doing?"

I should make something up, but I couldn't think of anything. "Trying to find your room."

"Oh." He frowned. "Was there something you needed?"

I shifted my weight to my other hip. What the hell was going on here? Why wasn't he showing me to his room? "I just...well...I was trying to find you because...because I wanted to explain more...more about my dad."

My heart rate spiked.

He shook his head. "Don't worry about it. You don't need to."

"No, I really do. I..." I looked around me, not wanting to say this in the middle of the hall, but I must. "You're the first person on campus I've told. No one knows except Jay because we went to high school together. I don't speak to my dad anymore. Basically, I've disowned him. Hence the new name."

He didn't say anything. He sucked in a deep breath and

released it. Then stared at me with a distant gaze, pondering something deep, something beyond me.

"I just wanted you to know that, because I don't want you to think…what he did…is anything I would condone. Also, as I said before, I'm asking you…no, begging you…to please keep this to yourself."

Suddenly, his eyes turned clear, like he'd made up his mind. He smiled wide and deep. Basking in his glow made my insides soften like cotton candy on my tongue.

"Okay, I can do that," he said. "My room's this way. You want to come in?"

I nodded then followed him, watching him closely. I was so into him. He had that high muscled hockey butt, but he wasn't bursting at the seams with brawn. His body was defined, yet lean.

He opened the door to room 227 and waved me in. It smelled a little like coffee and also his cucumber scent.

Except for a string of white Christmas lights, it was dark. Music was playing, but not loud. I glanced around again because there was no one else in the room and there was only one bed.

The door clicked shut behind me.

My back went rigid. "This is a single."

"Yep." He walked around me.

My stomach did somersaults. *This* was how it was possible for him to have so much sex. He never had to worry about a room-mate. Thirty girls might be an exaggeration, but there was no way he hadn't had a few.

He pointed to a futon folded up into a couch. "Have a seat."

I paused. How many girls had he screwed right there?

Stop it, Ade. Don't think about that.

He straddled his desk chair and placed his elbows on the back, looking relaxed. Sexually confident. My stomach turned over.

"You know what?" I started to back up. "It's late. I'll come over some other time."

He rested his chin on his arms and stared up at me. "You can go if you want, but you don't have to."

I halted. This was what I wanted. To be alone with him. So, I sat on the futon and put my toiletry bag next to me like it was my guard dog.

I slid my sweaty hands under my thighs. "I thought you were a freshman," I blurted out.

"I am."

"Then why do you have a single?"

"I was on the waiting list for housing. This was the room that was available when my number came up."

My shoulders relaxed. "That must have been hard. Waiting for a place."

"Sort of." He reached over and turned on a bedside lamp. "But it all worked out."

With the additional light, I started looking around his room, trying to get a feel for what he was like. On his desk, he had a laptop and the all-too-familiar textbooks. Chemistry, physics, calculus, biology. On the ledge above the books stood a frame with a photo. It appeared to be him in hockey pads, standing next to his mom and dad. But there were no other pictures. No friends. No siblings.

"Is that your mom and dad?" I pointed to the photo.

"Yeah, it was taken on parents' night my senior year of high school."

I spotted the large letter C on his jersey. "You were a captain?"

"Yeah." He shrugged.

Instead of taking the opportunity to talk about his family or his past, he said nothing more. I could press him, but I didn't feel like I should.

"Is that a smart coffeemaker?" I motioned to a stainless steel box where a coffee cup was already in position.

He nodded.

"I've heard you can control them from an app."

He nodded again and kept staring at me. It was like he was Superman, using his X-ray vision to see inside me.

My heart thudded. "Do you like coffee that much?"

"I'm addicted."

"Oh." No wonder he was at ease at Starbucks.

Silence followed. More looking around, more time for me to grapple for personal information. More time to feel the heat of his gaze on me.

Tucking my hair behind my ear, I swallowed down the lump thickening in my throat. "Didn't you think there was something off about the ending of our night tonight?"

Creases wove a pattern across his forehead. "Like what?"

I splayed my hand on the cushion and stared at the gray material between my fingers. A war ignited inside me. *Do I, or don't I?* I looked up at him. He was waiting.

But my gut knew. Contrary to Emma's opinion, he was the guy I wanted to send me into deep, blissful sleep after a round of exhausting sex.

"I wanted you to kiss me goodbye, and you didn't," I spoke softly but clearly. "And maybe it's because now you know about my dad, and I know what you must think about him and me and…"

He put his finger to his lips. "I'll admit, I was surprised, but what I think about your dad is not the reason I didn't kiss you."

"It's not?"

"No."

"Then why didn't you?"

He shifted, his eyes now focusing on everything but me. "Because I suddenly got this feeling that I'm not the best person for you to be kissing."

This wasn't happening. This *couldn't* be happening again. There was no way he could go from hot to lukewarm that fast. And him protecting me from his reputation? Bullshit.

"If it's because of the thirty girls, I don't care." I pushed myself forward, grabbed the back of his chair, and before I could take another breath or change my mind, I kissed him.

I ran my tongue over his lips. He opened them, inviting me

inside. And that was all I needed, all he needed. I was in—all in. There was no turning back.

He came out from behind the chair. I nudged him down on the futon and sat on his lap, straddling him. I buried my hands in his soft hair and kept on kissing him.

Taking control like this shocked me, but I wasn't going to play hard to get. I needed him to know I wanted him. Right now. Right this minute.

I pressed as much of myself against him as I could, needing to feel his hard body.

One of his hands skimmed up the side of my torso but stopped and didn't go any farther.

Was I not kissing him right? Was he not getting the proper signals?

I put my hand over his and dragged it up to my chest so he would cup my breast. My heart was pounding.

The kiss deepened. I heard a moan, and I couldn't quite figure out if it was him or me.

Okay. Now we were getting somewhere.

"Touch me," I whispered.

He ran his thumb over the outside of my tank and across my nipple, and it tightened instantly. I knew without a doubt the next moan came from me. I was quaking inside.

His lips left mine and trailed across my cheek to pull on my ear.

My hips gyrated against him. I couldn't help myself. I wanted him that bad.

His hand moved to my other nipple, and I couldn't help but press my fingers into his bicep. This was too good. He was too good. I couldn't have made a better choice.

"I...I..." My brain and my body were reconciled. I needed more.

But before I could say any more words of encouragement, he lifted me off and tucked me in beside him. His breaths came quick and short.

"Sorry," he said after gaining control over his breathing. "I think we're getting carried away."

Feeling the heat of him, I looked at his hand, still touching my belly. I wanted to guide it down a few inches, inside my pants, where my body was more than ready for him.

I started to do just that.

But he squeezed my hand. "Adriana, we should stop."

Stop? What did he mean stop?

"No." I shook my head. "We need to keep going."

I had a sense of urgency now. Like if we didn't keep moving full steam ahead, I'd be sleepless for the rest of my life.

He sighed and kissed the top of my head. The freaking top. What was going on here?

"I'm not having sex with you."

"Yes, you are." I stood up and pointed to his bed, warmth bathing me from head to toe. "You're going to take me over there and fuck my brains out."

He tried to keep his mouth shut, but he couldn't. He started to crack up, and my chest nearly exploded.

After he finished laughing, he stared at me with a serious expression. "You are cute."

"I am not. I'm wearing a thong. I am *sexy*."

He lifted his brows. "Can I see it?"

Turning, I pulled my yoga pants down so the string on my waist showed. I flashed him a seductive smile over my shoulder.

"Nice." He reached out and grazed my hip bone with his finger.

"If I show you the whole thing, then will you have sex with me?"

"No." He crossed his arms.

His response hit me square in the chest, heavy as a brick. He really didn't want what I wanted right now.

I was a loser. A pathetic, groveling loser. I pulled my pants back up. My face and neck were hot.

"I'm sorry," I said. "This is embarrassing. I better go."

I spun around and walked out the door. It shut automatically behind me with a clunk.

Shoot. My bag.

I cringed and covered my face with my hands. This was awful. Mortifying. And it wasn't over. I had to go back in there to get my stuff.

The door clicked open without me having to knock.

Dallas peeked out and then opened the door wide for me to come back in. "I think you forgot something."

I ducked underneath his arm and went straight for the bag. It had fallen off the futon during our hot but short make-out session. I picked it up and turned to leave again, but Dallas was blocking me.

"I'm sorry for laughing." His hands were behind his back.

"It's okay." I tried to find a way around him. "I just thought you were into easy fucks."

He grabbed my upper arm and stopped me.

I looked at him, my chin quivering. I really wish I hadn't said that. It was insulting to both of us.

"You and *easy* do not go together," he said.

I went limp under his grip. This was so confusing. I needed someone to point me to the beginning of the maze again and give me the directions.

"So, you do or you don't want to have sex with me?" I asked.

"I do. I'm just not going to ruin this."

"Ruin what?"

"Exactly." He opened the door and stepped aside.

I walked across the threshold and looked back at him.

He smiled, said good night…and shut the door.

I stared down the long, empty hallway, and an ache took root in my stomach. Where was I going to go now? Not back to my room. Luke was still there. Not to backstabbing Emma's room. No way.

I tapped on Dallas's door.

He opened it again, his mouth twitching. "Did you forget something else?"

"Um." I rubbed my lips together. This was awkward. "I know that you don't want to have sex with me, and we don't really know each other all that well, but do you think I could stay here tonight? On your futon?"

He squinted.

"My roommate's boyfriend is here, and…well…I sort of got into an argument with the other girl on my floor who I usually stay with when he's in town."

His brow unfurled. "Just to sleep?"

"Yes, I promise." I held my breath. An insomniac promising to sleep was like a toddler promising not to draw on the walls.

"Okay," he said, and I exhaled.

This was crazy. Totally bizarre. I'd all but walked out on the guy because he wasn't going to give me what I wanted. Now, I'd somehow managed to weasel myself back in for a no-nonsense sleepover.

Forget it. I was going to get him to have sex with me whether he liked it or not. Maybe not tonight, but soon. Very soon.

THIRTEEN
WALK OF SHAME

The next morning, I watched Dallas standing next to his fancy coffeemaker with his Minnesota University mug in his hand, his elastic waistband slung low on his hips. His white T-shirt had bunched high enough to show the bottom of his toned abs.

I rolled onto my side and sat up. The room looked different with light streaming through the blinds. A black hockey bag sat in the corner, slightly unzipped but no equipment poking out. A couple pieces of clothing were strewn across the floor. The top of a mini refrigerator held a few crumbs and unorganized snacks.

"Do you want a cup?" he asked.

"No thanks." I rubbed my eyes, sorting out what had happened last night. He'd been true to his word. He hadn't touched me. He'd stayed in his bed. I could attest to this. I'd tossed and turned while he'd lain over there in the deepest slumber I'd ever witnessed.

Now that I was upright and wishing I'd taken an Ambien, I remembered the worst thing about my decision to stay here. I didn't know how I was going to get back to my room without someone seeing me leave.

He sat on his desk chair.

I rolled my head in a circle to get the kinks out. "I'm sorry," I said.

"For what?"

"I probably shouldn't have stayed here last night."

"It's no big deal."

But it was big deal. It was huge. If anyone saw me leaving this room at this time in the morning, I would, without a doubt, be the talk of the dorm. And when people talked, they dug.

I glanced at his closet. "Do you have a hooded sweatshirt I can borrow?"

"I think so." He walked to a bank of drawers, rifled through one, and tossed me a hoodie. "Are you cold?"

He didn't get it. He didn't get it at all.

I put the oversized garment on over my head and pulled the hood up and as far over my face as it would go. I stuffed my toiletry bag in the front pocket and my phone in my pants. "If I walk out of here without a disguise and someone sees me, not only will I be the brunt of everyone's jokes, but people might figure out who I am."

"I doubt it. For all they know, your last name is Blankin."

I gave him a dead-on stare. "Remember what I told you. You have a reputation. When a person becomes associated with someone who has a reputation, people start gossiping, and they start asking questions."

"Hmm." He took a sip of his coffee. "Is it really that bad being Bianchini's daughter?"

"Worse."

"Do you want me to go with you?"

"Into the hallway?"

"Yeah."

"No." I wanted to scream. "I need you to stay right here."

He set his coffee mug down and came to me. He lifted the hood away from my face and kissed me. It wasn't like last night, when his kisses had sent me reeling. It was smooth, gentle, and sent rays of sunshine shooting through my heart.

He pulled the hood back down over my forehead. "Okay, soldier. Be brave, you'll make it."

A smile slipped across my face. I moved to the door, and just as I was about to turn the knob, someone pounded from the other side. "Dallas, wake up."

I darted into his closet, my breath lodging in my throat, my pulse thundering in my ears.

The pounding started again, and Dallas opened the door with his coffee in hand. "Hi," he said.

"Hey, bro. Thought we were going to play racquetball at the rec center this morning. Why aren't you dressed?"

"Sorry, I overslept."

"You got a chick in there?"

I buried myself behind Dallas's hanging clothes.

"Nah." Dallas cleared his throat. "But I am going to pass on playing."

The guy chuckled. "I knew it. You do have a chick in there. Awesome, man. Totally awesome."

My back slid down the wall, and I sat on a pair of shoes with my knees up.

"Sorry, dude," Dallas said. "Wish it were so."

"Whatever, man."

Dallas shut the door. He turned on his overhead light and came to the closet.

He separated the hangers, and his face appeared above me. "Sorry about that."

"And you don't think you have a reputation problem?"

"That guy thinks everyone is sleeping with someone." Dallas held out his hand.

I took it, and he pulled me up. "Right," I said.

Straightening his hoodie, I looked at the door, and my heart skipped a beat. It was like a war zone out there. Getting back to my room undetected was going to be difficult. And worse, I wasn't sure who would be waiting to interrogate me when I got there.

"Okay. See you later." I took a deep breath and exhaled.

Cracking open the door, I glanced down the hall to make sure it was clear. I slid out and walked with my head down as fast as I could. I didn't know if anyone saw me. I just kept going all the way up the stairs to my room.

Inside, I saw a lump in Priya's bed. Whew. She and Luke were still sleeping.

I went into my closet, pulled off the sweatshirt—which smelled like Dallas—and buried it deep in the back. I peeled off my yoga pants and put on my robe. A nice hot shower was what I needed.

"Where have you been?" Priya's voice stopped me in my tracks. She was on *my* side of the room, under *my* periodic table blanket, and sitting up on *my* bed.

"Why aren't you in bed with Luke?" I whispered.

"Oh." She brought her hands to her lap. "I was hot, then he kept rolling on top of me and I couldn't breathe. Since you were gone, I moved over here."

I thought when you had a boyfriend, you never wanted to be apart from him. Especially when you saw him only every other weekend.

Her eyes narrowed. "You didn't answer my question. Where have you been?"

I stayed silent. Mostly because I had nothing to say. I wasn't going to tell her I'd been in Dallas's room. I didn't want to go there. But then where had I been? Everything I came up with could be proven a lie.

"The lounge."

"You slept in the lounge?"

"Sort of. You know how I have trouble sleeping? I started reading one of those novels that are on the shelf, and I fell asleep on the couch."

"I'm sorry, Ade. That must have been really uncomfortable. I should have come looking for you."

"It wasn't bad. I'm fine. Just off to take a shower."

I walked out of the room, and an ache shot across the back of my throat. I hated lying to Priya. She didn't deserve that. Eventually, I would tell her the truth. As soon as I was ready. As soon as I had Dallas all worked out in my brain.

FOURTEEN
THE GIRL IN THE HOODIE

By the time I'd finished showering, wrapped my head in my towel, and cinched my terry cloth robe tight, I'd done my share of thinking about Dallas. Even though he'd outright refused me after I'd thrown myself at him, I was not having second thoughts. I still wanted him.

In the hallway I passed Priya, shower caddy in hand. "Luke's gone," she said, her voice sounding flat.

Hmm. I wondered if everything was okay.

When I got back to our room, I had it all to myself and decided to power up my laptop while I waited for Priya to return.

My mom had responded. She agreed to pick me up for an early sushi meal. Good.

I closed my email and opened my internet browser. It would seem after the previous night's debacle that just demanding to have sex with Dallas wasn't going to work. I needed a better plan. A strategy for Operation: Get Laid.

Somehow I landed on a wikiHow page titled "How to Start a Friends with Benefits Relationship." I didn't want just a one-night stand with Dallas. That wasn't going to be enough for me. He didn't need to be my boyfriend either. I wasn't looking for one.

What I wanted was something in between, and this might be the perfect solution.

The first step, the website said, was picking someone. Check.

When I scanned the details of the first step, I noticed some interesting points. I should pick someone I had chemistry with. I smiled, thinking of our conversation about aphrodisiacs. Dallas and I, we had chemistry.

The website also said to pick a person outside my social network. Another slam dunk there. Dallas would never be part of my circle of friends. Not when they distrusted him so much.

Lastly, the person should be experienced. I nodded and smiled again, remembering our first kiss at the party, outside the bathroom at the bar, and last night on his futon. Just as I'd concluded after I met him, he was such a good kisser. I couldn't have picked a better person.

The second step: hook up. Aha. This was the information I needed.

Start by flirting. Um. Dallas and I were beyond that.

Next, start kissing or doing more, which we had, but it also said to tell the person how attracted you were to them, but not to compliment their personality or say anything that would make it sound like you wanted to date.

I stared out the window and rested my chin on my hand. I loved Dallas's smile, his coyness, his touch, his belief that I was special.

Even if I'd said any of those things to him last night, I doubted that it would have made a difference. For some reason, he'd been adamant about not having sex. I looked back down at the screen. I needed the next point.

Set the ground rules.

And then it hit me. Why hadn't I thought of that before? We hadn't been on the same page, and if we'd come to a mutual understanding of the rules, of the expectations, maybe things would have gone differently.

As I scrolled, Priya came through the door.

I folded my computer shut just after I saw the next point: have hot sex.

My face heated. I was so close.

I put my computer in its case. "So, you slept in my bed last night and Luke left before having breakfast. Is everything okay with you guys?"

"I think so." She shrugged. "Maybe."

"Is it the stuff we talked about before?"

She sighed. "I'm hungry, and don't feel like talking about him. Let's just go eat instead."

"Okay," I said, because I got it. Sometimes you just didn't feel like rattling on about a guy. "Let me get dressed first."

Downstairs in the dining hall, Emma was there. She scooted her chair over to make room for me. It was quite incredible what she was doing, pretending like nothing had happened the night before.

Sandra, the infamous gossip, was sitting across from Emma.

"Hey, Adriana, I saw you make out with Dallas last weekend in front of a crowd of people." She lifted her eyebrows. "That must have been pretty embarrassing."

The muscles in my body tensed. "Not really," I said.

"But everyone saw you."

I ignored the feeling shooting across my chest. "A little love, Sandra. You should try it sometime."

Her mouth fell open. "I knew it. You're sleeping with him, aren't you?"

I wish.

"She is not." Priya spoke up in a terse tone. "I'm her room-mate. I would know."

I started to giggle maniacally because everything about this conversation was ridiculous. "I was kidding, Sandra," I said. "Lighten up."

Her shoulders drooped, and she frowned. "So you're not the girl in the hoodie, then."

My pulse sped up. "The hoodie?"

"A girl in a hoodie was spotted coming out of his room this morning."

Emma glanced at me with pained eyes.

At the same time, Priya flashed Sandra a look of death.

Neither Priya nor Emma knew that the elusive hoodie girl was me, and being the friends they were, they were trying to protect me. Even Emma, which was strange, given her present stance on Dallas. Maybe she regretted spilling my private information.

"I'm not sure why you think that's interesting," Emma said to Sandra. "When you first told me about him, it was amusing. Now it's just getting old."

"But that's the thing—before, his conquests didn't live here." Sandra sat up in her chair. "This girl must. She had no coat, no mittens, no hat. I just hope she doesn't get an STD. You know, Dallas must be like a petri dish."

I pushed away from the table. *Enough.* I went to go grab a tray and a bowl from the stack. Seriously. Dorm people were insane.

Next to me, Emma grabbed a plate. "I'm sorry about last night," she said softly.

I glanced at her.

"I didn't mean to tell Jay or Luke. It just came out before I could take it back."

My heart warmed. "It's okay."

"Really?"

"Yeah, sure." I mean, I was going to get laid any day now, so really, my lack in sexual experience was moot at this point.

After pouring cereal in my bowl, adding milk, and filling a glass with apple juice, I looked back at the table. Sandra was still there. But now so was Jay.

An image popped into my brain. Dallas coming through the doorway into the dining hall and stopping to talk to me while the entire room gawked and whispered.

No way could that happen. I needed to set those ground rules, and right away.

I set my tray down on the counter and pulled out my phone.

If you see me in public, ignore me.

A few seconds later.

DALLAS
Have you done your homework for physics yet?

What?

No... Please confirm, will you ignore me?

I tapped my foot on the floor, waiting for his answer.

DALLAS
You want to meet in Lund Hall tonight and work
on it?

Omigod.

DALLAS
Pretty please :)

I stared hard at that last text. He wasn't acknowledging my request. As I stood there in turmoil, I felt the heat of eyes on me, and I looked up. Dallas stood there in workout clothes, watching me, a cup of coffee in one hand and his cell phone in the other. He smiled with an amused glint in his eyes.

The noise in the dining hall grew in volume, assaulting my ears. He'd gotten the message. That was for sure.

I went back to the table and slid into my chair.

"He's here," Sandra whispered loudly to me. "Did you see him?"

I wanted to cover my ears. They were ringing.

I think the entire table stared him down as he walked past. Probably with different levels of loathing.

I was sure that Sandra hoped for a dramatic confrontation. Something she could talk about for the rest of the day.

I stayed focused on my breakfast as well as I could. But nonstop dinging was sounding in my pocket.

"Ade, is that your phone?" Priya asked.

I shrugged. My mom only emailed me; I wasn't speaking to my dad, and only on rare occasions with my brother. The only people I texted on a regular basis were sitting right here. So I knew that it was Dallas, but I wasn't going to take out my phone and see what he'd written.

That was what he wanted, and I wouldn't do it. I needed an addendum to my first ground rule: ignoring me when he saw me included texting.

Of course, he didn't seem like the kind of guy who did what he was told.

FIFTEEN
THE SHIRT OF TRUE RECKONING

Priya and I walked into our room, and the door shut automatically behind us. I needed privacy to read Dallas's texts, so I went straight to my closet.

"Are you good?" Priya asked.

I turned around and frowned. "Sure, why wouldn't I be?"

"Because of Sandra."

"What about her?"

"When she mentioned the girl in the hoodie, I wanted to staple her mouth shut. That's the last thing you needed to hear."

I shrugged, debating whether now was the time to tell Priya that the hoodie girl was me.

"Just so you know, Texas is a jerk." She put her hands on her hips. "I also think he sucks big-time."

I grimaced. It bothered me, her not understanding what was going on and coming to conclusions. The energy required to stay silent about it was exhausting. Like every time someone said something mean about him, I had to partake in an epic battle against myself to keep from screaming.

So I turned, dug through my closet, and pulled out his sweatshirt. No time like the present. I put it on and lifted the hood over my head. His smell was all around me.

I turned around.

Priya ran her fingers through her hair. "What are you doing?"

I stared harder at her, not saying a word.

She continued gazing at me, then her eyes widened, and she put a hand to her mouth. "You're the girl in the hoodie."

I took it off even though I'd have preferred to keep it on. His scent was intoxicating. I tossed it back into my closet. "Don't tell anyone, and for sure not Emma, Jay, or Luke."

"But you said you slept in the lounge last night."

"I lied."

She fell back onto her bed, placing a hand on her chest. "The girl in the hoodie. It's like the title of a movie." She rolled onto her side. "You know I won't be able to keep this to myself."

"Don't you even *think* about it."

She propped herself up on one elbow. "Fine. I won't say a word as long as you spill your guts. I need details."

My lips twitched. "No way. You're lucky I told you anything at all."

"How was it? I mean, how was the sex?" She fanned her face.

"I'm not talking about it."

She returned to her back and stared at the ceiling. "You have to tell me. I mean, roommates have to know about this kind of stuff. We *have* to. Especially it being your first time." She paused and looked at me again. "Is he as good at sex as he is at kissing?"

The back of my neck tingled. How embarrassing. The reason I couldn't talk about it was because, well…It. Never. Happened.

"I said I'm not talking about it."

"You're killing me, Ade. *Killing* me."

I grabbed my phone and started scrolling through Dallas's texts. *Ignore her. Ignore her.* The mantra kept repeating in my head so I wouldn't think about my real worry—that since he hadn't had sex with me yet, he never would.

She came up behind me and peered over my shoulder. "Is that why your phone was making noise in the dining hall? Was he texting you?" She backed away and started jumping up and down. "This is so exciting. I mean, dramatic, and a little scary because of his reputation, but so exciting!"

I shrugged. If only she knew. There was no drama here. Not even a little.

She stopped jumping and rubbed her hands together. "Okay, so what's next? When are you going to see him again? Do you think he'd go on a double date with Luke and me?"

I laid my phone down on my desk. "It's not like that."

"What do you mean?" She paused.

"We're not dating."

A gleam entered her eye. "But you went out with him last night."

"I wouldn't call it a date. We went to a bar and met up with some of his friends."

"But then you had sex with him."

I folded my arms, my face burning. In retrospect, showing Priya the hoodie might have been a mistake, because my confidence was plummeting. She was the reason I was now second-guessing my plan for Operation: Get Laid.

Suddenly, my head hurt. It was all becoming quite clear. He might pass my requirements, but I didn't pass his. No guy was given the green light and decided not to go for it. Especially someone like him.

She sat on the bed and squeezed her legs together. "Okay. You don't have to tell me about the sex. But you have to appease me with something—anything."

I dropped onto the bed next to her and slouched. "I can't tell you anything."

"Come on," she pleaded.

Just like I couldn't have her draw conclusions about the girl in the hoodie, I couldn't have her draw conclusions about my sex life. "I can't, because it didn't happen."

"What didn't happen?" Her eyebrows snapped together.

I held my head in my hands. "We didn't have sex. I wanted to, but he didn't."

Silence. Earsplitting silence.

Then her arm curled around me, and she hugged me. "Just because he didn't sleep with you last night doesn't mean he didn't want to. Did you guys make out?"

"Yes." I glanced at her. "And he wants to study together tonight."

Her eyes lit up. "Wow, Ade. He's totally crushing on you."

"You didn't hear me. He wants to do calculus-based physics problems together, not add the bed, subtract the clothes, divide the legs, and hope you don't multiply."

She laughed, grabbed my hand, and walked me to my closet. After shuffling through my clothes, she pulled out the lowest cut, tightest shirt she could find and held it up to me. "Tonight, when you get together with him, you're going to wear this."

I looked down at it. "You must be joking. It's freezing outside. I need layers."

"I'm not kidding around here. This, my friend, will be the shirt of true reckoning."

"What's that supposed to mean?"

"By wearing this top, you'll come to understand what kind of person he is. If he's confident enough to look directly at your chest and not be ashamed to appreciate it, then he's a bad boy and worth pursuing. If he boldly looks but also says something that makes you feel bad, like your boobs are too big or too small or saggy or something asshole-like, then he's a jerk. Not worth your time. If he glances but looks away fast, he's afraid of getting caught. That means he's a nice guy and also worth pursuing."

"What if he doesn't look at all, then what?"

She raised an eyebrow. "Oh, he'll look. He won't be able to help himself."

"I don't know, Priya. I still think there's a possibility he's not interested."

She shrugged. "Well, if that's the case, screw him. But I think that's impossible. He'd never have let you stay in his room or texted you this morning if he wasn't totally into you."

"Priya, you know how this works. Engineering students form friendships. We have this instinct to help each other out because otherwise no one would survive our torturous classes."

"Pshaw." She brushed lint off the shirt that had now been deemed sexy. "Have you ever kissed Jay?"

"No."

"Have I?"

She was also in engineering. Computer engineering. "No."

"See." She cocked her head and held out the shirt. "Now change."

I suppressed a low sigh. I didn't care if he was a nice guy, a bad boy, or even a jerk. I wanted to have sex with him. Still, I'd do it. I'd conduct Priya's experiment just to find out whether he wanted to be something more than my engineering study buddy.

But first, I'd have to get through dinner with Mom without being forced into a discussion about Dad.

SIXTEEN
MOM ISSUES

A little later, I jammed a bunch of pamphlets and internet printouts into my backpack along with my physics stuff and went to the lobby to wait for Mom. She pulled up into the loading area right on time, and I jumped into her sedan. I leaned over the center console and hugged her. The smell of her jasmine perfume comforted me.

She was tiny, my mother. Petite in stature, her features fine, and her hair always arranged with that fresh, recently blown effect.

"Hi, sweetie," she said. "I've missed you."

"Me too." I gave her a peck on the cheek.

Mom and I had always had a special bond that I'd never had with Dad. Probably because she was the one who encouraged me to do the things I wanted to do without interference or making me feel like a failure. The same could not be said for Dad.

My good relationship with my mom was why I was protective of her. Dad might have made our lives a living hell, but his fraudulent actions and subsequent arrest had taken the greatest toll on her. Eric and I had escaped from home. She was still there.

We drove to her favorite sushi restaurant and found a spot to park on the street. My mouth watered. You couldn't get this kind of food in the dorm.

The hostess sat us at a small table, and I took my jacket off.

"Don't you think that shirt is a bit…" Mom flicked her gaze downward.

"A bit what?" I asked as innocently as I could. Mom was always dressed in designer clothes with elegant accessories. She was posh—slutty was far beneath her.

"Revealing."

I looked down and saw the freckle that normally no one could see. *Maybe.*

"Adriana, I can see the top of your bra."

She was right, of course.

Just then, the hostess came back with a pot of tea and two cups.

"Is it caffeinated?" It was after four o'clock in the afternoon, and that meant no caffeine for me.

"It's green, so there's a little."

My mom raised an eyebrow at me. "You're not still having trouble sleeping, are you?"

I was happy for a diversion from my scantily clothed boobs. But this new topic might be just as uncomfortable. When I'd left for school last fall, I'd told her I was fine. I hadn't wanted her to worry. Even though Dad had caused some anxiety-induced insomnia, I'd wanted her to think I'd risen up and overcome it.

"No, I'm good." Another lie. Might as well. I was getting so good at it.

She lifted the pot and held on to the lid. "Do you want some?"

"No, thanks." I put a hand over the cup in front of me.

She poured her own and then folded her hands on the table. "Is your second semester going as well as the first?"

"It's going great," I said, and forced a smile. She also didn't need to know how poorly I'd done in my classes. She was used to me being a straight-A student—Cs and a D were not something I wanted to talk about, let alone admit to, even to myself.

The void in my stomach was not just because I was hungry.

"So, Mom, have you seen the news articles about the condos being built downtown and how empty nesters and retirees are gobbling them up?" I asked.

She shook her head. "No. I don't pay much attention to things like that."

"I've gathered some info." I unzipped my backpack, pulled out the brochures, and laid them on the table. "I think you should look into some of these. They're totally your style."

She stared down at the smiling faces and bright photos on the flyers. "Your dad would never want to move."

"I don't think he'll have much choice in the matter."

The waiter approached, and Mom rattled off to him the sushi rolls and nigiri we always ordered without even looking at the menu.

She looked back at me. "I'm confused. What are you talking about?"

"Dad has been charged with five felonies that he'll be going on trial for in two weeks. The maximum sentence for each count is ten years. If he's convicted and a judge decides to make those sentences consecutive, that's fifty years."

Mom gave me that deer-in-headlights look.

I reached over the pamphlets and squeezed her hand. "Mom, he might have to move to prison, without you. I just want to show you that you have options."

She pulled her hand back. "Well, if you were still talking with your dad, you'd know that his lawyer has some solid defenses that show he's not a criminal and won't be going to jail."

Ugh.

"In fact," she said, "I think you should work things out with him before the trial begins."

"No." My tone was sharp. Sharper than I'd intended. "Don't you remember high school graduation?" My heart drummed in my chest. Perspiration formed along the underside of my bra. It was difficult for me to breathe. "When I walked across the stage to receive my diploma and I was heckled?"

She frowned. "I know, sweetie. That was awful, and I still feel so horrible about it."

"I didn't dare go to the senior all-night party for fear of what people might do to me. That isn't something a teenager should have to deal with. Ever. My life was ruined, and he is to blame."

She sighed. "He made mistakes. He knows that."

"But he's never admitted to any wrongdoing."

Mom shook her head and said softly, "Just because you make mistakes that you regret doesn't mean those mistakes are illegal."

"Well, the government thinks they are."

"Your father deserves a chance to be heard, to defend himself. That's what our justice system is about."

I covered my face with my hands. Maybe I should cover my ears. I didn't want to hear this. I wanted her to be as upset as I was. "Guilty or not guilty, I'll not forget so easily. And neither will Eric."

"Actually, I think things with your dad and brother are better. Did Eric tell you that he signed with an AHL team in Canada?"

It was like a vacuum had sucked all the air out of my throat and choked me. "Since when?"

"Since the beginning of January."

I crossed my arms and tapped my foot on the ground. I couldn't believe Eric hadn't told me. I couldn't believe he'd been talking to Dad.

"I think connecting with Dad would help you too." She paused. "No matter how you look at it, he's your father—he'll always be your father, and you need him."

I put my hands back on the table. "I didn't need him before. I don't need him now."

"You don't mean that." She lowered her chin.

"Yes, I do."

"Well, he's paying for college, so, in fact, for now you do still need him."

"I thought they froze his bank accounts."

"They didn't freeze his retirement accounts. He's drawing money from them."

An ache swelled in my chest. I'd wondered about that. "Tell him to stop," I said. "I'll take out student loans, whatever."

The waiter appeared with bowls of miso soup and set them in front of us. I concentrated on the pieces of tofu suspended in the broth.

"You are *not* taking out loans."

"But I can."

She sighed again. "Ade, you need to hear him out. He's very sorry about what happened."

Mom retrieved a pad of sticky notes and a pen from her purse. After consulting her cell phone, she scratched down something, pulled the top note off, and set it on the table next to me. "This is his new cell number."

I clamped my mouth shut, but what I really wanted to do was laugh out loud. My dad had made our lives total shit, and yet she wanted me to reach out and make amends with him.

But I had things on my mind other than just Dad. So I searched my jacket pocket for my phone and brought it out.

"I'll put his number in here right now if and only if you take these flyers home with you."

She stared at me blankly. "Honey, I'm not going to move."

"Please," I said. "Keep them just in case."

She shrugged and started to gather them into a pile. "Okay, but you better start typing."

My fingers flew over my screen as I entered my dad's new number into my phone. It didn't make me feel good.

"Promise you'll read them," I said, watching my mom stick the pamphlets in her purse.

She looked at me. "Promise you won't delete your dad's number the second I drop you back off at school?"

I nodded.

She smiled. "Then I guess we have ourselves a deal."

SEVENTEEN
THE STUDY DATE

Dad might be responsible for my insomnia, but I knew who was going to cure it. Dallas.

Mom dropped me off as close to Lund Hall as possible. As I walked, I made good use of my smartphone gloves and called Eric.

It went to voicemail.

At the beep, I said, "I can't believe you didn't tell me about your AHL team contract! At Christmas, you said you were working for a youth development program, nothing about this. What gives? Call me…" I paused. "This is your sister, by the way, the only one you have, the one you obviously haven't talked to in weeks."

I walked up the front steps into the building, took a left down the hall, and entered the study lounge, a large room with a vaulted ceiling.

There he was. At a corner table.

Dallas was so dang hot my heart danced in my chest.

Okay, Operation: Get Laid, here we go.

I made my way to him and sat in the opposite chair. Who knew last week that we'd be sitting here, he and I, face-to-face, about to study together?

"Hi," Dallas said in a raspy voice.

My gaze dropped to his lips. *Mm.* I could almost taste them.

From my backpack I took out a three-ring binder with pocket folders, a notebook, my textbook, a calculator, and a pouch of pens and pencils.

He cleared his throat. "How do you fit all that in there?"

"Easily." I arranged everything in a spot on the table.

He looked at me with a furrowed brow.

"What?" I asked.

"Is this some sort of study ritual you have?"

"No." My ears heated, and I pushed everything to the side.

He slid a single sheet of paper across the table to me. "Is this the same physics problem your class has?"

I glanced at it. A magnetic-field question. "Yes."

He took his sheet back, and I pulled out my own from my binder. But I didn't pick up my pencil to begin. Not yet.

"You ready?" he asked.

"Actually, I wanted us to go over some ground rules first."

He did that trick I couldn't do, spinning his pencil around his thumb with his index finger. "What kind of rules?"

"Rules so we're both on the same page."

He lifted his piece of paper in the air and smiled with the corners of his mouth. "I thought we were?"

"No, I'm referring to my text message earlier—the one you didn't answer."

He wrinkled his nose. "The ignore-you-in-public one?"

"Yes."

"Don't worry. I got it. Loud and clear." His gaze remained focused on me. "I have some damage control to take care of on the reputation front, but I don't see it lasting. I'll fix it."

"And, of course, there are other rules."

"Like?" He lifted his brows.

At that moment, I decided that it was time to begin the Priya-induced-cleavage experiment. I took off my jacket, slung it over the back of the chair, and turned back to him. I didn't have to wait. He was already staring, his bold look branding me.

Finally, he slid his unabashed gaze up to mine, and his eyes glittered. "Nice shirt."

I warmed like an infrared space heater. I was sure my neck and face had turned the same orangish-red color as the heating coils. I needed no further experimental evidence. Dallas was a bad boy who thought I had nice tits.

Progress. Definitely progress happening here.

"So what kind of rules are you talking about?" he asked.

I looked down at my physics problem, unable to look him in the eye. "I think we should keep things between us...well...you know...like how you normally do things."

"Which is?"

"You know." Okay. Now I had to look at him again. Right into those bottomless brown eyes of his. "Just sex."

He froze.

"We keep things light, easy, fun."

He touched the base of his neck, not saying a word.

"Like this." I laid my palms flat on the table. "This is fine. We can still meet to study or whatever."

"Let me get this straight." His gaze was clouded. His face was blank. "Are you asking me to be your fuck buddy?"

My leg bounced. It wouldn't stop. "Isn't that what you do?"

"Adriana." He sounded like a parent scolding a child.

"Call me Ade. Remember? Light, easy, fun."

He leaned back. "Ade, I'm not sure what to say."

"You don't have to say anything more than yes."

He narrowed his eyes. "What makes you think fuck buddies is what I do?"

"Well, there's your reputation—"

"Which I'm going to fix."

"And you're a guy. I didn't think single guys wanted relationships?"

He swallowed, his Adam's apple bobbing. "Valid observation."

"So what's the problem?"

"Okay." He laid down his pencil. "Let's just say, as a hypothetical, we did what you want. No strings. No emotional commitment. What happens if one of us gets attached?"

"Then it's over."

"Just like that?"

I should probably tell him the real reason for all of this—I needed sleep—but I couldn't. I didn't want to scare him off.

"This isn't rocket science, it's called chemical attraction." I rested my chin on my hand. "If the forces between us become uneven, there's nothing we can do to prevent the bond from breaking."

He grew quiet—really quiet. I couldn't read him. He seemed to be processing, but even my solid-state laptop was louder than him.

Finally, he spoke. "Do you want to go ice-skating tomorrow?"

I glared at him. "Don't do that. Don't change the subject on me."

"Did I?" He smirked.

"Yes. Now stay on track. You're supposed to be considering my proposal."

"How about I think about it, and in the meantime, we go ice-skating?"

"Going ice-skating sounds relationship-y."

"No, it doesn't."

I was fuming now. This should be easy. A girl asks a guy to have sex, and he accepts. I mean, if it was him putting forward the same thing to me, then it would be a totally different situation. But we both knew he had sex—probably plenty of sex—with girls. And I knew he was attracted to me. So why wasn't he just saying yes?

I scanned the lounge. All males, of course. This was the main engineering classroom building. "I bet if I went up to any guy in here and asked him to have sex with me with no strings attached, he'd jump at it."

Dallas folded his arms and looked around. "Go ask that guy in the Jedi Knight T-shirt. I know that you like *Star Wars*. You'd have something in common."

I glanced over. The student he'd referred to was holding a pen in the shape of a lightsaber. His fingernails were bitten down so far they were raw, and his neck hair needed shaving. He might be a perfectly nice person, but I'd never be able to get over my other hang-ups.

"Seriously?" I looked back at Dallas.

"Yeah." He shrugged.

My neck steamed with scorching heat. "I'm not going to prove it to you when you know I'm right."

He leaned forward and lowered his voice. "I'm trying to make my own point. If all you wanted was sex, you could ask any Tom, Dick, or Harry."

The muscles in my face turned to stone. "That's not true. Picking the right person is a very important part of the process, even when there are no strings."

"So you have a method for this—a scientific method. Because if you do, we should also discuss STDs."

I froze.

"Are you clear?" he asked.

"Clear?"

"Have you been tested for STDs lately?"

I could feel my face go hot. I hadn't even thought about getting tested. Probably because no doctor had ever suggested it. Not when I'd never had sex before.

"I'm negative, and always use condoms," he said.

"Me too." I swallowed hard.

His eyes gleamed. "STD test results weren't part of your selection process, were they?"

"Yes. No." I covered my face with my hands and then dragged them down until the tips of my fingers were just below my eyes.

"STDs are an important topic. I'm glad you brought it up. But also, and to get less procedural, I'm attracted to you. I think you're attracted to me. It can also just be that simple."

He tilted his head. "You know I'm not going to be able to say no to you."

A rush of adrenaline shot straight to my heart. *Then he's saying yes. I think he's saying yes.*

"But I can't exactly say, 'Okay, let's have sex,' right now either."

Suddenly, I was an airplane signaling Mayday. My engines had died, and I was spiraling back to earth. "What's that supposed to mean?"

"Having sex should be..." A corner of his mouth tucked in, showing off his dimple. "Well, it should be spontaneous. But more importantly, I think my reputation will have a better chance of getting fixed if we don't hook up right away, don't you?"

"I was planning on making sure no one finds out what we're doing."

"So we'd just be good friends who like to sleep over in each other's room?"

"No." I rolled my eyes. "We would be so secretive that no one would ever see us together."

"We're together here."

"This is different. We're outside of the dorm. You don't have that same reputation in engineering classes. It's inside the dorm that's the problem."

I reached into my bag for my phone and woke it up. "How about next weekend?"

"That sounds like the complete opposite of spontaneous."

I resisted entering my password so I could schedule him into my calendar. "Oh."

"Besides," he said, "I'm busy next weekend."

"With what?" I asked.

"I thought you wanted no-strings sex?"

My throat went dry. *God, Ade. Get a grip.*

"Sorry." I put my phone back in my bag.

"No need to apologize." He shrugged. "I'm just taking your stipulations seriously."

"Fine," I said. "I get it. Impulsive. Impromptu. But what if this elusive moment never happens?"

"Don't worry." He spun his paper in a circle, his gaze slowly moving from my cleavage to my eyes, and he smiled. "It will happen."

EIGHTEEN
THE FLOOZY

We started on the homework, and it didn't take us long to finish the problem, which was a miracle. Usually, it took me forever, and I never knew if I had it right until I compared my answer to Jay's or found out in class that I'd done it all wrong.

We took it step-by-step. I'd start alone down a path, Dallas would rein me in, then point me in a different direction.

He was smart. Way smarter than me. Or maybe his way of solving a problem was more efficient than mine.

We packed up our stuff and headed back to the dorm.

A couple blocks away, he grabbed my hand and marched me into the snow behind the gigantic trunk of a cottonwood. He kissed me, making my heart pitter-patter.

No tongue. More like a nice-guy thing to do than a bad boy. This was confusing.

He pulled away, but hesitantly. "You go in first. I know that you don't want anyone to see us together."

I hooked my thumbs around my backpack straps.

He nodded. "Let's meet tomorrow at Linden Park to go skating."

"But we decided that would be crossing a line."

"No." He shook his head. "You decided that, I didn't."

I shrugged and left him there, leaning against the thick, ridged bark.

"Oh, come on," he shouted.

Looking over my shoulder, I grinned at him.

I trudged to the sidewalk and stomped the snow off my boots, knowing I'd go to the rink the next day. I wouldn't be able to stop myself. I'd take any opportunity I could just to be with him. Any opportunity that could lead to the spontaneous sex he wanted.

Inside the dorm, I pulled out my phone and saw that Eric had texted me.

ERIC
Sorry, Sis. Life's been hectic. Will call you soon.

You better!

I opened the door to my room and heard Priya's pop music playing on the speakers.

"The results are in," I called out over the beat. "He's officially a bad boy."

I let the door shut behind me and looked up. It was Jay staring back at me with a frown.

"Who's a bad boy?" he asked.

Dang.

"Where's Priya?" I dumped my backpack on my own desk and turned on my desk light.

"She left to watch TV."

I nodded. It was Sunday night. She was watching that horrible sci-fi show with the creepy-looking zombies.

"So who's the bad boy?" Jay asked again.

"Nobody. I thought I was talking to Priya." I hoped he'd let his question go unanswered. "What are you doing here?"

He pointed to a piece of paper on top of Priya's desk. "I thought we could do the physics homework together."

"I already did it." I glanced at his work.

"You did?"

"Yeah, and it looks like you finished yours too." I started digging through my backpack.

"When have you ever finished the physics homework by yourself?" Jay hung his arm over the back of Priya's chair.

I slipped the piece of paper out and waved it in the air. "There's a first time for everything."

"Not for physics homework." He squinted at me, his mouth in a straight line. "It's Dallas, isn't it?"

I wrinkled my nose.

"You did the homework with him." Jay made a clicking sound with his tongue. "He's the bad boy, isn't he?"

I continued to stay silent, now glancing over my work.

"So is that the way it's going to be now? You're one of his floozies?"

"Floozy?" I put my homework down. "Are you a grandma?"

"'Floozy' is a word."

"A stupid word. Besides, I'm not a floozy. We're just hanging out."

"Are you also hanging out with that girl in the hoodie who Sandra was talking about this morning?" Jay snickered. "Like a threesome?"

I unwound my scarf and threw it at him.

He ducked, but the fabric landed across the top of his head.

I wished it weren't soft and fuzzy. I wished it were a rock. A gigantic piece of granite. "Please stop being so ridiculous."

He pulled it off and tossed it onto my bed. "I'm not. Dallas is smoking hot. You'll have to beat people off to keep him to yourself, causing you even more anxiety."

Smirking, I went into my closet. But then I paused before I took off my jacket. *Wait a second.*

I backed out of the closet. "Did you just say that Dallas is hot?"

Jay's face went gray.

"You did. I heard you say it."

He shrugged. "So what? It's not like you don't think other girls are hot."

I shifted my weight. "I've thought girls were pretty or attractive, sure, but I don't think I've ever thought they were 'smoking hot.'"

"Whatever, forget it," he said. "My point is that history doesn't favor you and you're going to get hurt." Jay sealed his mouth shut.

"But I won't." Because I wasn't going to fall in love with Dallas. We'd established the ground rules. "Besides, last year I had the hundred-year flood of hurts and survived, so even if another flood happens again, it won't be as bad."

His eyes sparkled. "Did you know that a one-hundred-year flood doesn't mean that it occurs only once every one-hundred years? I think statistically there's a sixty percent chance of another hundred-year flood occurring in the same period."

I closed my eyes. "Jay."

"What?"

"Please stop being such a dork."

"Was that too nerdy?" He widened his smile.

"Yeah, you sound like a civil, not the material science engineer you want to be."

"Speaking of engineering," he said, "we should compare our physics homework."

I nodded, and we exchanged our problems. I sat down at my desk and glanced over his. We had the same answer. We even showed the same work to get there. My arms felt light and airy. I was getting this. I was doing better. *Dean's list, here I come.*

Jay let out a low whistle. "Wow, Ade. Looking good."

We returned our homework to each other, and Jay moved to the saucer chair.

"So about last night…" Jay folded his arms. "I just want you to know that I'm sorry I got caught up in Emma's little freak-out."

I breathed in and sighed. "It's okay."

"Really?" He tilted his head. "You seemed pretty upset, especially when she told everyone that you're a...a..."

"Virgin?"

"Yeah."

"You can say it, Jay. Vir-gin. It's not a hard word to pronounce."

"I know how to say it." He looked at the floor. "I just want you to know that *I* know that Emma was rude, and I'm sorry for any part I had in that."

"Are you a virgin, Jay?"

He glanced up. "Huh?"

"Are you a virgin too?"

He frowned.

Ha! I wasn't alone in this.

But then my neck tightened. He thought guys were hot, and he was still a virgin. Could he be closeted?

"You know what?" I felt bad for pressing him. "Don't answer that. I don't need to know."

Jay exhaled.

"What I do want you to know is that your apology is accepted."

"Good." He smiled slowly. "Thank you."

"So...moving on." I went to my closet, took off my jacket, and hung it up. "I need you to help me with something."

I looked down at myself. I still had on my low-cut shirt. I glanced behind me, at the top of Jay's head. It peeked out above the back of the chair. This shirt might be a good test for Jay. What kind of guy type was he? Did he think girls could be hot too?

"If it has to do with Dallas," he said, "I don't want to be involved."

"No, of course not." I stepped in front of him, my shoulders pulled back.

"Okay. Shoot." But Jay had laid his head back, and his eyes were closed.

Come on, Jay. Open them.

But he didn't move. He appeared to be content as he was.

"I need help with my grades." I paused, waiting for him to sit up and pay attention.

Nothing.

"What do you mean?" he asked.

"To recover from last semester, I might need straight As. But if that's impossible, I'll concede with a mix of As and Bs."

Finally, he opened his eyes. "How badly did you do?"

"Under a two-point-oh."

His brows shot up, but he wasn't even looking at my chest. Like he didn't even care. I drew my arms together to make my cleavage more pronounced.

"You need a two-point-eight to get into the third and fourth years of chemical engineering." His eyes didn't stray. He barely even blinked.

"Duh, I know that. Hence the plea for help."

He placed his arms behind his head, his elbows sticking up in the air. Still nothing. Not even a stealthy look.

"Doing old tests from previous semesters is a good way to study before an exam," Jay said.

"And where would I find those?"

He sat up. "The school has an online database."

"They do?"

"Yes, but I'm not sure how current they are. I could talk to some of the sophomores and juniors on the cross-country team who are in engineering. They might have kept theirs."

"That would be awesome, Jay."

"No problem." He grabbed onto the sides of the chair, pushed himself up, and then gathered his things. "I'll see you tomorrow."

"Sure."

And without glancing at me again, he left.

I stared at the closed door, then down at my boobs. Interesting. I mean, not Jay's willingness to help me with my classes or his concerns about my well-being, but his complete disregard for what any straight, horny male would like to look at without having to page through a Victoria's Secret catalog. Not that I wanted him to, because we were friends, but wow. I'd expected at least a snide comment, not complete indifference.

Back at my closet, I changed and then started digging for my ice skates.

I wasn't going to confront Jay about his sexuality. I wouldn't want to put him in an awkward position, and I didn't want to offend him if I was wrong. But I was going to have to pay more attention to the words I used, the actions I took. I wanted him to know I would be supportive of him no matter what.

My hand landed on my skating bag, and I pulled it out. I unzipped the top and lifted one of the boots out. The Vaseline I'd applied to the blades last summer to prevent them from oxidizing was still intact. I grinned.

It was going to be fun skating with Dallas.

NINETEEN
THE SKATE DATE

laced up my skates. They weren't as comfortable as I remembered, and the blades needed sharpening, but otherwise they felt all right.

I stood, my heart beating a little faster. It had been a while since I'd stepped onto the ice. Too busy with school.

After I did a couple laps, Dallas was still nowhere to be seen, but at that moment, I didn't care. The cold air whooshed across my face, and the edges of my skates carved deep into the ice underneath me. It couldn't get much better. I turned around and did some backward crossovers into a spin. I'd missed this. The feeling of flying.

Until Dallas whipped past and bumped my shoulder. That was the thing about hockey players. They always wanted to show off how fast they were, and how they could stop on a dime and switch directions. That trick didn't impress me. I was influenced by gracefulness. The movement from one technical element to the next with the ease of a plane lifting off the ground and into the sky.

To me, figure skating was the superior sport. Of course, I was biased because I was never good at stick handling. When I'd played hockey, I was the outcast. The shy girl who didn't play tough, who kept her angst inside and didn't have the internal desire to be the aggressive scrapper my father had wanted me to be.

I turned forward on one foot, gliding. Ahead, Dallas was holding the ledge behind him and leaning against the boards. I did a T-stop next to him.

"Hey," he said, slightly out of breath. "It's good to see you."

"Me too." I looked up at the spotlights above the rink. They were tall and massive. It would be fun if it were dark outside.

"You *were* a hockey cheerleader, weren't you?"

I looked at him. "Sorry to disappoint you."

If he'd known me in high school, he'd never have looked at me twice. I'd been awkward and nerdy. The girl who didn't talk to boys much and never attempted to draw their attention.

"Come on." He pushed off and looked back at me, his smile making the creases beside his lips run deep. I sighed, wanting to trace them with my tongue. And therein was the problem of all problems. My being so attracted to him didn't give me the upper hand.

We skated for a while, and it was wonderful. At one point, I started doing jump warm-up exercises. Of course, I didn't just want to go for something easy. I wanted to dazzle him, which quite possibly could lead to impetuous sex.

I did a single Axel-single loop. The Axel went great, and I landed it clean, but I underrotated the loop and fell on my ass. Pain ripped through my tailbone, and I winced, hard. The older, heavier me had arrived.

Dallas helped me up. "Are you okay?"

"I'm fine, but I think my skating for the day is over." We left the ice, and I eased myself onto a bench.

Sitting there, I wished I hadn't done the combination jump. I wasn't sure which was more bruised, my bottom or my ego. Hobbling back to campus wasn't going to be sexy. It was not going to result in me being pushed up against a wall with my legs wrapped around him. All it meant was I needed some ibuprofen.

"So are you going to the ice cross finals on Friday night?" He unlaced his first skate.

"The what?" I bent over to undo mine, and a stinging sensation went straight down my legs.

He was working on his second skate. "It's an extreme sport being hosted in the cities this weekend. Athletes race on skates down an ice track."

"Sounds dangerous."

"It can be, but it's totally awesome." He finished and put on his shoes. "They're setting up a village next to the course with tents for drinking and eating and other stuff too."

A fluttering filled my stomach. Another chance to be with him. Another chance at spur-of-the-moment sex. "Are you going?"

"Yeah." He stood up.

"You want to go together?"

"Oh." He frowned. "I can't."

His response hit me like a dozen tiny knives being thrown at my chest.

But seriously, what was wrong with me? Why had I asked for us to go there together anyway? It was in complete violation of my own ground rules—not to participate in anything relationship-y.

Actually, I knew why it hurt. Because I was trying to find that elusive moment when the "just sex" part of our deal would actually happen. Right now it seemed like an insurmountable peak that only an experienced mountaineer could conquer.

"Sorry." He examined me. "I was just mentioning it because I thought you'd have fun going with your friends. I'll already be there, but you can text me and we might be able to meet up."

I nodded as I finished taking my skates off. But all I heard was the word "might." I put the guards on the blades and put my skates into the bag. At this rate, I *might* still be sexless by spring break.

TWENTY
THE RACE

"Ice cross, huh?" the Uber driver asked.

"Yep." Jay sat in the passenger seat in front of me and fastened his belt.

"I'm not sure how close I'll be able to get, but I'll try."

I looked out the window to see if any other app-based cars had come yet to pick up Jay's cross-country friends from the dorm. But my breath fogged the glass and blocked my view. At least it wasn't frost. A warm front had moved in, and we were experiencing temperatures in the high twenties. When a January thaw hit, you went outside as much as possible. Everyone needed a surge of fresh air.

The driver took off and then jerked to an abrupt stop. The three of us in the back seat braced ourselves.

The car accelerated again.

Good thing my tailbone had stopped hurting from that fall I'd taken on the ice.

Priya pulled out her phone. "Emma, make sure you split the fare before we get there."

Seconds later, my phone dinged at me, and I accepted the charge.

I kept looking at my phone, hoping for a new text from Dallas, but there was none. This morning, he hadn't been in our chemistry lecture, and even though neither of us had attempted to connect in class before, I'd been disappointed. No fine shoulders to stare at for an entire hour.

I took a deep breath. Well, if he wasn't going to text me, I would text him.

> On my way to ice cross.
>
> Where are you?

I waited, but nothing. The message said delivered, but not read. I put the phone to sleep and put it back in my crossbody bag.

Priya was elevated on the center hump, inches taller than me. I was like a child stuck in the corner. With nothing to see out the window, I listened to her chatter, making sure to lean back whenever her waving arms got too close to my face.

"It's a twelve-hundred-foot track of ice and drops ninety feet." It almost sounded like Priya was out of breath. "There are turns and jumps and a hill to ascend. I read online that the skaters can reach speeds of over forty miles per hour."

I paused to listen closer, trying to glean as much information as I could.

She kept on. "They've been running heats all day to narrow it down to the semifinal pool of competitors, and from that number, the fastest will continue on to tomorrow's finals."

"Are you feeling okay, Priya?" Emma asked.

"Of course." She was smiley and bouncy. "Why?"

"I've never seen you this excited about...well, pretty much anything before."

I had. When she'd found out I was the girl in the hoodie.

Priya's eyes widened. "I love the Winter Olympics. When they're on, I'm glued to the television."

Jay cleared his throat. "This isn't the Olympics or an Olympic sport."

"I know that." Priya licked her lips. "But it's the closest I've ever come."

"Give her a break." Emma was tapping away on her phone. "From what I can tell, it's kind of like snowboard cross or ski cross. Those are in the Olympics."

Soon we were standing shoulder to shoulder among thousands of people. It didn't seem possible for us to find other people we knew, but somehow Jay's cross-country guys found us.

I was enthralled by the production of circling spotlights, the glistening serpentine track, and the roars and whistles coming from the crowd. Cowbells rang on all sides of me. I didn't have a drop of alcohol in me, yet I was dizzy.

The loudspeaker system echoed in my ears. Then over the shouts came "Racers ready. Five-second warning."

I rose onto my tiptoes. We still hadn't muscled our way close enough to the track.

"Can you see what's going on?" I asked Jay.

He pointed to a huge video screen. The camera zoomed in on the top of the track, where four riders were crouched behind gates, their names listed below them. There were female workers up there too, standing behind them, smiling, wearing cold-weather berets and black peacoats.

A long, high-pitched horn sounded. On the screen, the four competitors shot out of the gates and flew down the track on their skates.

I sucked in a breath, unable to tear my eyes away from the monitor. There were bumps and turns, jumps, and then the two skaters in front ascended a hill. The first threw a trick in the air at the top. The last two collided, and even though they tried to scramble up the hill using their blades, they slid right back down. The first and second skated through the finish line, the last two looking like ice crystals in their wake.

My heart raced. *Wow.* Completely reckless, but oh so thrilling to watch.

Emma whistled on one side of me.

Priya clapped and cheered on the other. "That was awesome. So awesome."

I was amazed. The race had started and finished so quickly that if it had been me, I'd still be at the top trying to muster the courage to start.

Priya grabbed my hand. "Let's get closer."

The four of us and the cross-country runners maneuvered as best we could, getting within fifty feet of the track. I glanced up at the screen again and saw the next set of racers finding their positions. There were those girls again in berets, each standing behind one of the four start gates, looking like female *The Price Is Right* models with their correct postures, beautiful smiles, and teased hair. Were they eye candy or did they actually have a job to do up there?

The next set of four was ready. The referee, in black-and-white-stripes, started announcing. But before the horn blew, one of the riders blasted through the gate. The crowd groaned. The disqualified rider skated the course to the end. From where I was, he looked like an ant falling down a sand dune made of glistening white fondant.

False start, and apparently there were no second chances in this sport.

"Come on." Priya was moving again, pulling me with her. "We have to get to the bottom, where the racers come off the track."

"Impossible," Jay said. "There are way too many people to get that close."

"Where there's a will, there's a way," Priya shouted.

Jay stayed with his friends, while Priya, Emma, and I plowed through the spectators and almost reached the spot she'd wanted.

Behind me, Emma let out a hollow breath. "Omigod."

"What?" I glanced her way.

She pointed to the screen.

I spun around but didn't see anything out of the ordinary, just the gates, the racers in helmets, masks, and pads and, of course, those girls behind them. Then a name jumped out at me.

Dallas Reynolds.

It was him. He was on top of that insane track, behind the fourth gate, pointed toward the very bottom. Only him and two other skaters left.

Well, I'd found him. Not where I'd expected him to be, that was for sure. I pushed closer to the track until I was able to stand at the rail. He hadn't told me. Hadn't said he was competing. My heart sped up. Why?

"Racers ready. Five-second warning."

I looked back for Jay and saw him about twenty yards away, staring at the screen.

I wasn't going to be able to see the skaters live until they got to the very last section, so I watched the monitor. The horn sounded, and I held my breath.

Dallas launched from the gate. He didn't make it to the front, but he was close behind the leader.

My stomach spun. I wanted him to win so badly that my insides hurt.

People cheered all around me, but I didn't make a sound. Dallas maneuvered the bumps and hairpin turns. When he reached the obstacle that the announcers called the volcano, my hands formed into fists. The uphill was so high. The racers needed a ton of momentum to get up there.

He succeeded, but the three of them were neck and neck, flying down the drop. They sped past me, and I could feel their drafts against my face.

Dallas finished last. Not enough points to move on in the competition. But it didn't seem to bother him. He was giving high fives to the other two, pounding them on the shoulders.

He took off his helmet. His hair stuck up in all directions, making him look sexier than ever. I wanted to shout his name, but I couldn't find the nerve or my voice.

He skated to the exit door and slid to a stop. My jaw dropped. Hanging over the barrier was Priya. How had she gotten over there?

She held out her fist, and they gave each other knucks. Priya was talking to him, and then she pointed at me. Before he even turned to look, my neck and face turned spicy hot.

We made eye contact, and a surge of energy sizzled between us, making my eyes water. He grinned and waved. I gave him a thumbs-up.

A thumbs-up. How lame.

He said something to Priya and then walked out the door and stopped, because one of those chicks in a black peacoat was standing right in front of him. His back was to me, so I couldn't see his face, but I could see hers. Bright, cheery, animated.

She twirled one finger through a long spiral curl, rose to her toes, and gave him a peck on his cheek.

I wanted to puke.

Stop it, Ade. Stop it. He wasn't mine. Yes, I wanted his body, but not his soul. He could flirt with whomever he wanted. The more the better. No way could I get attached to him, then.

For all of my mental reasoning, my heart still ached. Which meant I was in deep trouble. I'd talked the talk—no strings attached. But maybe I was a spider, living on silk threads, unable to survive without capturing him in my web.

TWENTY-ONE
DITCHED

A tap fell on my shoulder. It was Priya, breathing hard. "You're supposed to meet Dallas at O'Sullivan's."

"O'Sullivan's?"

"The Irish grill and pub down the road. They have a tent set up in their parking lot."

Emma pulled on Priya from behind her. "Would someone please tell me what's going on?"

Priya ignored her and turned back to me. "I'll go with you if you want."

"I don't know," I said. "I kind of feel weird about it."

"Wait a second." Emma stepped in between us now.

I looked straight at her.

"I thought we hated him," Emma said.

Priya glanced at her. "It turns out we don't. We're going to O'Sullivan's—are you coming with us?"

Emma frowned. "I guess, but I'm so confused, and what about Jay?"

He was still with his cross-country friends, watching the next race.

"Looks like he already ditched us. We'll text him." Priya grabbed my arm. "Let's go."

"Why are you doing this?" I asked Priya, keeping up with her as Emma trailed behind. "Why are you working so hard at making sure I see Dallas?"

I mean, I was happy I had a friend on my side, but at the same time, something was off. *I* was off.

"I'm living vicariously through you."

The muscles in my face slackened. "What?"

"My love life is boring, routine. Yours, Ade, is exciting, and I'm having so much fun!"

I narrowed my gaze on her. "Have you talked to Luke about how you feel?"

"No." She shrugged. "But I probably should."

I nodded. I really hoped she would.

The three of us made it to O'Sullivan's. Inside the tent, there was a music stage and long tables with benches set up. I almost turned around and went back outside. I was more nervous than I'd been the night I slept in Dallas's room. I think it was the four days that had elapsed since we'd last spoken. Four days was a long time.

Priya eyed me, as if she could sense that I wanted to get the hell out of there. "We'll stay with you. For as long as you want us to."

After Priya looked through the tent for Dallas and decided he wasn't there yet, we got some cocoa and sat at a table—Emma and Priya across from me. Propane heat lamps dotted the interior, but I was still cold. I kept my jacket, hat, and mittens on.

I took a sip of the hot liquid. When it reached my frozen stomach, it churned like milk being made into a brick of ice cream.

Emma wiped her fingers on a napkin. "So, can one of you explain to me how it went from Dallas is a complete jerk to let's-skip-the-rest-of-the-races-and-make-sure-Ade-meets-up-with-him?"

Priya rocked in her seat. "Since last weekend, when Ade told me that she's the girl in the hoodie."

"What?" Emma's mouth dropped open.

Both of their gazes fell on me.

I glared at Priya. "You *promised*."

She shrugged. "It's better if Emma knows. Otherwise, she won't understand."

I sighed and folded my arms on the table.

"Get out of here." Emma's voice seemed louder than it had before. "You slept with him?"

"No, nothing like that."

"But you were seen leaving his room in the morning."

"I know."

Emma's shoulders drooped. "I can't believe it's been almost a week and you didn't tell me until now."

My mouth pursed. I hadn't told her because she hadn't been able to keep her mouth shut of late. But I probably should have. She was my friend. A friend I didn't want to lose.

I took off my hat and mittens and unzipped my jacket halfway. I was getting a bit warmer. "Well, here's something I haven't told either of you."

"What?" they chimed in together.

"I've decided he's the one. He meets my criteria. He's going to cure my insomnia."

"That's awesome, Ade." Priya put up her hand, and I gave her a high five. "I'm so happy for you."

Emma, on the other hand, knitted her brows. "How do you know he's the one?"

Things got quiet around the table, and I gave Emma a hard stare. "Because I do."

"Because you totally dig him, don't you?" Priya's eyes sparkled.

My stomach wouldn't stop rolling. "Yes, but I'll admit I'm nervous too."

Petrified really. Our impromptu sex could happen at any time —it could happen tonight—and what if it wasn't perfect enough?

Emma started picking at threads on the sleeve of her jacket.

"Well, if either of you want my opinion, I'm still not totally convinced."

"I am." Priya was beaming.

Emma glanced at Priya. "But what about everything else we know about him?"

Priya raised her hands, palms up. "Who cares?"

"I don't know. I'm hesitant, and I think Ade should be too."

After a short lull, a tray of three creamy shots appeared on our table.

"Hi, ladies." It was Dallas, no longer in his gear but still wearing his racing jersey. He smiled down at us in that way that always made my insides feel like unset glue. "I thought you all could use a little something to warm up your cocoa."

"Awesome!" Priya watched him distribute the plastic tumblers around the table.

Emma lifted her shot to her nose and took a sniff. "Baileys."

Priya poured hers in and took a sip. "Mm, this is good. Really good."

Emma dumped the shot into her cup and swirled it around. "You're definitely getting points for being thoughtful."

I added my own, stacked the shot cups up, and put them back on the tray.

"I'll be right back." He picked up the tray. "My dad's here, and I've got to find him."

He walked away, and I almost choked. "Did he just say his dad?"

Both Emma and Priya nodded in unison, their eyes bright.

I watched Dallas go to the bar and return the cups. He glanced at his phone. Typed, and within moments, an older man carrying a half-filled pint of beer walked up to him and hugged him. He was the same height as Dallas and had a similar sloped nose, but with short silver hair and a thick waist.

I took a large gulp of my cocoa and Baileys. It heated a path straight to my stomach.

They talked for a little bit and then both headed in our direction.

"Dad, these are the friends from the dorm I was talking about. Ade, Priya, Emma, this is my dad, Mike."

Priya chimed in without missing a beat. "Hi, Mike, nice to meet you."

"Nice to meet you too." His dad smiled—the same smile as his son's.

Priya gave me a look and a slight nod.

But I still couldn't find words.

"Is it okay if we sit with you?" Dallas asked.

"Of course," Priya said, keeping the conversation going.

Dallas's warm body slid onto the bench to my left, smelling musky.

My heart slowed to a more restful pace. Funny how that happened. How being close to him relaxed me more than not. Even with one of his parents around. I wouldn't have thought it would be that way.

His dad sat on my right.

"You must have been watching Dallas race," Priya said to his dad.

"Yeah. Pretty great stuff. What did you all think of it?"

Dallas's hand found my thigh, and a tingle ran up my femur and into my hip joint.

I nudged his hand away. His dad was sitting right there.

"It's pretty incredible," Emma piped up. "How did you get into ice cross, Dallas?"

"In December, they set up a small training course at Buck Hill. I was looking for a new sport and decided to give it a try. I did it once, and I was hooked."

"Do women race?" Emma asked.

"Yeah, their championships are tomorrow." His hand was back on my leg, and he squeezed. "You want to try it, Ade? Get you back in some hockey pads and skates."

Dallas's dad, Priya, and Emma shifted their attention to me.

My neck steamed. I'd never told them about my skating past. It treaded too close to the stuff about my dad.

"You played hockey?" Dallas's dad asked.

"A little," I squeaked.

"I didn't know that." Priya leaned in.

"Yeah, it was a long time ago."

"She's better at figure skating," Dallas said.

"Figure skating?" Emma asked.

"Yeah, I was part of a club. Actually, I still am. I have a college membership now."

"That's really cool," Emma said. "You'll have to take us skating sometime."

Dallas's dad finished his beer and said he had to take off.

"Great to meet you all." Then he passed out his business card, explaining how he worked at a car dealership. "Any of you ever need a car, come find me."

"Dad," Dallas said with a sharp tone.

"You never know, son." His dad patted the back of his shoulder before he left. "Networking is key."

I inspected the card and then slid it into the zipped pocket of my jacket.

We finished our drinks.

"Your dad seems really nice," Priya said.

"Yeah, he's cool. Sorry about the business card though. He just got this new job, and he's taking it pretty seriously."

"You have any siblings?" Emma asked.

"Yeah, two older sisters."

My ears perked up. We had never talked about his own family, just mine.

"Do they live around here?" I asked.

"No, my oldest sister and her husband live in San Diego. My other sister is in the air force in Pensacola."

"Wow, I didn't know," I said. "How much older?"

"Six and eight years."

He, Emma, and Priya continued talking about how his sister ended up in the military.

I could feel the alcohol just a bit and needed to use the bathroom. So I excused myself and left the table, but halfway there, I realized leaving the three of them together might have been a bad idea.

I sped up, and of course when I got there, there was a line.

I waited and waited. Just as I became the next up for a stall, my phone dinged. I pulled it out.

PRIYA
Emma and I left. Have fun!

What?
I typed a furious response.'

Wait for me!

PRIYA
Stay. Dallas will bring you home. He promised us.

I went to the bathroom as fast as I could and ran back into the tent. Sure enough, there was Dallas, sitting by himself, Priya and Emma nowhere to be found.

TWENTY-TWO
THE VIEW

forced my legs to move even though it was like walking against a fast-flowing river. This time, instead of sitting next to him, I sat across from him, my stomach doing front flips.

"So I guess I've been ditched." I put my hands under my knees.

He smiled at me, his eyes alive and sparkling. "I wouldn't say that. More like you've traded up."

"You think I'll have a better time with you?"

"Of course." He stood and held out his hand. "Let's go."

I stared at his hand, then back up at his face. "Go where?"

"Not sure, but I think it has something to do with my car, a bottle of wine, and a view."

It was the view that got me. I couldn't imagine a better one than staring at him. I put my hand in his.

His car was parked a few blocks away on the street at a meter. It was a blue Subaru Impreza. We got in, and I looked around. The interior wasn't spotless, but it was orderly and empty of belongings. He warmed up the car, and we took off.

"I have an important question for you," I said.

"Ask away." He made a turn.

"Why didn't you say that the reason you couldn't go to the ice cross event with me was because you were in it?"

"I had no idea how qualifications were going to go today, so I didn't want to make plans. Like I said, a new sport."

"And if you sucked at it, you didn't want me to know."

"Maybe." He smiled. "Guys have egos, you know."

We pulled into a parking lot at a liquor store.

"I have another question."

He parked the car. "What?"

"How do you purchase alcohol when you're underage?"

He laughed. "How old do you think I am?"

"You're a freshman. So, nineteen. Maybe twenty if you took a gap year."

He grinned and opened his door. "I'm twenty-one."

I tilted my head. "But I thought—"

Dallas shut the door, leaving the car running for me. It didn't take him long. Soon we were back on the road with a glass bottle in a brown bag.

"Okay. You need to explain. How can you be twenty-one years old?" I asked.

He switched lanes. "I played juniors for two years after high school."

"Junior hockey?"

He nodded.

"Which league?"

"The USHL." He looked over his shoulder and switched back.

"That's tier one."

"I guess so."

"Which means you're really good."

He shrugged. "I haven't played a game since the season ended last April, so probably not."

"I don't understand. Usually tier-one hockey players go on to play some level of college hockey. Why aren't you?"

He parked on an incline and cranked the emergency brake into place.

"Well" I urged.

He didn't move, just stared down at his hand gripping the stick shift. "Sometimes things don't work out and you have to start down a different path." He glanced at me. "But then sometimes the new path intersects with the old, and it's hard to know which path you're supposed to be on."

Dallas popped the trunk and got out of the car with the bottle of wine.

Hearing him rummaging in the back, I sat still. Old path. New path. He was really good at speaking in riddles. Especially when it came to preserving his male ego.

I got out and came around the car. Dallas had pulled out a bright orange sled and a blanket.

"We're going sledding?"

"Maybe. It might be a good way to get down the hill after we're done seeing the view."

He put the wine and the blanket in the sled, and we started up the sidewalk. It curved around until we reached some partially cleared steps leading up to the top of the hill. We made it, and embarrassingly enough, I was out of breath. He wasn't. Now that I thought about it, when we'd gone skating the other day, I hadn't heard him huff or puff once.

There was a bench at the top of the hill. He brushed it off and laid out the blanket, and we sat down next to each other. He'd been right. The view was incredible.

Tree branches framed the night sky. In the distance, I could see the lighted skyscrapers. Each building had its own shape and size, and observing them like this, all together, I felt small. Insignificant.

"It's gorgeous," I said.

He nodded while twisting the cap off the bottle, which he'd left in the bag.

"Here, ladies first." He handed me the wine.

I took a sip. It tasted like the complete opposite of wine. "Is this Boone's Farm?"

"What?" He grabbed it from me and took a gulp. "Ew, that's way sweet."

I took the bag back and lifted the bottle out to inspect the label. Arbor Mist. Same thing. "You don't know much about wine, do you?"

"Not really. I just grabbed the first thing I saw in the cooler that didn't have a cork. I probably should have done some research."

I bumped his upper arm with mine. "What kind of engineer are you?"

He smiled. "One who likes beer."

"Well, we can't let it go to waste." I took another mouthful.

Together, we cringed our way through the bottle. He told me about his preparation for the race that day. Our shared magic of being on the ice, whether it was a rink or an ice cross hill. I knew he was being genuine because while I might not be an expert on girly wine, I did know there wasn't enough alcohol content in it to make us even the slightest bit drunk.

I shivered. Partly from the chill and partly from the cold liquid in my stomach. Dallas pulled the blanket around us, and I cuddled up against him. His warm breath thawed my nose and my cheeks. I looked up at him, and we kissed. He tasted sweet and fruity.

Soon, I was in his lap, the heat of him all around me, but the bulkiness of our jackets created an irritating barrier. I wanted to get closer to him, to feel my skin against his.

His lips found my forehead, and he tucked my head under his chin. "I think we should go. Being naked outside in January was not in my plans."

The word "naked" made my throat burn. This was it. Our moment had come. I was going to get laid. I waited for my heart to go into a frenzy with nerves, but it didn't. Dallas was right, sex should come naturally. Not be preplanned.

He set up the sled with the blanket and the bottle and climbed in, leaving space for me between his legs. I tugged on the ends of my hair and secured my hat in place. This might be just the opportunity I needed to make sure I'd get what I wanted this time.

I stepped in, lifted my jacket, and sat down, then shimmied up against his crotch. Just enough pressure for him to notice, not enough to hurt.

"Hey," he whispered into my ear.

There was nothing he could do about it. His hands were grounded in the snow, keeping us steady and in position to head down the hill.

I did it again, rubbed my ass against him, right where it would count. And then I felt it. His growing need pressing against the seam of my jeans.

"Fuck." He let go, and we started flying down the hill.

I laughed, the cold wind burning my face.

The sled pulled a bit right. Then so much it started to turn. Dallas was trying to redirect it, but before I knew it, the sled leaned so hard it dumped us right out. I skidded to a stop, my cheek dragging against the icy snow. The sled was now turned backward and going down the hill all by itself. I turned over, wiped the cold water from my face, and found Dallas spread-eagled on the hill, staring up at the sky.

I crawled over to him and sat beside him on my knees. "Are you okay?"

He turned his head and looked me straight in the eyes. "I'm going to get you back for that."

I smiled so hard the muscles in my face hurt.

He scrambled up, and I took off, screaming, trying my best to plow through the knee-deep snow back to the car. He grabbed me from behind, and the next thing I knew, I was on my back being kissed so thoroughly, the world faded from existence. His silky tongue, the heaviness of him on me… He didn't even have to touch me; I wanted him.

I tried to wrap my legs around him, but it was awkward and impossible with our boots.

We stopped kissing, and he arranged my hair, his gaze brushing across my entire face. "Let's get out of here."

"Okay." But I didn't move.

"I mean right now." He pulled me up.

Somehow we unglued from each other for as long as it took us to get the blanket, the sled, and the bottle back in the car and us into our seats. One more kiss, and we were back on the road and stopping at the front entrance of our dorm.

"Don't you need to park your car?"

He took a key off his ring and handed it to me. "Let yourself into my room. I'll meet you there."

I took it, but hesitated. "I can go with you."

"No, this is better." He gave me a little nudge with his shoulder and raised an eyebrow. "Wouldn't want anyone to see us together, now would we?"

"Oh, right." I let myself out of the car.

He sped away, his red taillights disappearing.

I winced. Now that my friends knew I was hanging with Dallas, and they had given me their stamp of approval by leaving me with him at the pub, this whole not wanting people to see us together seemed foolish.

In the lobby, it was still early in the night, and there were people milling around, socializing.

I aimed for the hallway, but a clacking sound followed me.

"Hi, Adriana." It was Sandra in her flip-flops, flannel pants, and a university sweatshirt. "I heard that you went to ice cross. How was it?"

"It was fun." I tried edging away from her, but she wouldn't let me—she'd boxed me in.

"Cool." She jutted her hip out and shifted her weight to one leg. "Didn't you go with Priya and Emma?"

"Yeah."

"Where are they?"

"I don't know." My gaze shifted to the front door.

"So what are you doing for the rest of the night?"

"Nothing."

"Oh, come on, it's still pretty early. You must be doing something?"

God, she was so nosy. She must make multiple passes by the lobby every day just to see who was here. It was annoying.

The front door opened, and a breeze of cold air swooped in. It was Dallas.

I looked at her. I looked at him. But I didn't have that uh-oh feeling inside me. Instead, there was something glowing. Hot and burning. I didn't care about what she would think or say about me if she knew I was with Dallas.

A grin spread across my face. "Actually, Sandra, Dallas and I are doing something together tonight. Have you two met?"

It was one of those moments where one revealed they'd murdered Professor Plum in the library with the lead pipe.

Dallas frowned.

Sandra gave him an intense, feverish stare. "We know each other, don't we, Dallas?"

He flinched back slightly. "Sure."

My smile wavered. She was the one. The revenge-seeker who'd started the rumors about him. I just knew it.

I swallowed slowly. I didn't know what to do, what to say.

The only thing I knew was I disliked her immensely. From her blonde hair to her cute, upturned nose, to her tiny ass and purple-painted toenails. But I wouldn't let her ruin this night.

I grabbed Dallas's hand. "Sorry, we have to get going."

He nodded. "You're right. We do."

"Good night," I called to Sandra as we stepped away. My palms were sweaty and my stomach felt like a mass of buzzing honeybees.

Dallas squeezed my hand as we walked together through the hall to the stairs. I paused at the bottom and let go.

"Are you okay?" he asked.

"Sandra's the one who started the rumors about you, isn't she?"

His shoulders sagged a little. "Yeah, she's the one."

I squeezed my eyes shut. Which also meant he probably had slept with her, and for whatever reason, she was making him pay for it. *Stop it, Ade. Stop it. Remember, you don't care about that stuff.* And even if they did, it was before I even knew he existed.

"Ade?" Dallas's voice was strong.

I opened my eyes and found him staring at me.

"I thought you didn't want people in the dorm to see us together?"

I started up the stairs, and he followed. I glanced at him sideways. The answer to his question was clear, but I wasn't ready to say it aloud or even admit it to myself. I didn't want us to hide anymore, because somehow, somewhere, and contrary to the voice in my head, this thing between us had become about more than just sex. I wanted to be with him. I wanted people to know. I wanted to be just a regular girl attracted to a guy who made me feel special. Was that so horrible?

Stopping at his room, I passed him the key. "I guess I just don't care about the not-being-seen-together thing anymore."

"Really?" He lifted an eyebrow.

"Let people talk. It'll be fun to find out what they say."

"Sounds good to me." He unlocked the door and let us in.

"But there is one thing…"

The door closed behind him. "What?"

I didn't really want to ask him. But I had to. I had to know. "Sandra said that the night of that party, the one when we…when we first…"

"Kissed?"

"Yes, when we first kissed, you took home a different girl and fucked her. Is that true?"

TWENTY-THREE
IT FINALLY HAPPENS

allas snapped his head back and froze.

I waited.

He sighed and then flopped onto the futon. "Did Sandra really say that to you?"

"Well." I sat next to him. "Kind of. She told Emma, and Emma told me."

"Okay." He sat straight. "First, I need to do some explaining, and then I can answer the question." He took his jacket off. "The truth is, last fall, Sandra had a—"

I clapped my hand over his mouth. "If you're about to tell me that you slept with Sandra, I don't want to know."

I felt his lips move into a smile under my hand.

"Sorry." I lifted my palm away from him. "There are some things I just can't handle."

He kept smiling. "Are you jealous of Buford Hall's gossip queen?"

"No. Never." I rubbed my hands together. "Well, maybe."

He put his hand on my thigh. "I didn't sleep with her."

Whew. Turns out the thought of it made me want to gag.

"What happened was she had a thing for me and I knew it." He paused. "And this is the part where I admit I was a prick. I sort of led her on. I didn't really mean to, but I didn't quash her fixation either."

I slipped off my jacket, reached for his hand, and put it back on my thigh.

"Needless to say, one night she was all over me, and I ended up hanging out with a different girl. It was a dick move, I know, but I thought it was a way to make her understand that I wasn't interested without having to tell her. Now Sandra despises me."

"But you still haven't answered my question."

"Oh. Sorry, no. The answer is no. How would I have thought about someone else that night when all I was thinking about was my next move with you?"

"Your next move, huh?" I threaded my fingers through his. "What was your next move?"

"Reconnaissance."

"When you asked Jay if I was dating him?"

He nodded.

I smiled. "Then what?"

"Do you really think us talking in the laundry room was an accident?"

"It wasn't?" The pitch of my voice rose. I hadn't expected him to say that.

He shook his head. "I wasn't going to leave things to chance."

"I thought guys didn't get worked up about that kind of stuff." I squinted.

"We don't, but we do understand the concept of making our own luck."

From the futon, Dallas tossed both of our jackets onto his desk. He picked up his computer and opened it. "You want to pick out a movie to watch?"

I stilled. "A movie?"

No. There was one thing that was going to happen in this room right now, and it had nothing to do with a tomato-meter or popcorn.

He glanced at me.

"Um…" I said.

He grinned, setting his computer back down. "You don't want to watch a movie, do you?"

"No." My heart pumped, and my feet numbed.

He closed the distance between us. "Me neither."

His mouth was on me, and I slid my arms around his neck. I hadn't realized it, but he'd taken his shoes off when he entered the room, and I still had my boots on.

I tried my best to kick them off, but they were the kind that zipper up.

"What are you doing?" Dallas mumbled against my mouth.

"My boots."

He pulled away and looked down.

"I need to take them off."

He bent down and unzipped them. I watched him intently, his shoulder blades moving in his back. I ran my hands over them. They were perfect in every way.

With the boots off, he sat back up.

My hands were still on his shoulders, so I moved them down to this waist. "Can I take your shirt off?"

He nodded, one corner of his mouth rising into a half grin. He helped me pull it off, but I still had to contend with another layer —one of those performance shirts. *Grr.* So I took that off too. Underneath was much more than I'd expected. It wasn't that he had bulging biceps or pecs or a giant six pack, but he had just the right amount of toned muscles.

I ran my fingers over him. His skin was hot, and I wanted to press my cheek against it. "How about your pants too?"

He rested his finger under my jawbone and lifted my chin. "I think we need a different game here. I feel like I'm losing."

"What kind of game?"

His eyes glinted. "Like I took off my shirt, now you take off yours. I take off my pants, you take off yours."

"That's doable."

Before I could take a breath, he already had the neck of my

shirt over my head. *Shoot, my bra.* This one gave me nice cleavage, but it wasn't the lacy black one I'd intended for this moment.

He groaned, sliding a finger under a strap. "Have I told you how beautiful you are?"

"Yes, actually you have. The night at the house party when you wanted to get in my pants."

He paused. "That's not exactly how I remember it."

"Yes, it was. You were totally hitting on me."

"Actually, I wanted to make sure that when you went home you wouldn't forget me."

I swallowed hard, gooseflesh traveling across my bare skin. "I'm cold, and you're a furnace," I said. "I think you owe me some heat."

He obliged without complaint, pulling me into his chest and nibbling on my ear.

A shudder went straight into my pelvis.

"The pants," I whispered. "Don't forget your pants."

Soon we were both down to our underwear. Mine bikini. His boxer briefs. He pulled me into his bed, and I wanted to celebrate.

The kissing went into full force. I could have made out with him for hours and hours and not minded. His kisses weren't the stuff of boys, slurp and tongue. They were all man. Warm, skillful, teasing. His mouth was everywhere and then again nowhere at all.

A tingling sensation started in my core and spread all over my body.

But making out wasn't why I was here. Well, maybe it was, but we needed to stay on track. We needed to get rid of the rest of our garments, the ones that were just getting in the way, before I chickened out and lost the self-confidence I had.

I put my hands behind my back to unhook my bra.

"Hey." He pulled his mouth away. "That's my job."

"Then what are you waiting for?"

His face turned a little redder than it already was.

It didn't take him much to get my bra off. My breasts were

free, and I gasped, in a good way. I'd gone this far before, in high school, but it had been weird and awkward. Now it felt right, natural, like my breasts were there purely to be cupped by Dallas, worshiped with his tongue.

I arched my hips against him. His torso was hard, and underneath his boxers, he was harder.

He coaxed one of my nipples to a peak, and a delightful ache traveled straight to my groin.

I couldn't stand the anticipation any longer. I needed him completely naked *right now*. I tugged on the elastic at his waist, over the ridge of his tapered hips. "Can we get these off?"

He helped me, all the while staring down at me with eyes that wanted to gobble me up. It made my heart warm and mushy, my lungs panting for breath.

Then he was naked, and I couldn't stop looking, at his rigid abs, the deep vee just below them.

On the bus, before the girls and I had plunged, I'd made a joke that everything in Texas was bigger. But Dallas wasn't huge, and he wasn't little. He was perfect.

He rested on his side next to me and started tracing circles on my stomach. "Ade," he said.

I liked him looking at me. The appreciation, the fervor in his eyes.

"Mm," I mumbled.

"We don't have to go any further than this. Us having sex is not the only reason I want to be with you right now."

I pushed him over and crawled on top of him with my underwear still on.

He groaned.

I couldn't believe how good it felt, having him right there, underneath me. I leaned over, laying my heart on his chest, creating friction between us as I moved. "But I want to."

A pain shot through me. I'd just lied. Yes, I wanted sex. But I also wanted him in every possible way. And the more time I spent with him, the more I reveled in this feeling of being entangled with him.

I moved up and down along the length of his body, kissing him.

He moaned into my mouth. "So sexy. You're so sexy."

His hands rubbed my thighs, my butt, and then he was guiding me along him like I was a train engine and he was my track.

Then a thought came whizzing into my brain. Condoms.

Glancing around the room, I looked for my purse. I had some in my purse. The ones I'd taken from the RA on my floor.

"What's the matter?" Dallas's hands were still gripping my hips, but we'd both stopped moving.

I looked down at him. "I think we should get a condom."

He smiled, rolled me over, and laid me down on his bed. "Good idea."

The fact that he had to get out of the bed made me feel better. He didn't keep a pile of them right next to the headboard.

He set the wrapper on the mattress and leaned over me, kissing my belly button and trailing his tongue all the way down to the top of my underwear. I squirmed as a shiver went straight down my legs to my feet, making my toes curl.

Resting his chin on my pelvis, he stared up at me. It was enthralling to see him from this angle, his mouth so close to the heartbeat of my desire. I didn't want to buck him off, but it took superhuman strength for me not to move my hips.

"I'm going to take off your underwear, and then I'm going to kiss you down there." He glanced down to the spot between my legs and returned this gaze to me. His eyes were deep and bottomless, and I was falling into them. "You okay?" he asked.

I couldn't speak, couldn't make a sound. Kiss me? There? I thought I might faint. Not only from embarrassment, but because the mere sound of his voice speaking those words sent me into a throbbing mess. I couldn't imagine what having his lips on me like that would feel like, but I wanted it. Desperately. So I nodded.

He pulled down my underwear and tossed them aside. His thumb touched me, and my hips thrust skyward. *Breathe. Just breathe.*

My hips gyrated in the same rhythm, and my head crashed back into his pillow as I whimpered. I peeked down at him and saw him moving lower...and then a flood of sensations almost suffocated me. *His tongue. On me.* It was hot and breathy, wet and soft. My insides were pulsing, and as much as I wanted to keep moving my hips, I restrained myself, afraid he couldn't stay latched on if I did.

The headiness inside me grew stronger, the weightlessness of my body more prominent.

But then he sat up and fumbled for the condom. "I'm sorry, Ade, I can't wait."

Yes, I wanted to scream. *Yes.* He'd already waited far too long.

He tore the foil wrapper, and I got a quick glimpse of him rolling on the condom. "You want to crawl up on top of me?"

I swallowed. There was no way I was going to get into the saddle when I'd never had a riding lesson in my life. I wasn't sure it was going to work. I wasn't sure how to make him fit.

So I grabbed his waist and pulled him to me. "Next time."

He didn't protest. Especially when I wrapped a leg around his waist.

Then he entered me, slowly and achingly. My body stretched around him, and he moaned.

I expected a sharp sting or a stabbing pain, but there was nothing like that.

We were kissing again, moving together. He was thrusting deep inside me, filling me with a need I'd never felt before.

"You feel so good, Ade," he whispered against my mouth. "So tight."

I was grinding against him, wanting as much as I could get.

He withdrew so only his tip remained inside me. He sucked on his thumb and then slipped it in between my legs.

"Yes," I pleaded. "Yes."

He plunged back inside me.

I was on the edge. Hot pleasure kept growing.

He sped up.

I tried to catch him, but I was too far behind.

His last strokes were reckless, and then he shuddered inside me.

My heart was beating so loud it roared in my ears.

So close to the release of oxytocin and prolactin that I needed. But not quite.

TWENTY-FOUR
EPIC FAILURE

While Dallas breathed heavily next to me, I remained wide awake. *So much for sex equals sleep.*

I didn't blame him. I blamed myself. I probably shouldn't have expected my first time to be good enough to work magic. I guess I should have taken his offer to ride him and maybe that would have helped me.

I untangled myself from Dallas's arms and put on my clothes and his flip-flops. Maybe it all was a bust, because I had to pee. I clomped to the door.

Dallas's voice stopped me. "Where you going?"

"To the bathroom," I said.

He sat up, the sight of his chest giving me a hot flush of desire. "But you're coming back, aren't you?"

"Of course."

I went quickly, not because I feared someone would see me, but because I had to go that bad.

Back in Dallas's room, I stripped everything off again and got in beside him.

He put an arm underneath me. "I'm going to ask you a question, and while I don't think you'll get upset at me for asking, I just want to warn you that it's personal."

I inhaled a gulp of air and prepared myself. "Okay. Go ahead, ask away."

"Was that the first time you'd ever had sex?"

I buried my face into his shoulder. "Yes," I mumbled.

He moved my head away from him so we were eye to eye. "You don't have to be embarrassed about it."

"I'm not, but I probably should have told you up front," I said. "Was it that obvious?"

"You were really tight. I mean, it felt totally awesome for me, but I got the feeling that it might not have been that way for you."

"It was okay. I think maybe I need some practice."

He frowned and smoothed my hair away from my face. "I'm sorry."

"Don't be. It's not your fault. It's no one's fault. It just is."

"I'm going to make it up to you."

My body clenched. "Right now?"

He nodded and went down to the bottom of the bed, taking the covers with him.

His gaze fixed right between my legs, and my face flushed.

Before he dipped his head, he glanced at me and smiled.

I closed my eyes.

A throbbing inside of me started to build and build. I heard myself beg, "More. Please. More."

He nudged a finger inside me, still licking, still sucking.

Electricity shot right up my spine. I moaned in ecstasy.

The pulsing was getting faster, closer together. Then a moment of reprieve, like when an aerial shell is sent hurling through the air, and I waited… But this was no dud. The firework burst open, lighting the sky in awe.

After I came down, able to breathe again, he crawled up to me and kissed the throbbing artery in my neck.

I smiled slowly, lazily. It was going to work. Just as the internet had said. I was going to fall asleep in his arms and not wake until morning.

But even with my head tucked into the crook of his arm and my wet, hot sex pressed up against his thigh, sleep never came.

TWENTY-FIVE
THE MORNING AFTER

Dallas and I walked into the cafeteria together for breakfast. Not holding hands or arm in arm—instead, he was pinching my ass. I hadn't expected this crackling energy between us, but I loved it. We went our separate ways to grab food and then joined back up to find a seat together.

"She's the one," said a female voice to my right. "She's the girl in the hoodie."

"It won't last," said her friend.

I looked at Dallas, but he didn't seem to be paying attention. I threw back my shoulders and remained strong. I had to get over this fear of being ridiculed. And there was no better time to start than right now.

"Where should we sit?" I asked him.

"With your friends is fine." He headed in their direction without hesitation.

Priya and Emma scooted over to make room for us, their mouths twitching, and I wondered if they were going to burst out in a contagious laugh. So far, so good. I hadn't known how they were going to act when Dallas and I showed up together.

"Ade, no energy drink this morning?" Priya had a twinkle in her eye.

Dallas looked at me strangely. "I thought you didn't drink caffeine?"

"I do energy drinks, just not coffee," I said to him. But then I focused back on Priya and winked at her, even though I probably could use some. "And no, no Red Bull this morning."

Priya lit up like the string lights we'd hung up in our room in December. Her glow touched me, warming my insides.

Emma nudged me and smirked.

I smiled back at her.

I might not have slept like I'd wanted to, but I still had a surge of energy from just being with Dallas. He made me feel like I was capable of being the person I wanted to be. It could be that we simply needed to have more sex—a lot more sex—before it was *good riddance, insomnia*. Dean's list, here I came. Unfortunately, I sensed that it was going to take some other personal feat to make my inability to sleep go away.

We finished eating, and after bussing our trays, we walked out of the cafeteria together. In my mind, I was figuring out what I needed to get ready for work when my phone rang.

Weird. No one ever called me, so I let it go to voicemail.

Dallas glanced at me. "Aren't you going to get that?"

"Nah."

"Not even going to see who it was?"

Crap. Eric still hadn't called me back.

The phone started ringing again.

Dallas stopped.

I pulled out my phone and looked. The name "Dad" was in large font at the top.

My shoulders dropped, and I let out a sigh.

Nope. Not going to answer that. I declined the call and slid it back in my pocket. Good thing Mom had made me put his contact information in my phone—at least I knew that it was him.

I started up the stairs, but Dallas didn't move. I looked back at him. "What?"

"It's your dad."

"So?"

"I thought you said you disowned him?"

"I did. I don't talk to him anymore. That's why I didn't answer." Not that Dallas would understand. He didn't have a dad like mine. The kind who would make their kid a public laughing-stock. There was a line between people of decency and those who had none.

Dallas's face pinched, and he folded his arms across his chest. "But you have his number in your phone."

"My mom made me take it. She probably gave my new number to him."

"*Made* you?"

"You know how moms are—how good they are at pushing you into doing things that you don't want to do even when you're officially an adult."

He winced, like I'd just slapped him upside the cheek.

"Come on, I bet your mom does the same thing."

The pain across his face was still there.

"She does, doesn't she?"

"I don't know." It took some effort for him to say those words.

A knot formed in my gut, cinching tighter and tighter. "What do you mean you don't know?"

"I don't know what she would do now that I'm an adult, because she's gone. She passed away."

My throat closed. I couldn't breathe. *Oh shit. Oh, double shit.*

The skin on my face and neck felt like I'd brushed against a stinging nettle.

My stomach was doing somersaults now. "I'm sorry...but I thought...because there's that photo of her in your room, with both of your parents."

Dallas cringed. "Yeah. That's one of the last good photos I have with her."

My knees went weak. My heart hurt.

This conversation was nothing like a fight, but it felt weird. I should ask him more questions to ease the awkwardness. Or at least say something more to show him I cared. But I didn't know how to go there. Where to start.

"I'm sorry," I said.

An ache swirled in his eyes, clouding the spark that was usually there. I'd brought back memories of his mother, and I wished I'd never gotten that call from my dad.

"It is what it is," he said.

We continued up the stairs in silence. This was not how the day was supposed to go, especially after how it had begun. In these past twelve hours together, I'd been as close to Dallas as humanly possible, but now, I'd never felt so far apart.

TWENTY-SIX
THE NIGHTLY NEWS

To my dismay, Dallas also enjoyed the zombie show that Priya liked, so on Sunday night, after doing our physics problems for the week and avoided talking about his mother, we watched it in the fourth-floor lounge with a bunch of other people.

I kept my earbuds in to dampen the sound. The music always did me in. If they'd just get rid of the creepy sounds, I might actually enjoy the show. There were interesting characters, high stakes, and the need to work together to survive. All elements of exciting television.

At the climax, the tension got to me. Blood and guts were everywhere. I was white-knuckling the chair and at the point where I really hated this program. Like I'll-never-watch-it-again kind of hate.

Dallas put a hand on my leg. "You okay?"

"I just don't have the stomach for this."

He squeezed. "Don't worry, there can't be much left. We can leave if you want."

"No, I'll make it." I shut my eyes again and waited.

Finally, the show ended, and I sighed in relief.

"That was so awesome." Priya was bouncing. "Did you see

that one zombie with half a body?"

My insides lurched. Good thing my eyes had been closed tight for quite a bit of the show.

The credits sped by, and then the local news blared. Two anchors with perfectly ironed suits and teased hair started with a report on the ice cross competition. No photos of Dallas, but they showed aerial views of the crowds, and it was breathtaking.

They moved on to a more serious issue, a demonstration at the State Capitol. Then once more they changed gears.

And there, on all fifty inches of the flat-screen television, was my father's mug shot from last year, with his thick, dark hair dusted with flecks of gray, his wide hazel eyes like mine, and his face devoid of expression.

My stomach clenched so hard, I almost doubled over. The room grew silent. This one bit of old news had captured everyone's attention. Of course it would. He was the university's ex-coach. Loved and cherished until he'd effed it all up.

I wanted to throw up. Retch right there. I swallowed saliva just to keep the bile down.

His photo zoomed out, and the camera focused again on the anchorwoman. I could barely digest any of her words. Something about his trial starting next week. The charges against him.

I was frozen to my chair, but Dallas wasn't. I didn't realize he'd gotten up until he was standing in front of the TV and changing the station. Instantly, the faces and voices on the screen disappeared, replaced with something else.

"Hey," Priya shouted. "If you hadn't noticed, some of us were watching that."

My head started throbbing.

Dallas turned around, and he looked at me, his eyes soft. "I'm not sure who even watches the news. I don't."

"David Bianchini screwed over the whole university athletic department." I could almost see steam coming out of Priya's nostrils. "Did you hear how much they had to pay him to sever his contract? And now I've heard that the NCAA might hand down even more sanctions. It's total bullshit."

My heart thudded and seemed to skip a beat.

Everything that had happened to me last year was suddenly pouring into me like water through a leak in the hull of a boat. I needed to get away. Now.

So I walked out. In the hallway, I was disoriented. I didn't know which way to go. Back to my room? Maybe, but I wouldn't be alone for long. That was the trouble with the dorm. There was no place to hide. No place to tuck yourself away to have a good cry or scream. No place to rein in your feelings and put on a game face.

The door to the community bathroom beckoned, and I pushed through it. I went straight to the last stall, locked myself in, and sat on the toilet seat completely clothed, crisscross apple saucing my legs so no one would see me under the stall door.

I cradled my face in my hands and tried to breathe. But it was hard, especially with my throat closing around a volcano of emotion. I wouldn't cry, not here. I'd already shed enough tears about my dad. I was past this.

The door creaked open.

"Ade," Priya's voice called out. "Are you in here?"

I wasn't ready to face anyone yet.

"Dallas is looking for you."

With the quietest of motions, I pulled my cell phone out of my pocket and flipped the switch to silent. In seconds, the phone lit up.

DALLAS
Where are you?

I held my breath.

Then a squeak and Priya said, "She's not in there, Let's—"

The door slammed shut, and I missed the rest.

My heart was beating wildly. I needed more time to recover. That was all.

I went to the voicemail my dad had left for me, which I hadn't listened to yet, and pressed play.

"Hi, Ade." My dad's baritone sounded authoritative and soothing all at the same time. It reminded me of the days when he'd talk me through lacing up my skates before hockey practice. "It's me. Your mom gave me your phone number. Please don't be mad. I just want to see you. This week would be best. I miss you. Call me."

The voicemail ended, and my heart squeezed tight, pain swelling in my esophagus. Why had he screwed everything up?

Tears welled in my eyes, but before they could spill, I wiped them away with my arm.

I pictured his mug shot. The same one I'd seen thousands of times last year. It was a horrible depiction of him.

I supposed I should break the silence and meet with him. It might be the last time for a while, if he was actually convicted and had to go to jail. And I definitely wouldn't be visiting him there.

I typed a message to Dallas.

> I'm fine. I'm in the building.

> **DALLAS**
> You coming over tonight?

I stared hard at his text, and my chest flooded with warmth. I wanted to be with him. And if I did, I'd be giving myself another shot at getting a night of sleep. But given his reaction to my dad calling me, I wasn't sure Dallas would give me the best advice about how to handle him. That left Jay, who was the only other person in the dorm who knew who he was.

> Not tonight. But do you want to walk to class together tomorrow morning?

> **DALLAS**
> Sure.

I left the bathroom and went downstairs to the first floor, to Jay's room. I knocked. It was sort of late for a Sunday. Ten-twenty-two at night, to be exact.

The door swung open, and I met his friendly eyes.

"Hi," I said. "Are you alone, or is your roommate in there too?"

He opened the door wider to let me in. "Come on in, I'm by myself."

I walked in. The room was tidy, but it smelled like boys—cross-country-runner boys. Dirty socks and sweaty polyester running shirts. How did they live like this?

I sat on his couch.

Jay sat across from me on his desk chair. "What's up?"

"My dad left me a voicemail. Can I play it for you?"

"Sure." He crossed his arms.

I took out my phone and played the message. Jay leaned forward to get closer to the speaker. The sound of my dad's voice made me all squishy inside again, and I remained that way even when the voicemail was over.

"Are you going to call him back?"

I shrugged. "I'm not sure. What do you think?"

Jay shifted in his seat. "Interesting that he called you."

"No, it's not. My mom is behind this, and the trial starts next week. Haven't you seen it on the news?"

He shrugged. "I don't watch TV unless I'm streaming something."

"Well, it made the headlines tonight. I was hoping the media didn't care about him anymore, but they're probably even more excited now that there'll be more drama."

"Maybe," he said. "Or maybe there was nothing else to report on."

"So..." I folded one leg under my thigh. "You think I should meet up with him like he wants."

"Yeah," Jay said. "I think you should."

"But it's so complicated." I nibbled on the inside of my mouth.

He stared at me. "Life is complicated. But sometimes you need to suck it up and face it. You'll be better off."

"Face it, huh? Like face the source of my anxiety and maybe, just maybe, it will go away and I'll finally sleep well?"

Jay gave me a knowing look and chuckled. "Does that mean Dallas hasn't been the fix you thought he'd be?"

"For your information, he's good." I folded my arms together.

"Just good?"

"Very good." I kicked his foot. "But as it turns out, sex as a remedy was like all the other ones I've tried. A total bust."

He laughed.

"What's so funny?"

"I find it hilarious that you spent all that time obsessing about how sex would cure your insomnia and then in the end it didn't work."

"It's frustrating, that's for sure, but Dallas and I are...well... we're having a great time together."

He nodded. "That's good. I'm glad to hear it."

"Back to my dad. What you're saying makes sense. But what if reconciling with him doesn't work to cure me either?"

He shrugged. "At least you'd have a dad again. Don't get me wrong, he made some really awful, terrible choices. And he's going to have to deal with the consequences. That's for sure. But are you going to refuse to talk to him for the rest of your life and never have any resolution for yourself?"

I sighed. This was why I'd come to Jay. I knew he'd lay it out for me. And deep inside, I knew I needed to move on and start the life I was trying to create for myself. The baggage wasn't helping. And at this point, I'd try anything to help me get some sleep.

"Okay, I'll do it," I said. "But if things get ugly, I'm blaming you."

TWENTY-SEVEN
DAD ISSUES

The next day, between classes, I searched out a vacant corner in the student union and called my dad.

"Hey, sweetheart."

His voice sent a sharp, painful twinge right through me.

"I'm so glad you called," he continued.

My jaw stiffened. *Glad.* That was his response to our first exchange of words in months. My feelings were bigger, much bigger. As big as discovering a new chemical element on the periodic table.

"I'm not busy during lunch on Thursday." I sounded a bit cold. "We could meet then."

"Great," he said. "How about that sub shop I love so much?"

"Huh?" I had no idea what he was talking about.

"The place with the fresh-cut deli meat and the good bread and dressing."

"Do you mean Big Mike's?" I asked.

"Yes, that's it. I love that place."

My heart started beating faster. My phone was slippery in my hand. "But aren't you banned from university property?"

"No, I'm not, and besides, Big Mike's isn't on school property."

"It's really close. Across the street."

"Oh, right."

I wasn't sure what was going through my dad's brain. He couldn't possibly go to a restaurant by campus. People would recognize him and cause a scene. And I'd be there. What a mess.

"All right, how about I put in an order for Big Mike's, you pick it up, and I drive by and get you in the car?"

All I could imagine was walking in there and asking for David Bianchini's sub order and everyone looking at me like I was a monster.

"How about *I* put in the order at Big Mike's, I pick it up, and then you drive by and I get in your car?"

He went silent.

I waited.

"All right. I'll pick you up at noon."

I let out a large breath. "Sounds good. See you there."

And it was over. The first real conversation I'd had with my dad in months. Strange how anticlimactic it had been. Like no time had passed at all.

———

Three days later, when I arrived at the sandwich place, I got our order easily. No looks. No nothing.

I stepped outside…and Dad was already there, waving to me. I crawled into the car and held my breath, not really knowing what to expect.

"Hi, Ade!" Dad leaned over and gave me one of his bear hugs. Reluctantly, I patted him on his back before he pulled away from the curb.

My dad had always been in shape, and that hadn't changed. But today his clothes got my attention. He looked fancy. A collared shirt, a tie, a sweater vest, and a blazer over it. All coordinated. The only time I'd ever seen him wear suit-type clothing was on game days.

His face looked the same. Not bad, like his mug shot, but what my dad normally looked like. Cool and collected. That Italian Mafia charm that made people of any age hang on to his every word. He was even chewing gum like he always had. It smelled like his usual, sweet mint Orbit.

"Did you get me the roast beef?"

"Yep." I nodded. "Why are you all dressed up?"

He shrugged. He put on his blinker and merged into traffic.

"How's school going?" he asked.

"Good," I said.

Then silence. Lots of silence. Certainly he wasn't expecting me to give him a play-by-play of my classes and my grades?

I broke the quiet. "I saw you on the news."

He flinched. "You did?"

"On Sunday night. They were reporting on your upcoming trial."

His chin dipped down, and he grimaced. "That's disappointing. I thought the press had grown tired of me. Now it means they'll be there, at the courthouse, hounding my lawyer for interviews."

"Mom says you have a pretty good case."

He perked up a bit. "I do, and actually the trial is one of the reasons I wanted to get together with you this week."

And not the week before or last month or any other month during the months we hadn't spoken.

Stop it, Ade. Stop it right now. I was here to listen to what he had to say, receive some version of an apology, and see if we could patch things up, not become more irritated, more bitter.

"Dad." I took a deep breath and let it out. This was it. I was going to get right into it.

He reached out and touched my hand. "The reason I'm dressed up is that we're going to take our sandwiches to my lawyer's office and have lunch there. He wants to talk to us."

"What?" My stomach did a somersault.

"It's not far. Just about five minutes away."

My neck tensed. I ground my teeth so hard my jaw hurt. I couldn't believe it. My dad was treating our reunion as less important than a meeting with his lawyer.

I squeezed my hands into fists and looked out the window. I wanted to yell at him. I wanted to jump out of the car.

But I couldn't get myself to make him pull over. Instead, I remained still, quietly seething.

Inside the law firm's conference room, Dad put the sandwiches on the table while the lawyer reached his hand out to shake mine. "Hello, Adriana. My name is Gray Horton."

How was it that so often a person's name described them perfectly? The man was bland. Generic. I glanced down at his hand, at the neatly trimmed fingernails that looked like something out of a cosmetology handbook. But I didn't grasp it, because my dad had invited *his* lawyer to *our* lunch. The *first* lunch, the first *real* conversation we were supposed to have in months.

We all sat down.

"I've heard a lot about you, Adriana," Gray said. "A chemical engineering student. Wow, that's pretty difficult coursework."

"Yeah." My voice had no strength, no vibrance.

"But not for my Adriana." Dad's spine straightened, and his chest expanded. "She's a straight-A student, always has been."

Not anymore. Not since he'd reduced me to a sleep-deprived, dysfunctional mess. I placed my palms on the table and bit my bottom lip. It hurt like hell, but I had to do it because I wasn't sure what might come out of my mouth if it opened.

"That's great," Gray said.

A second later, a legal assistant came in with a tray of different drinks. Dad took a Coke. I grabbed a bottle of one of those fancy sparkling waters. Might as well. Dad was paying for it.

"So, Adriana, I'm not sure how much detail your dad was able to go into so far, but I wanted to explain to you a little about his case."

"My mom mentioned it, but I don't need to know details." I took a sip from the bottle of water.

"Actually, we think you should."

I knew that this guy was a lawyer and I should be respectful, but I was beyond that. Not only had he ruined my day, but he must not understand that I didn't care about the trial. I just wanted it to be over. Every loose end tied up, so people would start forgetting about what had happened.

The lawyer and I locked gazes.

Then he blinked. "You need to know about the case because we want you to be an exhibit at the trial."

My stomach shrank. I was no longer hungry. I was ill. "A what?"

"An exhibit. That's what we call the family members who are in the courtroom supporting the defendant. We can't call character witnesses to testify, because there's no he-said-she said at issue, but we can make sure the family is there sitting behind your dad. This will speak volumes to the jury."

I glanced at my father. He was leaning in, his lips parted, waiting for my reaction.

In that moment, I sort of felt bad for him, but as quick as the feeling came, it disappeared.

I looked back at the lawyer. "As my dad already knows and should have explained to you, I've started a new life with a new name so that I could attend Minnesota University in peace. Going to the trial would ruin everything I've done to put last year behind me. So no, I will not be attending."

Gray squinted at me. "Your dad has told me this, and I don't think you going to the trial will ruin your new identity. Video cameras are not allowed in the courtroom, and your presence could mean the difference between a guilty and a not-guilty verdict."

I stared at the wood table. My heart was pounding, my muscles quivering. He was giving me a guilt trip, which made me dislike this guy even more. "Why don't you ask Eric to go?"

Dad's expression was unreadable. "We tried. He can't come."

"Oh, that's right." My shoulders were tense, and I knew that what I was going to say next was going to be petty and hurtful. But I didn't care. "He's probably busy with his AHL team, not the NHL draft team who dropped him...because of *you*."

Dad grimaced.

The lawyer piped up again, his voice full of authority. "Eric would be a great option, but he can't be here because of his commitments. That's why we need you."

A bitter taste rose in my throat.

My family and I had been on a camping trip once and gotten hit by a severe thunderstorm, the rain coming at us horizontally because the straight-line winds had been that bad. That was how I felt now. Like I was being blindsided. I couldn't orient myself. Couldn't keep myself upright.

My father dug into his lunch, but I couldn't imagine taking one single bite of my sandwich. I'd probably throw it up the moment I tried to swallow.

I had to leave.

So I put on my jacket and grabbed my backpack.

"Ade, where are you going?" My dad almost sounded like he was choking.

"I can't do this." I put on my backpack. "I'm getting an Uber."

I turned and left. I walked faster and faster, opened my Uber app, and ordered one.

Good. Only two minutes away. I needed to create space between myself and him before I flipped out completely.

In the vestibule to the office building, I stared out the window, waiting. My muscles wouldn't stop quivering.

I just wanted a father. One who wasn't a narcissist. One who could try to understand what I'd been going through this year. But even that must be too much to ask.

The interior door burst open.

"Ade," my dad sputtered, out of breath. "Please don't leave like this."

"What other choice do I have?"

"Stay."

"Stay and what?" My nostrils flared. "Be treated with more disrespect?"

He shook his head. "Disrespect?"

"Today I thought we were supposed to have our first lunch, our first *conversation,* since the arrest, and instead you brought me to see your lawyer. Then your lawyer tells me that you need my help and that, while you know my situation, you need me to do it anyway. That's what I call disrespect."

He came toward me, trying to bridge the distance between us, but I stepped back.

"My God, Ade, I'm sorry. I didn't mean for you to feel this way. You have my utmost respect. You always have."

"Like when you went behind my back and tried to use your influence to get that hockey cheer coach to put me on their team because you didn't think I was good enough to get on it by myself?"

His arms fell to his sides. "I wasn't thinking when I did that, honey. It was a mistake. I made a lot of mistakes."

The Uber car pulled up in front of the door.

"You've always been good enough," he said. "I've always been so proud of what you've accomplished."

I was shaking now, uncontrollably. Part of me wanted to sink to the floor and let him console me. To convince me that all the pent-up, hurtful feelings I had about him right now were wrong.

The other part of me wanted to run. As far away as I could get. But there was one thing I knew with certainty.

"I can't sit there, Dad." Tears brimmed in the corners of my eyes, and I fought them. "I can't sit there during your trial. And you know exactly why."

"Okay." He nodded and kept nodding. "I understand."

I exited the building and jogged to the Uber, opened the door and collapsed into the back seat. Only then did I let the tears slide down my face.

I couldn't go to the trial, because it would mean publicly admitting who I was. That I was Coach Bianchini's daughter. And that I wouldn't do.

TWENTY-EIGHT
DAD ISSUES CONTINUED

I wiped my cheeks with the back of my hand. All I wanted was to go back to my dorm room and bury myself in my bed. Pull the covers over my head until the trial was over. Until my father's fate was decided.

But of course, driving to my dorm meant having to pass the building where my class would be held. And I knew I couldn't afford to miss it. Not with the current state of my grades. I was early, but I stopped the Uber, went into the building and kerplunked myself into a desk far away from where I usually sat.

I probably should have pulled out my books and used the extra wait time to get in some studying, but I didn't. I sat there in a daze, staring straight ahead, shrinking inside myself.

The scrape of metal against vinyl tiles pulled me out of my stupor. A tall body moved the desk with its attached chair closer to me and sat.

"Why are you sitting over here?" It was Jay. He shimmied out of his jacket.

He sat back, and I eyed him. I wondered what it would be like to be him. To have a normal family, one without constant drama.

Better than being me. Way better.

"I'm sitting here because I need a change," I said.

"What's that supposed to mean?"

I shrugged because honestly I didn't know what it meant either.

"Your advice, by the way…" I leaned over and unzipped my backpack. "It was terrible."

"What advice?"

"The one where you told me to go see my dad."

His brows furrowed. "That was good advice."

"No, it wasn't." I took out my notebook. "Get this. My dad brought me to meet his lawyer."

"Interesting." Jay slid backward.

"And guess what? The lawyer proceeded to ask me to be an exhibit at the trial next week." I paused and looked Jay in the eye.

"An exhibit?"

"Sit in the audience behind my dad, day in and day out. I'd be a prop in a theatrical performance. I wouldn't have to say anything, I'd only have to smile and look empathetic."

"Well, aren't you going to go to the trial anyway?"

"Nooooo." I held the vowel for longer than I should. "I've never planned on being anywhere close to that courtroom."

The classroom was filling up. The TA had come in and was taking questions at the front.

Jay reached into his backpack and began pulling out materials. "Here." He flopped stapled pages onto my desktop. "I found some old tests and printed them for you."

"Wow." My body warmed. "What subjects?"

"Calc and physics. I'm having a harder time finding chemistry tests."

I paged through them. They appeared to hold a wealth of information. "Thanks. This is great."

Class began, and the teacher went over sample problems on the board. I followed along as best I could, trying to focus.

Afterward, Jay and I walked out together. "You going back to the dorm?" he asked.

I heard him, but I didn't respond. I couldn't stop thinking

about my dad, imagining him sitting at the defendant's table in a courtroom.

Ugh. I needed to get that image out of my head.

"Ade," Jay said, a little more urgently than I thought necessary. "Are you okay?"

"Sorry. Yeah, that's where I'm going. Back to the dorm."

"All right." He waved at me, but it was weak, his eyes all-knowing. "See you later."

I needed a distraction. Something bigger than class, something that would make me completely forget about Dad.

My phone dinged, and I fished it out.

> **DALLAS**
> You busy tonight?

I smiled for the first time that day.

> No. Except I need to start getting ready for the chemistry test next week.

> **DALLAS**
> Want to study?

> Where?

> **DALLAS**
> The engineering building again?

> The hallway to get there is too cold.

> **DALLAS**
> My room?

> Ha! I don't think I can study in there. Too many other things to do.

> **DALLAS**
> Agreed

> 4th floor lounge?

DALLAS
So you really don't care if anyone sees us,
do you?

Right

DALLAS
See you there

And it was settled. A productive night with Dallas was on the menu, and I had a feeling that my angst over my father would disappear. I just had to stop thinking about him and concentrate instead on the hot guy who, for reasons beyond sensibility, was totally into me.

TWENTY-NINE
THE BOY APPROVES

My study date with Dallas didn't last long. Not even an hour went by before we moved to his room and took off all our clothes. For me, it wasn't so much about sex or sleep. It was being with him, connecting with him. He helped me forget about all the crap in my life.

Later, when I was thoroughly relaxed and Dallas had fallen asleep, I began drifting off with my fingers crossed, but then suddenly, out of nowhere, my head exploded. A flash like a bomb detonated in a blinding light and, seconds later, released a deafening bang.

I jolted straight up, my chest thundering, electricity running through my body. I was gasping, hardly able to breathe.

"Ade." Dallas put a hand on my back. "Are you okay?"

I looked down at him, my heart thrashing so hard I couldn't speak.

"Ade?"

I nodded, trying to swallow, trying to form words. "I'm good."

"Were you having a nightmare?" he asked.

I lay back down and pulled the covers up to my shoulders. That had been crazy. The noise. The shock. The only logical thing I could come up with was I'd had a hallucination—an audible one.

Exploding head syndrome. I'd had it one other time last fall. The internet said it was something people with sleep disorders got. But I wasn't about to tell him my whole sleep problem or the original reasons I had for having sex with him.

"Yeah." I nodded. "It must have been a nightmare. Not sure how I'll fall asleep now."

He pulled me close and tucked my head into his shoulder. "I could talk you through that yoga thing. Where you concentrate on relaxing each muscle from your toes all the way up to your neck."

"I don't know. It probably won't work."

"It always works for me. Let's do it."

And he did. He used his deep, calming voice and started at our feet. I tried to focus on tensing a muscle and then relaxing it, but it wasn't working. I was still wide awake. Of course, it worked for him. He only made it to our abs before his breathing evened out and turned heavy.

In the morning, I lay in his bed, still fatigued, while he stood in the middle of his room drinking coffee. "Hey, I've been meaning to tell you, I'm leaving today to go out of town for the weekend."

His words made my stomach cramp. Then a jumble of questions rained down on me like pellets of rock, but I couldn't sort through them or place them in a queue for processing. There was only one thing I could spit out. "To go where?"

"Another ice cross competition."

If I hadn't been in his bed with the covers over me, the heaviness in my chest might have made me collapse to the ground. I needed him. I had to get through this weekend and the rest of next week in a state of distraction before my dad's trial was over.

Maybe if I went with him, I'd be okay.

But he didn't say anything more. Didn't follow up his announcement with a much-needed invitation. Instead, he walked to his closet and picked out something to wear.

Suddenly, the girls in the peacoats and berets jumped into my overworked imagination. Maybe he wasn't asking me to go because he was meeting up with another girl or girls.

Stop it, Ade. You're freaking out for no reason.

I made a grab for my underwear and bra and put them on underneath the sheets. Then I stood and donned the clothes I'd been wearing the day before. "But you'll be back Sunday, won't you?"

He turned. "Maybe. I'm not totally sure. I could be gone through the beginning of the week."

My heart started beating faster. It might be as many as a handful of days until I saw him again. *Please stop panicking, please.*

I sat on his futon and dug through my pocket for lip balm, then popped off the cap and lubed up my chafed lips.

Well, if he could lay a surprise on me, I could too, though mine wasn't even close to being as hurtful. "I saw my dad yesterday."

Dallas jerked back. "You what?"

My muscles stiffened. I hadn't expected my announcement to shock him that much. "We ordered Big Mike's."

He clamped his mouth shut and opened it again.

Strange.

"But I thought you weren't speaking to him," he said.

"I wasn't, then I did, and now I'm not sure if I am again."

He rubbed his forehead, then smoothed out his brows with his fingers. "I'm confused. Just the other day, you wouldn't even answer his call."

"I changed my mind and called him back. But it was all for nothing."

"What's that supposed to mean?"

I paused. I didn't know if I should explain it to him. Mostly because I didn't know which camp he would align himself with. The you-should-be-nice-to-your-dad camp—the one Jay belonged to—or the I-can't-be-seen-with-my-dad camp that I belonged to.

"He wants me to be at the trial."

His face turned red. Now I was the one who was confused.

"Are you...going?" he asked.

"No," I said. "No way."

"Oh." His shoulders relaxed. "That's good."

My eyes narrowed. "You think so?"

For some reason, I'd expected him to share Jay's opinion. Not mine. I should be happy about this—that he was supporting me— but something didn't feel right.

"Yeah, I mean, you want to keep your identity hidden here on campus, and if you go, your secret might be in jeopardy."

He went back to his closet, and I stood to leave. A rush of blood went straight to my head, forcing me to regain my balance. There was something I wasn't picking up on here. He agreed with me about my dad issues like a supportive boyfriend would, but he hadn't invited me to come with him to his race.

He came up to me, kissed me on the forehead, and stepped back. "What's wrong?"

"Nothing," I said. But of course I'd lied. There were millions of things I wanted to say to him, but I wouldn't. I couldn't. It was just too soon to put a label on our relationship or for me to nose around in his business.

I forced a smile. "Good luck this weekend."

"Thanks."

I left without kissing him back. I wanted to, but I didn't, because I thought maybe, just maybe, I would lose my composure. I didn't want to become a pathetic heap on his floor. I wanted to be the cool chick who didn't care that I'd just been relegated to the back burner on the stove.

Back in my room, Priya was awake and getting ready for class.

"Hi-ee," she said in a singsong voice. "How's your boyfriend?"

"I don't have one." I sounded stiff.

"Oh, come on, you do too. I can't remember the last time you actually slept in our room."

"Sunday." My voice sounded flat.

She glanced at me and raised an eyebrow. "Is something wrong?"

"No." I headed to my closet. "I'm fine."

Why did everyone keep asking me that?

I stared at my hanging clothes. Nothing appealed to me. The colors were too bright. I needed something drab.

"Do you…do you want me to wait for you and we can walk together?" she asked.

"Nah. I still have some time."

"Okay. See you later." Priya left.

I picked something out and dressed slowly. I didn't know what I was going to do now. I didn't know how I was going to get through the weekend.

Since Dallas wasn't going to ask me to go to the race with him, I needed some other diversion.

I speed-dialed Mom.

She picked up right away. "Hi, sweetheart. Great to hear from you."

"I'm scheduled to work tomorrow, but do you think you could pick me up after class today and we could go do something?"

"Of course, dear. Oh, this will be fun. How about a movie?"

"Sure, that sounds great." I hung up.

I should be happy that I had a plan now, but I wasn't. My mom might distract me for a little while, but then I'd go back to thinking about my dad…or what Dallas was doing without me.

THIRTY
FINAL DECISION

My mom and I stopped at a Vietnamese restaurant near the movie theater. I got my favorite, shrimp chow fun with baby bok choy. My intestines were going to pay for it, but for now I reveled in the chewy texture of the large, flat noodles.

My mom got a bowl of pho and was sitting across from me, mixing more herbs into the broth.

My brain hummed like I'd put a song on repeat. It kept playing and replaying the tune called "Dallas." So I decided that now was as good a time as any to tell her about him. I was ready.

Before I could think of the best way to start, she said, "Your dad wanted to come with us tonight."

I paused and placed my elbows on the table.

"But I told him that he needed to give you some space."

I stared at her. "He took me to see his lawyer yesterday. Did you know that?"

She nodded and poked at her soup. "Probably not the best way to restart your father-daughter relationship."

"No." I picked up my chopsticks and gripped them hard enough, they pinched my fingers. "His lawyer sure had a lot of nerve, asking me to go to the trial like that."

"Dad said you walked out before you even started eating."

"I was mad. Really mad. But then Dad caught up to me, and now I'm just confused."

"He feels bad for putting you in that situation. He wishes he hadn't." She tilted her head. "In fact, there are a lot of things he regrets. It seems never-ending…"

I moved the noodles around on my plate and nodded. At least he was trying to show some remorse.

A quiet settled around us. An awkward silence.

I glanced at my mom. Her eyes were glistening, and her nose had turned pink.

"Mom, please don't cry."

"I can't help myself." She sniffled. "I just don't know what I'm going to do if your dad is sent to prison."

"I doubt he'll go to prison," I said.

"But you said it yourself. Five counts. Maximum sentence for each is ten years."

"I've done some research since that night I gave you those pamphlets. In the cases I've found of college athletic bribery, the coaches got two, maybe three months tops and a year or two of probation."

"I suppose that makes me feel a little better." Mom's voice went back to being as steady as she could make it.

She stirred her soup and blew on it. "Your dad said you're not going to come to the trial next week. You haven't changed your mind?"

I didn't say a word. Mostly because I didn't know what to say. I wasn't going. That decision was final. Actually, it had never even been a decision. It was a nonnegotiable given.

Finally, I said, "It's true. I'm not going. It could jeopardize my situation at school. Where I am Adriana Blankin and not Adriana Bianchini."

Mom nodded. Seconds later, she whispered, "Okay."

I breathed in, but my lungs wouldn't fill all the way.

Mom hadn't yelled at me or reprimanded me for it, and Dad had accepted it. They were treating me like the adult I was. Yet still my chest was heavy with the burden.

THIRTY-ONE
OR NOT

On Monday morning, in the middle of chemistry, I woke up my phone. The screen said nine thirty in the morning. Dad's trial must be well underway.

A picture of him in orange flashed like a beacon in my mind. An image of a prison cell with metal bars came next.

Stop it. Just stop it. You are not going to the trial to be an exhibit. You're just not.

I glanced at Dallas's empty seat. It shouldn't bother me that he was a no-show. He'd told me that he didn't know if he'd be back by Monday, but his absence and lack of contact hurt. He hadn't bothered to text me all weekend.

After class, Jay and I walked together to our next one. I was having a hard time keeping up with him. My legs just wouldn't cooperate.

"I take it that you still haven't been sleeping very well." Jay blew another bubble with the gum he was chewing, and I grimaced. The popping sound was driving me crazy.

"Do I look that bad?"

"No, not bad. Just more tired than usual."

I sighed. He was right. My insomnia hadn't relented.

"Doesn't your dad's trial start today?" Jay asked.

"Yes." My shoulders tensed.

"And you didn't go?"

I tried to relax. "No."

"Why?"

But me trying to stay calm was difficult. "You know why."

"If you're worried about missing classes, you know I'd take good notes for you, and the chemistry test later this week is early in the morning and won't last more than an hour."

I stared at him and sighed. "I don't want anyone to know who I am. And if I go, I could be found out."

Jay slowed his pace. "But he's your dad. The only dad you're ever going to get."

An ache swelled in the back of my throat. *Ugh.*

"Besides," I said, "if I went, Priya and Emma would wonder where I was going every day."

He halted. "Wait, are you saying that you haven't told Priya and Emma who your dad is yet?"

I shrugged. "You should have seen Priya's reaction the other day when she saw my dad on the news."

He moaned, loud and hard. "It's official. I don't get girls at all."

"Even if I thought I could unload all of my baggage on them like that"—I sucked in my cheeks—"their perception of me would be forever changed."

"You claim them to be your best friends, but when it comes down to it, you've never shared with them anything that's really important about yourself. Including the one thing they should know."

We arrived at the entrance to the building that held our calculus class. Jay ascended the concrete stairs, and I followed behind.

He started into the lecture hall, and I grabbed him by the elbow. "Obviously, you never noticed how my high school friends stopped talking to me after they found out about my dad. I never want that to happen again. Ever."

"I didn't do that."

"You don't count. We weren't friends in high school. We were classmates, but we didn't socialize outside of that."

His brows drew together.

"The summer after graduation, the girls I used to hang out with stopped talking to me."

"Even your best friend, Sarah?" he asked.

"Yes."

"That sucks." His lanky posture stooped. "I'm sorry."

"Me too. We all went off to different colleges, and we would have grown apart a little anyway, but still. They just cut me off."

"Those girls," he said. "If they abandoned you, they were never your friends to begin with. Priya and Emma, they wouldn't do that."

We sat down in class, and I thought back to the fall of my senior year, when my friends and I had toilet-papered another girl's house—a girl who'd had the audacity not to invite us over for a gathering, so Sarah had decided we'd play a practical joke on her. It wasn't a moment I was proud of. It also should have been the moment I realized that Sarah wasn't a kindhearted person.

Jay was right. Priya and Emma wouldn't abandon me.

That afternoon, I met them at the rec center to run the indoor track. We changed, stretched, and started jogging. Me inserted between them, keeping pace all together.

Two laps in, my heart pounded, my legs were weak, and I was dizzy enough that I kept thinking I might fall flat on my face.

On the third lap, I took a deep breath and said, "Do you remember the other night...when the news came on...and they mentioned Coach David Bianchini?"

"The night we watched my zombie show with Dallas?" Priya asked.

"Yes." This time I caught my breath and let out a long exhale to prepare. "Okay, so I need to tell you both something important about Coach Bianchini that I don't want you to tell anyone else."

Emma locked in her pace to mine. "What in the world, Ade?"

I squeezed my eyes shut and grimaced. "He's my dad."

Emma halted with a gasp.

Priya stopped midstride. Her face contorted.

Since I was still jogging, I pivoted backward and paused.

I held my breath and waited for them to say something, anything.

"I thought…" Priya said. "I thought you said your dad lived out of state, and that's why we haven't met him."

"Yeah, I'm really sorry about that. I lied."

They began to walk hesitantly, and I dropped in alongside them. I told them the entire gut-wrenching story. From the news reporters that had camped out on the street in front of my house trying to get a statement from anyone who would stop, to the last months of my senior year falling apart, to graduation day, when I'd been so badly humiliated that I'd gone home and taken a Vicodin, the ones prescribed to me back when I'd had my wisdom teeth pulled out, and then my mom finding me drugged out in my bed.

There had been so much pain inside me, and I'd just wanted it to go away.

Then I brought them up to the present—the trial having started, my mom being there, and Jay telling me I should go because my dad is the only dad I'll ever have.

After all that, I half expected them to turn and run from me as fast as they could. But like Jay promised, they didn't. They were true friends.

"This is so horrible." Priya's eyes were still wide in shock. "I don't even know what to say."

"I know I should have told you both sooner, but I've been trying really hard for people not to find out. Jay knows, of course."

"And your brother—is your brother Eric Bianchini?" Emma asked.

I nodded.

"He is so hot," she mumbled.

I laughed out loud. "I was expecting you to get all judgy on me, Emma, not obsess about my brother."

"I can't believe I've known you since August, and all of this time, I could have met your hot hockey-playing brother and you kept this from us!"

Priya nodded. "Not only that, but the fact is, you're famous."

"You mean famously hated."

"Back to your brother." Emma held her chin high. "They shouldn't have taken him off the list for the Hobey Baker Award. It wasn't fair."

"I wouldn't worry about him. He's doing fine." I waved my hand. "Way better than me. He's playing for the AHL in Canada."

"So why aren't you at the trial?" Priya asked.

"Honestly?"

"Yes. What's holding you back?"

I chewed on the inside of my cheek. A difficult question. "At first, I thought it was resentment. Because I was angry at my dad. But now...well...I think the truth is I'm afraid. I'm afraid of people finding out who I am. I'm afraid of being judged all over again. I don't think I can take it a second time. Being the target of so much hatred." A shiver went down my arms. "I have PTSD just thinking about it. It must be the reason I can't sleep."

"I'm so sorry, Ade," Priya said, hugging me. "So very sorry."

Emma joined us, putting her arms around both of us. "Me too."

Their unexpected show of love made the tension in my muscles release. I should have told them the truth about my dad long ago.

"Thank you," I said.

"You're welcome," Priya said.

"We're here for you, Ade." Emma smiled.

Together, we went into the locker room and changed back into our street clothes.

"How do you think your mom is holding up?" Priya asked.

I winced. That same thought had been popping into my brain all day. "Not sure. I'll text her."

Priya and Emma left to get to their next classes, and I sat on a cushioned seat in the lobby, staring at the ceiling.

I pulled out my phone and sent a text.

> Hi, Mom. How's the trial?

I didn't know how long it would take her to respond, or if she'd respond at all, but right now it was really important to me that she got my message.

I waited and...nothing. So, I turned off the screen and put the phone in my back pocket.

When I got back to the dorm and was walking down the hallway to my room, my phone dinged.

MOM
Jury selection today and probably the rest of tomorrow.

> How are you doing?

MOM
It's hard.

Then came a slight moment of hesitation. I knew what I needed to ask her. I knew that it was what I should do, what I needed to do. I had to get rid of this fear. It was all-consuming.

> Do you want me to come sit with you?

MOM
I thought you were a hard no.

My gut squeezed.

> I'll come.

MOM
Oh, sweetie. You don't have to. Your dad and I
will survive.

Don't talk me out of it. I'll come tomorrow.

MOM
Wednesday morning would be better. After the
jury is selected.

We'll pick you up.

We?

MOM
Yeah, your dad and I.

Is there any way you could drop Dad off first
and then come get me?

I just couldn't stomach it. Dad in the car in the parking lot of
my dorm. Dad walking with Mom and me from the car to court.

MOM
Oh. Sure. I guess that would work. How about
8:30a?

Sounds good.

Whew.
Next stop: Dallas's door and a knock that went unanswered.
Where the hell was he?

THIRTY-TWO
BOY IS BACK

I t wasn't until Tuesday night that I finally saw Dallas in the dining hall. His back was to me as he ate dinner with some guys from his floor.

Before that moment, I'd been fine, maybe a little nervous about going to watch the trial, but fine. After I'd noticed him, even the noise echoing off the high ceiling made me cringe.

He'd come back, and hadn't told me.

I *should* be okay with that. We weren't an item. There was no understanding between us. So I tried to stay positive while sitting with Priya, Emma, and some of the girls from my floor, but it was hard. When I'd last seen him, something had felt off between us. A tectonic shift in plates. I hoped they were back in alignment.

I bussed my tray, and just as I was setting it on top of all the others, a hand snaked around my waist and pulled me close. *Dallas.* He smelled like spring, like planting ornamental grasses in a rain garden.

"Hey, hot stuff." His breath tickled my ear. His chin brushed my shoulder.

And just like that, *poof.* I was back to good. I sort of hated myself for it. It shouldn't be so easy for me to change my feelings about him. But I couldn't help it. I'd missed him. I wanted to be with him.

"How was your weekend?" I tried to stop my smile from stretching too far.

"Good." We walked out of the cafeteria together. "Great actually. I qualified for the semifinals."

"Awesome. Congratulations." Oh, how I wished I'd been with him instead of sulking here.

"I didn't get any further than that, but it was a blast, that's for sure. Met some other athletes in the sport. What did you do this weekend?"

"I went to a movie with my mom."

"Cool."

I supposed it was best that he hadn't invited me along, but at the same time, I'd give practically anything to have been there to see him get as far as he had in the competition. *Ugh.* This wasn't good. I was falling hard. And I didn't like how it was making me feel. Lonely. Desperate.

"I didn't make it to classes yesterday." He changed the subject.

"Yeah, I know. Your usual seat was empty."

"Did you take notes in chemistry?"

"Of course." When it came to school, taking detailed notes was the one thing I was good at.

"Could we go grab them and make copies in my room on my printer?"

His room? *Yes, please.* "Sure."

We grabbed my chemistry binder first and then we trekked to his floor. He stood over his printer, and I sat on the futon. I could watch him all day and never get bored. He had jeans on with a long-sleeve T-shirt. His ass filled out his pockets perfectly, and his shoulders had just the right amount of definition. The cute dimple at the corner of his mouth sucked in as he gave his full concentration to the task at hand.

It was funny how this worked. How much I wanted to have sex with him right this second. I needed to do something about it.

Make my intentions known. Maybe I should drape my naked body across his couch—that might give him a hint.

The copier made scanning noises as he turned to me. "So are you ready for the test?"

My face heated. Good thing he couldn't read minds, because mine had been on his groin rather than his brain. "I studied over the weekend, and Jay got his hands on some old tests, so I think I'm in pretty good shape. Are you?"

"I think so."

"So you've been studying?"

"Nah."

Seriously? So this was what it meant to be on the dean's list. He never had to study, because he already knew how to solve all the problems.

Sigh.

I wished I were that smart.

He finished up and gave me back my binder. "I need to go down and get a load of laundry. You want to come?"

"Sure thing. On the washer or the dryer?"

He narrowed his eyes and then opened them wide.

"Yes, thank you very much, I would like to come, soft and wet, please." I tried to stop myself from giggling.

That deep grin of his appeared on his face, the kind that made me want to jump into his lap.

He started toward me, but then stopped. "Hold it—give me a couple minutes to get my laundry and I'll be right back."

I sat back on his futon while he headed for the door, but then over his shoulder, he said, "There's beer in the refrigerator if you want one."

Beer. Definitely not what I wanted right now. I wanted *him*.

I took off my clothes, left them in a pile on the ground, and slipped into his bed. The smell of him surrounded me, and I lay there, breathing him in.

I'd been worried about us, but now I thought we were fine. And we'd be even better after some time alone together.

He came back with his basket, saw me in the bed, and dropped it in his closet. With every step he took toward me, he lost an article of clothing until there was nothing left on his body and he was naked. He crawled in, and I wrapped myself around him, his skin hot against mine.

We lay like that for a while. Doing nothing but listening to each other breathe, feeling the thudding of our hearts against each other. He picked up my hand and caressed my fingers, tracing every line, rubbing every crevice. He put one of my fingers in his mouth and sucked on it. I was getting as gooey as a roasted marshmallow.

He brushed innocent kisses against my temples, and I buried my head in his neck.

"I missed you," he whispered.

A rainbow lit up my heart. "Me too," I whispered back.

I'd never felt like this before. So attached to a person that pieces of me were melding with pieces of him. I wouldn't think about the future, not even a little.

The next morning, after a mediocre night of sleep, I rolled out of Dallas's bed and dressed. I didn't like the chill after soaking in the heat of his body.

I didn't want to leave him.

He slept on, and I stared down at him, my chest swelling with a scary amount of adoration. I kissed him, and then almost said it out loud. I almost told him that I loved him. But I stopped myself. He might actually be awake, and my declaration would be too soon, too much.

I exited his room and shut the door softly behind me. I felt lightheaded, and I inhaled a sharp breath.

That was unexpected. Love was not on the agenda. My heart had turned as fragile as one of the glass figurines in my mom's curio cabinet.

Calm down, I told myself. *Calm down.* People have fallen in love before.

Just not me.

THIRTY-THREE
OPENING STATEMENTS

I dressed myself in the dark. In a pencil skirt and cowl-neck sweater. I wanted to look respectable for the trial and, at the same time blend into the background. Be invisible. If only I had a cloaking device to activate. Like the spaceships in *Star Wars*.

Outside, my mom was waiting for me. When we arrived downtown, we parked in the courthouse's underground parking garage.

We took an elevator and stepped out. A glass-ceilinged atrium spanned the distance between two building towers. In the center, a water fountain surrounded by spaced-apart trees burbled steadily. An indoor oasis in contrast to the Minnesota tundra outside.

Mom headed toward the tower to our right, where a line of people waited to get through security.

My stomach rolled.

"How long do you think the trial is going to last?" I asked Mom.

"I'm not sure. The lawyer said it will take the rest of the week, maybe more."

We took the elevator up, and as we stepped out, there was

Dad. He was dressed in one of his game-day suits, his hair neatly arranged, debonair and stately.

There were other people too. Some with bound notepads.

Dad took a sip of his coffee and noticed me. "Ade." His deep voice sounded bright, cheerful, and he walked straight over to give me a hug. "I'm so glad you're here."

I gave him a stiff hug.

"So sorry about the other day," he whispered into my hair. "So sorry about everything I've made you live through this past year."

My heart leaped, and I squeezed him. So was I.

Gray Holton appeared next. Taller than my dad, he looked regal in a gray suit that matched his hair and, of course, matched his name. He patted my dad on the back. "Are you ready, Coach?"

Gray took my dad aside and started talking to him in a low tone. Mom went in search of a bathroom, so I was stuck all by myself.

The people with the notepads kept staring at my dad, so I drew back into the corner. I didn't like them.

My mom came back from the bathroom.

"Who are those people who keep looking at Dad?" I asked her.

"Reporters. They've been lurking all week."

A slight chill crawled up my arms. "They don't have cameras, do they?"

"No. Cameras aren't allowed."

That was right. Gray had told me before. Thank God. The last thing I needed was to be plastered all over television or in a newspaper.

"Also, Gray told your father and me that we—the family— should not speak to the media at all. Even if they ask questions. We need to walk away or say 'No comment.' Gray has told them that we are hands off, but he says to be careful. He'll be our spokesperson if he has to be."

Fine by me.

Finally, we—Gray, Dad, Mom, and I—walked into the court-room together. Two bailiffs were already inside and barely glanced at us. A clerk sat at a desk to the side of the bench, typing away on a computer. Gray and Dad headed to the defendant's table to take a seat. My mom and I settled in directly behind them.

The notepad lurkers sat behind us.

When I'd imagined attending the trial, this wasn't what I'd pictured. The courtroom was smaller, more intimate. Like a classroom, not a place to decide a man's fate. Even the jurors' chairs—two rows, one behind the other—were not so far away from us.

I saw movement out of the corner of my eye and looked to my left. The prosecuting attorney was standing next to her table. I hadn't noticed her walk in. She was young and gave off a type A vibe with her small, eagle-like features, boring black pant suit, and intense expression.

A bailiff called out, "All rise."

I looked around as everyone got to their feet, and I scrambled to mine.

The deep voice spoke again. "The Honorable Eleanor Thomas presiding."

A woman in a black robe came floating in, her glasses sitting low on the bridge of her nose. She sat down with a sigh, tucked in her chin, and scanned the room over the top of her lenses. "Please be seated."

She was probably in her mid to late fifties and seemed no-nonsense, but at the same time, I could see some warmth in her eyes.

"Today we start with opening statements, and hopefully we can make good headway into testimony. Before I let the jury in, I want everyone to understand that this is a court of law. Please keep quiet during proceedings and out in the hallway during recesses. We do not want any of the jurors hearing something they should not. Also, make sure your cell phones are turned off."

She paused.

I pulled out my cell and turned on airplane mode. It was nine-oh-six a.m.

"Good, please let the jury in."

My mouth went dry. Things were moving too fast.

Dad was writing down notes. Gray stood and tapped him on the shoulder. My dad joined him, and as the jury filed into the room, both Dad and Gray smiled at them, Gray even nodding a hello to each juror before he and Dad sat back down.

I scanned the seven men and five women who held my father's fate in their hands. They would decide his innocence or guilt. It made me feel faint.

The judge spoke to the jury, and then the prosecutor stood to give her opening statement.

I chewed on my hangnails. *Ick.* I knew. I was just that nervous, and I didn't understand why. I wasn't supposed to care about any of this. My dad's future didn't matter to me.

But it did.

The prosecutor began, her voice monotone and slow. "Deep down inside us, in the moral fiber of our community, we believe it to be true that athletic coaches are role models who hold important positions in schools and universities."

She was hitting on the point that had kept me up at night all these months. Unable to fall asleep, tossing and turning because I'd always believed my dad to be that kind of man. Even if he had found himself in a desperate situation, didn't he have the kind of embedded moral code that would tell him bribing people was wrong?

"But this is not what the defendant, Coach Bianchini, embodied in his tenure," she continued. "What he did was conspire to funnel money to families of recruits, and then conceal the scheme."

I slid down in my seat. Put that way, it sounded bad.

"Members of the jury, you will hear testimony and evidence proving guilt in the charges of bribery conspiracy, solicitation of bribes, honest services fraud conspiracy, honest services fraud, and conspiracy to commit wire fraud. The defendant"—she glanced my dad's way—"was a popular university hockey coach for over ten years. He wasn't just popular within the university, but also statewide, where he had, in his relatively short career, won more games season over season than any other coach in school's history. But how he won those games, it was discovered, was more than on his coaching talent—he won those games by bribing the best hockey players and their families to come play for him."

Mom looked at me, her face pale. I was trying hard not to feel anything, but there was no denying the nausea churning in my stomach.

"You will hear testimony that Mr. Bianchini directed payments to be made to families of recruits from a booster group and had the money wired to families as a consulting fee. Then he would instruct the families not to say anything to the university."

I couldn't imagine what was going through my dad's head. But somehow he appeared unaffected. Solid, statuesque. I wondered what Gray had up his sleeve, because if I were a juror, I'd believe everything the prosecutor was saying.

She kept talking, hashing and rehashing the points she'd already made. I thought if she'd stopped earlier, her statements would have been more effective. But how should I know? I was no lawyer. I was an engineering student on the verge of failing.

Finally, she ended by telling the jury, "This, members of the jury, is what corruption in college hockey looks like."

Gray stood, and I straightened.

He buttoned the top button of his jacket, came out from behind the table, and stood there, somber, engaging. He had a presence about him. A you-can-trust-me-to-tell-you-what's-really-going-on-here posture.

"Thank you, members of the jury, for coming today." Gray took the time to make eye contact with each person in the jury box. "We know there are other places you would rather be, but your service this week is greatly appreciated and wholly recognized." He paced away from the lectern and then back again. "Let me start this morning by stating something that needs clarification. I'm not going to waste everyone's time pretending that money was never wired to families of athletes. Because it was. There is evidence. What I am going to explain to you is that the NCAA has rules, created by members of their organization. But these rules—these NCAA-derived rules—are not the laws of our country. The NCAA is run much like a youth soccer league, if that soccer league brought in millions of dollars each year. Millions of dollars they have no interest in sharing. And these rules...they are equivalent to the rules in your homeowners association. If you break them, you haven't broken the law."

I straightened a little. It was a good start. I'd give him that.

As I scanned the jury, I noticed they were all middle-aged except for one girl who looked like she'd just stepped out of an EDM nightclub with her fake-animal-fur collar, tight dress, and dark eye makeup.

"Because, members of the jury"—he raised a hand in the air and shook it—"that is exactly what happened here. My client, David Bianchini, may have broken the rules of an athletic organization, but he did not commit a crime." Gray walked to the table and picked up a white sheet of paper. "The boosters who were mentioned by the prosecution just now weren't from a youth booster club raising money from raffle tickets. The mentioned booster is a billion-dollar company. While the NCAA allows colleges to be sponsored by Fortune 500 athletic companies, they do not allow athletes being recruited by the college to be paid by the sponsors to play. Sure, there are the name, image, and likeness contract rules now in place, but those NIL rules cannot induce an athlete to enroll in or stay at a particular school. So, let's sift through this. What kinds of companies are we talking about here, who sponsor colleges?" He looked down at the piece of paper to read names. "Nike, Adidas, Under Armour. As you very well know, these companies are interested in the athletic success of the colleges they sponsor."

He waved the paper in the air. "What happened here is exactly that. Achilles Incorporated, a billion-dollar company and sponsor of Minnesota University, wired money to families of top players so they would attend a specific school. It was a win-win-win situation that benefited all parties involved—the university by securing highly ranked athletes, Achilles Incorporated by placing top players at Achilles-sponsored schools and the athletes and their families by receiving the money."

He returned the paper to the table.

The jury stared back at him, seeming mesmerized. He really did know how to speak to them to keep their full, on-the-edge-of-their-seats attention.

"Of course a coach might appear to be culpable in some way. Coaches are the ones trying to find talent for the team, but they're also the ones who care deeply about the welfare of their players."

He paused and shifted his weight from the front of his toes to his heels. "Let's be clear here, folks. The money given to these families wasn't David Bianchini's money. He never asked anyone for money. It wasn't university money. The evidence will show that the money that was wired or attempted to be wired to the families of players was from Achilles Incorporated."

My face was burning, hot and steamy. *Wow.* Could the overachieving prosecutor be wasting everyone's time and public resources on my father? Could it be the big, bad, wealthy corporations that were to blame?

"Members of the jury"—Gray's voice was louder now—"if my client never gave his recruits money, never asked anyone to give his recruits money, then how can he be guilty?" He lifted his arm and pointed at Dad, which also meant he was pointing at me and my mom. I sank back a little.

"Rather, he is a loving husband, a supportive father, and a devoted coach."

I kept my face as motionless as I could. *Supportive father* was debatable.

Gray squared his shoulders and turned back to the jury, who were now looking at me as I shrank in my seat. "My client isn't guilty of a crime. The only thing he is guilty of is trying to be the best coach he could possibly be."

He walked back to his chair and sat down with a flourish.

Dad pulled his shoulders back into place.

My immediate instinct was to stand and cheer. Let loose a shout and a whistle. I loved Gray.

But wait. I didn't want to draw attention to myself. Quickly, I tamped down my emotions like I was being rolled over by heavy machinery used to flatten dirt.

There was a lunch break. The jurors retired to whatever room existed behind the wall, and the judge went to her chambers.

Mom whispered to me, "I think things are going really well."

I nodded. I didn't know what to think, what to feel. The district attorney's opening had been convincing, but Gray's had been so good.

After lunch, court resumed. The jury looked refreshed and ready to do their job. Judge Thomas looked on passively.

The prosecutor stood up at her table. "Your Honor, the US would like to call our first witness to the stand."

The judge nodded.

I heard the doors creak open.

"The prosecution calls Mr. Dallas Reynolds."

THIRTY-FOUR
THE WITNESS

I t must be my ears. I must be hearing things.

But when I looked behind me, it was Dallas—*my* Dallas—walking through the door wearing nice pants and a jacket cut to emphasize his shoulders and tapered waist.

A woman with a badge hanging from her waist followed him in and stayed at the back of the room. He passed by and stood before the witness box facing the judge, his back to me.

My breath came short and fast. My heart pounded so hard my rib cage hurt.

"Please face the clerk and raise your right hand," the judge said.

"Do you solemnly swear that the testimony you are about to give is the truth, the whole truth, and nothing but the truth, so help you God?" the clerk asked.

"I do."

The sound of Dallas's voice sent a sharp pain through my lungs.

"Thank you. You may be seated," said the judge.

He went around the stand and sat in the chair.

The clerk continued. "Please say and spell your name for the record."

He looked at her. "Dallas Reynolds. D-A-L-L-A-S R-E-Y-N-O-L-D-S."

Sweat started dripping down my back. None of this made sense. I didn't know what to do with my hands, my legs, my body.

Expression blank, Dallas looked first at the rows of jurors, then glanced at the district attorney, then the defense table where my dad and Gray were sitting. Finally, his gaze trailed behind them and onto me.

In that moment, time stopped. It seemed like every person in the courtroom froze and it was only Dallas who had not. His eyes —the same eyes that had looked at me with reverence the night before—held mine. At first his brows rose, but then they furrowed into a tight frown.

I died a little inside. Dallas was on the stand at my dad's trial. It was disorienting, discombobulating. Had Mars crashed into Venus?

Still worse, he wasn't testifying on behalf of my dad. No. Dallas was here to help prove his guilt. Send him to jail. I might choose to be a critic of my father, but I wasn't that awful of a daughter. I wasn't that horrid. I still wanted him to put this part of his life behind him. Rid himself of the lawyers, judges, and be free.

The district attorney stayed seated behind her table, a binder in front of her.

"Mr. Reynolds, do you play hockey?"

He said nothing. He was still looking at me, his face flushed, his eyes trying to read me. He shouldn't have much difficulty. He'd known who I was. He knew that my father was on trial. But he'd failed to tell me anything about himself and why he was sitting on that stand.

Bastard.

"Mr. Reynolds?"

He inched closer to the microphone, his glossy brown eyes still glued to me. "Yes."

"How long have you played?"

"Since I was five years old."

"And what team did you last play for?"

Dallas looked away from me and at the district attorney. "A USHL team called the Storm."

"Were you being recruited by any college teams during your time as a USHL player?"

"Yes."

"Was there a particular coach that was recruiting you who is in this room?"

My heart thumped like a bass drum.

"Yes."

"His name?"

"David Bianchini."

"If you could, please point this person out to us."

Dallas paled, almost as if he didn't want to do it. Like if he did, it would mean more than just answering one of the prosecutor's yes or no questions. It would be evidence of his betrayal. He glanced at the defendant's table and, with hesitation, pointed at my dad.

I looked away. I couldn't watch his condemning finger angled right at Dad. It physically hurt.

"Let the record show that Mr. Reynolds has indicated the defendant." After a pause, the district attorney continued. "Mr. Reynolds, I would like for you to explain to us what happened to you and your family leading up to your dealings with Mr. David Bianchini, the defendant."

Dallas looked directly at me again.

"Mr. Reynolds?"

He glanced away. "The year after I graduated from high school, my mom's cancer returned. After six months, the medical bills were piling up. At the same time, I had multiple colleges pursuing me to play hockey. But then she passed away, and everything fell apart."

My chest ached. Cancer. He'd never told me.

"Everything fell apart in what way?"

Dallas's voice was clear and steady. "My dad got laid off from his job. We had to organize and pay for the funeral, figure out where we would get the money to cover her medical bills and end-of-life care. When you play in the USHL, you're an amateur. They don't pay you. They only pay for your expenses."

A heaviness grew inside me.

"Did you figure out where the money would come from?" the district attorney asked.

I was having trouble breathing.

"Coach Bianchini set it up. He would give us enough money to pay for the funeral, the unpaid medical bills, and then some."

"Do you remember the exact sum?"

"Two hundred thousand dollars."

Omigod. Omigod. Omigod.

"And how do you know that the two hundred thousand dollars was from Coach Bianchini?"

Dallas rearranged himself on the chair. Then he swallowed hard. "He told me that as soon as I signed my letter of intent, we would get it, how we would get it, and that we shouldn't mention anything to the university."

Blood rushed to my head. The pressure in my ears was like an emergency descent in an airplane.

"And then what happened?" the attorney asked.

Dallas fidgeted. It was as if he suddenly didn't want to go on.

His voice lost all of its power. "I signed the letter. I took the money."

I sucked in a breath and slowly let it out.

"Thank you, Mr. Reynolds. A couple more questions and then I'm done. Do you play college hockey now?"

"No."

"Why not?"

"I am NCAA ineligible."

"Because?"

"It is a violation of NCAA rules to accept money to sign with a specific school."

"So your dreams were dashed."

"I suppose they were. At least, the dreams I had in that moment."

"Thank you, Mr. Reynolds."

There was silence. Some paper shuffling. I gazed at the floor because I couldn't—*couldn't*—look at Dallas.

None of this had anything to do with me, but every muscle in my body quivered. My head was woozy. I couldn't believe he hadn't told me about his deal with my dad, about his ineligibility.

The judge nodded to Gray.

He got up from behind his table. "I have only a couple of follow-up questions, Mr. Reynolds."

Dallas sat a little straighter.

"How can you say the money was from Coach Bianchini if you didn't actually get it directly from him?"

"Because I gave him my dad's bank account information."

"But he didn't actually hand you a check, is that correct?"

"No. It came as an electronic deposit."

"Did you ever meet with representatives of Achilles Incorporated?"

Dallas paused, then leaned into microphone. "I spoke with them on the phone."

"Did they talk about money with you?"

"They did."

"And what did they say?"

"That they were working with Coach Bianchini to help me out financially because of my mother's death."

"So, did you think the money that you were going to get was going to come from Coach Bianchini or from Achilles Incorporated?"

"Well, it must have been Achilles because—"

"Thank you, Mr. Reynolds. I didn't ask you to explain."

"But I need to. I want to. It must have been Achilles money because my dad gave it back to them."

"Thank you again, Mr. Reynolds."

Gray walked to the stenographer. "For the record, the witness said he believed the money was coming from Achilles Incorporated.

"I have nothing further." Gray walked back to his seat.

The prosecutor shot to her feet and moved around her table. "Mr. Reynolds, is the money that Achilles Incorporated discussed with you the same money that Coach Bianchini was referring to?"

"Yes."

"How do you know?"

"Because Coach Bianchini set up the conference call with Achilles. He was also there during the conversation."

"That's all I have, Your Honor." The prosecutor sat right back down and started scribbling away.

I had to get out of here. I had to get out now.

"Mom," I whispered, "I need a break."

She nodded.

"Can I have your keys?"

She dug in her purse and handed them over.

I got up and walked as normally as I could down the center aisle. But after the door to the courtroom closed behind me, I ran.

I pushed the call button for the elevator over and over. It dinged. Inside, I pressed the button for the main floor then hit the door-close button. Just before the elevator shut, I saw Dallas, jogging straight at me.

"Ade," he shouted. "Wait."

THIRTY-FIVE
THE PANIC ATTACK

was panting, hyperventilating. If only I had a small brown paper bag.

The elevator kept stopping—on every floor. People entered, and then at the next stop, they'd exit. I should have taken the stairs.

My nose started running, and I wiped it with the back of my trembling hand. My stomach ached. Dallas had known. He'd known weeks ago who I was. But he hadn't said a thing. Not a thing.

The night we went to Sporty's and played pool, I'd told him about my dad. And he'd said *nothing*.

My lungs were caving in.

Finally, the elevator made it to the second-floor atrium, and I ran. I dodged past people as they read or typed away on their phones. I didn't look back. I just kept going. Heading straight for the elevator that would send me down into the attached parking garage.

But I wasn't fast enough. A hand pulled me to a stop.

"Ade." Dallas's face was splotchy, his eyes feverish, hot. "I need to talk to you."

The pressure he had on my arm was like a vise. "Let me go."

"I can't." He breathed hard. "I'm afraid you'll run again."

I stood motionless. My eyes were tearing up. "You're hurting me."

"Oh God!" He released me. "I'm sorry, so sorry."

I hugged my arm. There was a war going on inside of me. I didn't want to talk to him, because I was so confused, so hurt. But I also did. I wanted to tell him exactly what I thought of how careless he'd been with me, with my heart.

A person bumped into me, and Dallas pointed me to the center of the atrium, to the circular water fountain. "This way."

He looked miserable. I *was* miserable.

We walked across the atrium together but far enough apart from each other that a couple of hockey players in their pads could have fit between us.

When we reached the slabs of granite that made up the border of the fountain, we faced each other. But damn him, I had to look away.

I gazed up through the glass roof at the two looming towers, and my heart broke straight down the center. This was it. We were done.

Over.

"In the courtroom." He swallowed. "I didn't think you were going to be there. You told me that you weren't coming."

I stepped farther away from him. "But he's my dad."

The corner of his mouth twitched.

I folded my arms, wondering exactly how long his Pinocchio nose really was. How many more lies had he told me that I'd been oblivious to?

"In fact"—I squeezed my arms together—"you've known my secret for weeks, that I'm his daughter, yet you never told me who you were."

He winced then scrubbed a hand down his face. "It wasn't like that."

"It wasn't?"

"You have to believe me." He glanced up with pained eyes. "I thought it would be better if you didn't know. I was going to tell you after the trial."

"Seriously?"

"Who I am, what happened in the past, it has nothing to do with what's going on between us. It's an unlucky coincidence, and it shouldn't affect how we feel about each other."

"Oh, I get it." I nodded.

"You do?"

"You wanted to have sex with me. No, not just sex—you wanted to have *revenge* sex with me. To get back at my dad for ruining your dreams."

"*What?* No. I—"

"It's so obvious." I was shivering so hard I had to tighten my grip on my arms. "If you felt anything for me at all, you would have told me who you were. It's as simple as that."

He slumped. "I know how it looks, but it *wasn't* that way. I promise."

"Then what way was it?"

"I thought if I told you, you wouldn't have given me...you wouldn't have given yourself a chance to get to know me."

I pressed my lips together. God. This shit was complicated.

His gaze hardened, then softened, changing right in front of me. "Please. Ade, you're killing me." His voiced sounded anguished.

Walking away from him was going to be hard. So hard. My heart might be telling me that it didn't want this to be the end. For us to be done. But my brain was telling me something else, that I was doing the right thing. There was no other choice.

I took a deep breath and exhaled. "It's over. We're finished."

With those words, I walked away.

"Ade," I heard his raspy voice call out.

But I didn't look back. I owed him nothing.

I made it to the parking garage and found the car. I got into the driver's seat and crouched over the steering wheel.

My legs jiggled. My insides burned. I breathed in and out, in and out. *I'll get through this.* I had to. I'd pretend I hadn't fallen in love with Dallas. Pretend I'd never met him. That he was the stuff of a make-believe land.

I tried hard to hold it back, but I couldn't. I didn't have enough strength. I screamed at the windshield and sobbed.

Without Dallas, there'd be no more mornings skipping from his dorm room to mine with a glow in my chest. Without Dallas, my insomnia would worsen. Without Dallas... *Get over yourself, Ade.*

I gasped for breath.

Without each other, we'd both be better off.

THIRTY-SIX

ROCK BOTTOM

dried my face on the front of my shirt and checked my phone.
Mom had texted me.

MOM
Are you coming back?

No. I'll wait for you in the car.

MOM
Are you okay?

I was going to type back that I was fine, but I wasn't. I was far
from that.

No

MOM
What's wrong?

I'll tell you when you get here.

MOM
Another recruit is testifying and then they'll
adjourn for the day. I'll be there as soon as
I can.

I turned on the car to warm it up, and while it was past my allotted time for drinking caffeine, I wanted a Red Bull so bad. I needed something, anything, that would give me comfort.

Resting my head on the steering wheel, I closed my eyes...and went numb. Almost like I was in a trance. I breathed in and out. In and out. Oblivious to time. Unaware of space.

A rap sounded on the window, and I jumped.

It was Mom.

I opened the door and got out.

"Hi, sweetie." She gave me the biggest, strongest hug. Then her hands fluttered up to brush pieces of my hair aside. "Oh, honey, it looks like you've been crying. Should we talk in the car?"

I nodded.

She got into the driver's side, and I went around to the passenger side. She blasted the heat, threw the car into reverse, and away we went. She paid at the attendant kiosk, and the next thing I knew, we were winding through the one-way streets of downtown Minneapolis.

"What's going on?" she finally asked.

I cleared my throat. I needed to choose my words wisely. "Lately, I kind of sort of started hanging out with a guy at school."

Her brow creased. "That's great, Ade, but what does that have to do with this afternoon?"

I paused to collect myself, taking a deep breath and exhaling. "This guy, his name is Dallas. Dallas Reynolds."

Mom frowned. "Isn't that the name of the witness who testified today?"

I nodded.

She sucked in a breath, but still managed to check her rearview mirrors, toss a glance over her shoulder, and change lanes. After she was done, she looked at me. "That poor young man who lost his mother to cancer?"

"Yes. Him."

"Did you know he was going to be a witness?"

"No."

"Oh," she said quietly.

I clenched my teeth. She wasn't freaking out like I had.

Maybe I needed to tell her more. That he'd broken my heart. Actually, it was worse than that—he'd pulled my heart apart like monkey bread, and now it was sticky and getting all over everything.

Putting my face in my hands, I used all my willpower to keep myself from crying again, but I couldn't control my trembling shoulders or my whimper.

She put her hand on my knee. "Sweetie, I'm so sorry. I hate seeing you this upset."

I dragged my hands over my face. "He knew." My voice sounded like cracking ice. "He knew exactly who I was and that he would be testifying against Dad, but he didn't tell me."

She placed both hands back on the steering wheel. "He knew?"

"Yes, and he didn't say a word." A flood was building inside me.

"That doesn't sound very honorable, but, Ade, maybe there's a reason he couldn't."

The waters were pressing against my heart, trying to find a way out. "What do you mean?"

"Maybe he signed a document that bound him to secrecy."

"That can't be true. If you watch any courtroom show or read any books, both sides know who's on the witness list."

"Maybe he just recently got subpoenaed and he hadn't been able to tell you yet."

"Impossible. We slept together last night."

Silence filled the car interior.

"Then you're not just hanging out with him."

"Right."

Mom stared straight ahead, gripping the steering wheel harder. "I hope you two are using protection."

"Of course we are."

"Should I take you to the doctor so you can get on the pill?"

"Mom!"

She flinched. "Sorry, I'm just processing over here."

"Well, you don't need to, because it doesn't matter anymore. It's over between us."

She glanced at me. "Are you sure?"

I nodded. He was a fraud. Just like me. Both of us trying to be someone we were not.

Because who was I kidding? Even if I could sleep, I was never going to be on any dean's list. I was never going to have the GPA to get into upper division chemical engineering.

I was never going to be good enough.

An ache the size of a watermelon swelled inside my throat.

"Oh, honey." Her hand was back on my knee and squeezing. "I know how horrible you must feel, especially with"—she cleared her throat —"how close you must be with him, but I think you should also look at it from his perspective too. He lost everything. First his mom. Then hockey."

I rested my arm on the door and stared out the window. A tear slid down my cheek as I looked at the people on the sidewalk, going about their business, waiting at bus stops. I wiped it away.

Mom might be right about Dallas having suffered. But he hadn't shared that pain with me, and because he hadn't, he felt like a stranger. Like I hadn't known him at all.

THIRTY-SEVEN
THE TEST

Early the next morning, I flew out of one of the dorm's exit-only side doors and into a snowdrift. The automatic lock clicked behind me. I trudged to the sidewalk and stomped clumps of snow off my boots. With my winter gear in place, I was ready to make my trek to chemistry to take this week's test.

Ahead, Jay was waiting for me at the street corner.

As I approached, he tilted his head. "I almost didn't recognize you all bundled up like that."

"Good." I pulled my scarf up a little higher.

"A bunch of residents watched the news last night in the main floor lounge to get highlights of the trial. Is that why you texted me to meet you on the street rather than in the dorm lobby? Because you've taken hiding to a new extreme?"

"Thanks, Jay." I raised an eyebrow. "I didn't know that, but now I do and it doesn't make me feel good."

"All right, all right. I'm sorry." He started walking. "Spill it. What's going on?"

"Long story."

"Good thing you can talk and walk to class at the same time."

He checked the time on his cell phone. "But we better hurry because we're running late."

I wasn't sure why I was being evasive with Jay. I'd eventually tell him everything. I always did.

"The truth is"—I took a deep, cold breath as we scooted along —"I never knew who Dallas was at all."

"What?"

"It turns out he's one of them."

"One of who?"

"One of the recruits my dad is accused of bribing."

All I got in response was Jay's breathing, his Adam's apple moving up and down as he swallowed.

"That's...that's unexpected," he finally said.

I tried concentrating on him, but I couldn't stop my arms from waving in the air. "It's not just unexpected. It's an explosion. It's like a hydrogen balloon turning into a firebomb, and now my eyebrows have been singed off." My heart was doing palpitations. "I told him weeks ago who I really was. Trusted him with my secret, but he didn't say a thing about himself. Then he showed up in court yesterday to testify against my dad, thinking I wasn't going to be there."

"Wow." Jay's eyes were wide, unblinking. "How many Red Bulls did you have this morning?"

"None. I downed two of those five-hour energy shots. Extra strength."

"Holy balls, Ade."

"Anyway, now I have to avoid him, because if he finds me, I'm afraid I'll punch him." My fist went flying in the air. "I'm afraid I'll knee him in the groin." I acted out that maneuver too. "And when he's writhing on the ground, I'm afraid I'll crush his hands with my feet."

"Whoa, Ade. Settle down."

I froze midstomp and cocked my head. "I can't. This is the kind of danger he'll be in if I run into him, that's all. That's why I had to meet you outside."

"You do realize he's in our class right now. He's going to be taking the test too."

The wind sent us sailing through the door of the building.

"I know," I said. "Which is why I made sure we'd get here just as the test was about to be handed out."

"Also, you said you don't know him, but I hope you've realized that he doesn't know you either."

"Yes, he does." I peeled off my layers. "I told you. He knew my secret. He knew who my father was."

"He didn't know your other secret."

In the lecture hall, we sat with an empty seat between us— test-taking protocol.

"I don't know what you're talking about." I set my calculator on the corner of the foldout desk. "I don't have another secret."

Jay tapped his pencil on the desk, then leaned over and lowered his voice. "That you were using him to cure your insomnia."

My heart stopped. Or maybe skipped a beat. Jay sure had a way of making me sound like the evil one here. Because I wasn't, was I?

My right leg started to jiggle. But it was true. I'd never told Dallas. Not even the night I had the auditory hallucination.

I tried not to look for him. Not to find the back of his head. But I did. He was sitting at the bottom and to the right of the large auditorium room.

The ache in my chest intensified. I could hardly breathe. Hardly see straight. Jay was right. *Both* Dallas and I had been insincere to each other.

Jay squinted at me. "Are you okay?"

But I couldn't respond. My heart was beating too fast. A whooshing sound kept crashing in my ears. I couldn't find words or figure out how to get them out of me.

"Ade, you've got to stop taking so much caffeine, and stop hiding behind all of these secrets. You need to embrace the life that you were born with. I promise you that it will be okay."

The room was full now. Tests were being passed down the row, and I took one. I placed my hand on the stapled packet lying upside down, and I knew without a doubt that I was going to fail. No amount of studying or practicing, no amount of energy supplement, was going to get me through this. Not today.

I glanced around the room at the other students, but they all had deadpan faces. I was the only one about to break in half. Even Jay was calm and collected. I should just leave. Call my mom and tell her I'd meet her at the courthouse earlier than I'd thought. Even though she told me last night that they'd delayed court this morning until ten, making my eight a.m. exam occur at the perfect time.

"Ade," Jay said, "you can do this. As hard as it sounds, you need to block out everything else and concentrate."

I nodded in panic.

"Breathe, Ade. Breathe."

So I did. And it helped. A little.

After the teaching assistant gave us the cue, I flipped over the packet and dug in. I read the first question, and a cylinder fired in my brain. Aha. I knew how to solve this problem. I hunched over and started scratching away, showing my work.

When I got to the last question, I looked up to check the time. Less than two minutes left. Dang. I hadn't finished. And I wasn't going to have enough time to look over my answers to make sure I'd done the math right. I scribbled as fast as I could in the time left, making some educated guesses.

The tests were collected, and all I wanted to do was steal mine back.

I sulked out of class and into the hall, and standing there, waiting for me, was Dallas. His brown eyes searched mine, his backpack slung over one shoulder.

I was in no shape to talk to him. Especially now, after realizing that I was partially to blame for our dysfunctional relationship. I only had enough kinetic energy to keep on walking. To put distance between us. So that was what I did. I kept moving.

Dallas stepped in front of me. "Hey."

"Ade," Jay said from behind me. "Don't do anything stupid."

I walked around Dallas.

Jay had taken me seriously about beating Dallas up. *No need to worry, my friend. I wasn't going to do anything. Not now.*

"Ade, please." Dallas's voice sounded louder. "I need you to listen to me for just a second."

His familiar voice made my insides hurt, but I didn't stop. I couldn't.

"Not cool, dude," Jay said. "Not cool."

"Ade." Dallas's voice echoed in the hall. "Have you talked to your brother?"

My heart sped up to double time, but I kept going forward, moving away from him. What was he even talking about?

I glanced behind me and saw Jay holding on to Dallas's arm. "You need to give her space. Wait until the trial is over."

Once outside, I fled straight for the station to catch the train to the courthouse downtown. When I got to the platform, I stood under a heat lamp, gasping for air. My head hurt. My stomach ached. Like someone had kicked me in the gut. My hands were shaking. So much was wrong with me, I didn't know whether to attribute it to the five-hour energy shots or everything else.

"Are you okay?" asked a female voice from next to me under the heater.

I glanced up. My gaze met a girl's, and at the same time, our eyes widened. It was her. It was the EDM juror with the black makeup.

"Oh shit," she choked out. "I'm not supposed to talk to you."

"You're not?"

"The judge told us that we couldn't talk to any lawyer, party, or witness in the case."

"I'm not any of those."

"But you're...you're David Bianchini's daughter, aren't you?"

I paused, letting her words soak in. Steep a bit. And I was fine. No panic. No nothing.

"I'll go stand over there." I pointed down the platform. "By the other heater, and make sure we get on different cars."

"Wait," she said. "Do you go to school here?"

This strange sensation crawled up my spine. Normally, I would have lied to her. Denied my enrollment. But not now.

I nodded. "I do."

Her features softened. Even with the dark makeup on. "Has it been awful for you? People knowing who you are?" Her eyebrows drew into a frown. "Actually, don't answer that. You shouldn't answer that. I shouldn't be talking to you."

I glanced away and then back to her. "I had been keeping my identity a secret."

Her eyes widened again. "I won't say anything to anyone. I promise."

"You don't have to promise. It's a secret I no longer want to keep."

Right then, the train came to a flying stop. The brakes squealed so loud that even if she said something more, I wouldn't have heard it. The doors opened, and she got into the last car. I turned, jogged to the front, and jumped in.

I settled into a seat. Secrets. My secrets. Dallas's secret. They made one's life miserable. Two five-hour-energy-shots miserable.

Jay was right. The time had come to stop hiding. I needed to be the person I was born to be, even if it meant unloading all of the baggage that came with it.

THIRTY-EIGHT
BIG BROTHER

I walked alone from the train stop to the courthouse. It wasn't until I was inside the glass-covered atrium that I noticed the EDM juror again. She was in the security line to take the elevator up.

Instead of getting into the queue, I veered to a café kiosk for a bottle of water.

Best not to find myself near her. I wouldn't want her to get in trouble or give anyone the wrong idea.

I took my time and started to people watch. A man in a suit running to the elevator bank. A security guard looking bored. A reporter and her camera operator setting up by the fountain, the camera painted with a local television station logo.

Hm.

Maybe that was it.

Maybe that was a way for me to efficiently let the world know who I was. And I didn't have to give an interview. All I'd have to do was stand by my dad while Gray talked.

I glanced at my phone. *Shoot.* It was past the ten o'clock scheduled start time.

I rushed to get through security and up the elevator. When the doors slid open, they revealed an empty hall. Except there on a bench, sitting against the wall, was my brother, Eric.

My heart filled.

"Ade." His thick brown hair was longer than I remembered. Light stubble covered his jaw.

"What are you doing here?" My voice cracked.

"My team has a short break, so I flew in last night." He stood up. "Mom begged me to come."

I hugged him, and my entire body relaxed into his folded embrace. Sometimes a girl just needed her big brother to take the weight of the world off her shoulders.

"You never called me back." I stepped back.

"Sorry." He grimaced. "I've been meaning to and never got the chance."

"It's okay." I hugged him again. "I'm glad you're here. But why are you not inside the courtroom?"

He looked at the door. "Plunkett is testifying."

My shoulders sagged. I'd figured the district attorney would bring in people from the university to testify, but I was hoping one of them wouldn't be George Plunkett, the athletic director. He'd always butted heads with my dad.

"I don't have the stomach to listen to him. So I decided to wait for you."

"I get it," I said. "Plunkett...he's...well...he's..."

"He can be an asshole." Eric raised an eyebrow.

I gave him a huge smile.

"He walked right past me earlier and pretended he didn't know me," Eric said.

"How rude." Eric had been selected Minnesota Mr. Hockey, awarded to the most outstanding high school hockey player in the state. "Think about how much prestige you brought to the school."

Eric shrugged and sat back down on the bench. He scooted over to make room for me.

I plopped down next to him, and my heart continued to burst. We hadn't had any type of real togetherness for a long time.

"The thing is"—Eric leaned back against the wall—"Plunkett is the one person you should be nice to no matter how he treats you."

"Even now, with your college career over?"

"Things have a way of circling back."

I laid my head against the wall too. I guessed his theory made sense. But it didn't mean *I* had to like Plunkett.

"And that goes for recruits too."

I looked at Eric. "What?"

Eric sighed. "Ade, I know about you and Dallas Reynolds."

I sat straight. My face turned hot. "Who told you?"

"Dallas."

I almost slid off the seat. *"What?"*

"He called me."

Dallas mentioning Eric earlier now made more sense, but still. "Dallas has your number?"

"Yeah. Dad had me meet with him back when he was being recruited."

"Omigod."

"Omigod, what?"

"Well, first, I wish I'd known that. Second, you didn't...you didn't know about the money, did you?"

Eric's eyes widened. *"No.* I had no idea about any sort of financial transaction. Dad just wanted me to talk to recruits about my experience as a hockey player at the university and give them a tour. I did that sometimes."

I exhaled. "That's good."

"Anyway, there's something you need to know about Dallas."

I sat still and didn't move. Since seeing Dallas this morning, I'd erected a temporary dam, and I wasn't sure how long it was going to hold. I feared that thinking about him would cause tiny fissures, and I needed to keep myself together right now, not be susceptible to collapsing into a crumpled heap. But who was I fooling? What was it that Eric thought I needed to know?

"Go ahead," I said. "I'm listening."

Eric sat still, not moving a muscle. "After he found out who you were, he told the prosecutor he was no longer willing to testify. The attorney then made a deal with him. She said that if he testified, she'd get him his NCAA eligibility back."

I swallowed. Hard. "And?"

"And nothing. She's done nothing. The school's done nothing. He couldn't get a straight answer out of anyone, and he's pretty pissed off about it. Now the attorney is telling him that he misunderstood. She never promised him his eligibility back, only that if he testified, it might make him look better to the NCAA."

A sinking feeling spread through my stomach.

"I feel really bad for him," Eric said. "His whole life, his whole career completely effed up because of all of this."

"Me too." My chest pulled taut. My ears grew hot with embarrassment. Me and my insomnia paled in comparison to that.

I'd been so mad at Dallas after he'd testified that I hadn't bothered to listen, and then I'd avoided him after the test today even when all he wanted was to explain it to me.

Eric put an arm around me and squeezed. "Normally, the idea of a hockey player dating my little sister wouldn't sit well with me. I know what they can be like. But this Dallas kid, he seems okay."

I frowned. "Eric, I know you're well intentioned, but whatever *was* going on between Dallas and me, and I'm not sure I'd call it dating, it's…well…things are complicated, and it's over."

"Oh." Eric flinched. "Sorry. I didn't realize."

The elevator popped open, and a tiny woman with long blonde hair dressed in a pantsuit came out, along with another woman with a court badge hanging around her neck. The tiny woman made eye contact with us and hesitated.

"Who's that?" I whispered to my brother.

"I'm not sure," he said. "But she looks familiar."

The woman kept her distance from us.

"Do you think she's testifying?" My voice was quiet.

"She must be," Eric said.

The blonde kept eyeing us. She wrung her hands and glanced at the closed courtroom doors.

I couldn't fathom what she was so nervous about. She wasn't the one on trial.

The doors opened again and out strode Plunkett. He didn't give us a sideways glance, not until Eric got up and intercepted him.

Abruptly, he stopped.

Eric shook his hand. "Nice to see you again, George."

I got up from the bench and stood next to my brother.

"Hi, Eric, Adriana." His voice sounded like he had a frog in his throat. "You two are looking well, considering the…circumstances."

"Yep." Eric stood straighter. "We're here to support Dad."

"Heard you signed with the AHL."

Eric nodded.

"Always good to see our players continuing on with professional careers."

Eric kept nodding.

"Well, if either of you need anything, you know where to find me."

"Thanks," Eric said.

Plunkett hurried away as fast as he could. Like if he lingered too long, he might catch something from us.

Mom appeared at the doors. "Are you two coming?"

We nodded and followed her in.

I took a seat between Mom and Eric.

Dad rolled back his chair and leaned over the guardrail. "Hey, kids."

"Hi, Dad," Eric and I said in unison.

"I just want to thank you two for coming. It means a lot." He reached over and covered my hand with his. "I'm sorry for not being the kind of dad I should have been these past months. From now on, I'm going to do better."

I gave him a weak smile. "Okay, Dad."

The judge struck her gavel, and Dad rolled himself back to the table.

I whispered into my mom's ear, "How are things going?"

According to her, Plunkett's testimony went poorly for Dad. I was glad I hadn't been here for that. Instead of just feeling sick, I would have gotten sick.

The blonde woman, whose name, I learned, was Melanie Burch, was called to the stand.

"Ms. Burch," the prosecutor said, "please state your position at the university and explain your job description to us."

"I'm the head hockey cheer coach."

A sudden jolt of cold went through me.

"Each year, we recruit members to try out for our cheer squad, and then we hold a full season of workouts, performances, and cheer."

"So, hockey cheer is a separate tryout from other cheerleading squads?"

"Yes. Hockey cheer is its own quite unique separate group because of the skating components involved. We have high standards for those on the squad in terms of technical skating abilities."

The prosecutor stood. "Your Honor, may I have permission to approach the witness?"

The judge nodded. "Permission granted."

The prosecutor came around the table and handed Melanie a piece of paper. "Do you recognize this?"

Melanie took it and looked it over. "Yes."

"What is it?"

"An inquiry I received in February of last year."

Oh no. It couldn't be. This really was happening.

"Please read the message to us," the prosecutor said.

Melanie scanned the page, and then she began. "Dear Ms. Burch, I am reaching out to you regarding hockey cheerleading. My daughter is a figure skater, quite an accomplished one, having obtained her gold medal in Skating Skills and being close to completing her Free Skate tests. She has been accepted for enrollment at Minnesota University next year and is interested in information about how to try out for your team. Best regards, Coach Bianchini."

The gazes of the jury slid my way, including the EDM juror.

My face turned hot. I'd known that my dad had contacted the head coach about me, and I'd been mad about it. But now, having heard what the email said, I couldn't believe how innocent it was. He'd even used the correct figure-skating lingo.

I raised my chin. My lungs expanded with deep, satisfying breaths.

"Did you know who Coach Bianchini was at the time of receiving this message?"

"Yes, of course. Everyone knows Coach Bianchini."

"Did you send him any information?"

"I did. I sent him a link to our hockey cheer tryout packet and application."

"So, this packet and application are readily available on the internet?"

"Correct."

The prosecutor crossed her arms. "And easy to find?"

"Relatively easy if you know how to navigate the website."

"Ms. Burch." The prosecutor's tone sharpened. "Explain to me about a call that you received one week later."

Melanie sat up straight. "Yes. I received a call from a representative at Achilles Incorporated."

"And what did this representative say to you?"

Melanie scooted closer to the microphone. "He understood

how little funding there is for college cheer teams. He said they would be happy to make a financial pledge to my hockey cheer squad as long as some particular people made the team."

Suddenly, my ears became hypersensitive. Black spots appeared in my vision.

"Can you please tell us who those people were?"

"Well, I shouldn't say 'people' in the plural. It was really one person."

"Who?"

"Coach Bianchini's daughter."

This was craziness. Lunacy. I had never ever wanted to become a cheerleader, let alone try out for the team.

"Did you receive any of this money from Achilles Incorporated?"

"No."

"Why not?"

"I assume because the investigation broke before they could send any money."

Crap. That sounded terrible. It sounded like all my dad did was direct bribes at people. I eyed Gray, but he was just sitting there, observing.

He needed to fix this.

I grabbed my bag and fished out a pen and a scrap of paper. I wrote on it as quickly as I could.

"Thank you, Ms. Burch. I have nothing more." The prosecutor returned to her chair.

Gray stood and turned toward us while he buttoned his jacket. I leaned forward and handed him my note.

He narrowed his eyes but took it and read it. He looked back at me once before stepping out from behind the table to move to the podium.

"Ms. Burch, you said that this message came to you in an inquiry. What does that mean?"

"It means that Coach Bianchini was on our cheer home page and filled out a form that gets sent to my inbox."

"So, this message did not come from, say, his personal or university email?"

"No."

"How can you verify that Mr. Bianchini submitted the message?"

"Because he signed his name to it."

"But couldn't someone else have sent the message and put his name on it?"

"I suppose, but I don't know why they would."

Gray paused, looking straight at the jury and letting her words sink in.

"Okay," he continued. "You also said that you sent Mr. Bianchini a link after you received the message. How did you do that?"

"I emailed him."

"So you looked up his email address and emailed him the link?"

"Correct."

"Did he ever email you back?"

"No, I don't believe so."

Gray paused again.

"Ms. Burch, when do you make this tryout packet and application available to the public?" he asked.

"February." A piercing sound from the microphone filled the room. Her lips had come too close, and she leaned back. "In most cases, February for the following season."

"And when are the applications due?"

"In March."

"And when do the tryouts take place?"

"April."

"So, Ms. Burch, let me get the course of events straight. A message was sent to you in February that we can't verify was actually from Mr. Bianchini. In response, you sent Mr. Bianchini a link to the publicly available tryout packet and application with no confirmation of receipt. One week later, Achilles Incorporated offered you financial support if Coach Bianchini's daughter was placed on the squad."

"Correct."

"Did Coach Bianchini's daughter ever turn in an application?"

The woman sat silently in her chair, staring at Gray but not flinching. "I don't know."

"Did Coach Bianchini's daughter ever come to tryouts?"

"I don't believe so."

"Have you ever spoken to Coach Bianchini's daughter?"

"No."

"Ms. Burch, do you know the date that the defendant was charged with his alleged crimes?"

"No."

"Since you haven't had the benefit of watching the entirety of this trial, I will tell you. It was May twenty-third. My client, Coach Bianchini, was relieved of his coaching duties two days later, on May twenty-fifth. So, my question to you is, do February and March come before May?"

"Objection," the prosecutor said. "Harassing the witness."

"Overruled." The judge raised her head. "The witness is capable of answering the question."

Gray repeated himself. "Ms. Burch, do February and March come before May?"

"Yes, they do."

"So, we can safely assume that the reason Achilles never sent you any money is not because an investigation broke before they could send you the money?"

"Yes, that is probably true."

"In fact, was there ever any indication from Coach Bianchini's daughter that she wanted to be part of your hockey cheer squad?"

Melanie paused for a while, staring into space. "No."

"And if she didn't want to be part of a hockey cheer squad, there's no reason Mr. Bianchini would need to induce you to ensure that she was?"

"I suppose that makes sense."

"That's all I have, Your Honor. Thank you."

I stared at Gray, understanding, but then again not totally understanding, what had just happened or what impact, if any, it'd had.

Gray winked at me before he sat.

At least *he* seemed to think something had just gone right.

THIRTY-NINE
HOME SWEET HOME

After, the judge adjourned for what would likely be the second to last day of the trial. The prosecution had rested their case, and Gray had decided not to put my father on the stand.

Before Gray left, I pulled him aside. "Do you plan on granting an interview to the media?"

"Hadn't thought about it. Should I?"

"Part of the reason I've been coming to court is that I'm done hiding. But the thought of having to tell an entire dorm about who I am, or even people in my classes, is too much. I saw a reporter and a camera operator this morning in the atrium, and I realized that being on camera with you and my family might be the best way to let it be known and be done with it."

He squinted. "Interesting thought." Gray patted me on the shoulder. "I'll run it past your dad, but I'm sure he'd be on board."

Eric and I stayed at my parents' house that night. My mom made her famous Valentine's chocolate and cherry layered cake in the shape of a heart. I hadn't even realized that the following day was February fourteenth.

We played cards. We had a few good laughs.

After my parents went to bed, Eric and I sat in the living room. He streamed Netflix, and I texted.

PRIYA
Where are you?

Home. With my parents

PRIYA
You coming back tonight?

No. Tomorrow is the last day of the trial and probably the verdict. I'm going to spend tonight and tomorrow with my family. BTW, Eric is here!

PRIYA
Your brother?

Yes. He flew in last night!

PRIYA
I promise I won't tell Emma or she'll rush to your house to meet him.

Haha. You're right. She would do that.

PRIYA
Keep me posted tomorrow.

Sounds good

I slept horribly that night. I was nervous for Dad and what he would face the next day. And then, as much as I tried not to, I kept thinking about Dallas. Dallas and his ineligibility.

A memory came back to me from the night we'd gone to Sporty's. When I told him who my dad was, and he clammed up on me. He'd gone from a pursuer to an avoider in mere seconds. And if I hadn't cornered him later that night and forced myself on him, our short relationship would have run its course and I wouldn't have been mad at him now.

Damn it. I didn't want this turmoil.

There was a rock in my stomach. And because of that, I wanted—no, needed—to fix things for him. Make them right. He deserved that.

FORTY
THE VERDICT

The next morning, both sides gave their closing arguments, and the jury was excused to decide the verdict.

I texted Priya an update.

Gray put us in a small conference room adjacent the courtroom to wait. I wasn't sure how many times Dad stood up from the table, paced to the window, wrung his hands, and then came back again to sit with Mom, Eric, and me. A dozen at least.

Waiting was horrible. Especially when it was to find out whether he'd face jail time or not.

An hour went by. Then another.

I pulled Eric aside. "I've been thinking, and I have an idea."

"About what?"

"I was doing some research, and it's the university who has to request that an athlete's NCAA eligibility be reinstated. Then the NCAA reviews the case on its merits and makes a decision. So you're right about Plunkett. About things having a way of coming full circle. He's the one who would have to submit for Dallas's reinstatement. Do you think we could convince him to do it?"

Eric paused, stared, and blinked a couple times. "That is a good idea. He did tell us to come to him if we needed anything."

After one of his laps, Dad sat and stared at his hands, clasped together on the table. "I want to thank you all for being here with me through all of this. It's been rough and nerve-racking, but you've stood by my side, and I'll be forever appreciative."

Mom moved behind him and put her arms around him.

Dad moved his hands to her arms. "I'm sorry. Really sorry. For the mistakes I made. How what happened and what I did affected more than just myself." He looked at Eric and me, his eyes red and watery. "I love you all so much."

Eric reached out and put his arms around Mom and Dad. I got up and did the same thing.

My family and I were all wrapped in this gigantic family pretzel when Gray entered the room.

"Well, this picture warms my heart," he said.

We pulled apart, laughed, and dried our eyes.

"Especially since I'm here to tell you that it's done." Gray put his hands on the table and leaned against it. "Court is to resume in fifteen minutes. The jury has reached a decision."

We all inhaled.

Finally, it would be over. Almost a whole year of trauma, almost a whole year of heartache, so many sleepless nights I couldn't begin to count them, and it came down to this. Twelve people were about to speak my father's fate.

"Oh, Ade," Gray said. "There's someone asking for you in the hallway."

Every raw emotion hit me at the same time. Dallas. It had to be Dallas. On Valentine's Day.

Eric opened the conference room doors, and I rushed out.

Standing there was Priya in her puffy winter jacket.

I didn't know what I was thinking when I thought it was Dallas. He never once tried to declare his undying love for me.

"Priya!" I hugged her. "I had no idea you were thinking of coming. How'd you get here?"

"The train."

Then Emma walked out of the bathroom.

Tears clogged my throat, and my mouth tipped into a smile. I hugged both of them at the same time. "I can't believe you two are here."

"We can't let our bestie spend Galentine's Day without us." Priya beamed.

"Especially when she needs us for moral support," Emma said.

Unlike the rest of my body, my voice came out steady and strong. "You two are the best friends a girl could have."

Emma's gaze flickered to the right.

Probably to check out Eric. I sighed. Poor thing was going to have her hopes about my brother crushed. He was secretive about the girls he dated, and it wouldn't surprise me if he had a girlfriend that none of us knew anything about.

"You've met my mom before, but let me introduce you to my dad and brother." I gestured to them. "Dad, Eric, I'd like you to meet my roommate, Priya, and my friend Emma."

Dad scanned the group of us and grinned. He knew that this was a big deal. I was letting him into my new life. Letting him meet my new friends.

He shook both Priya's and Emma's hands. "So nice to meet you ladies. Not, of course, on the greatest of occasions, but no matter. This is long overdue."

Eric punched my arm. "Thanks for befriending Ade here. We know how difficult she can be—"

I shoved Eric back.

Gray clapped his hands. "Come on, gang. We need to be in our seats before the judge appears."

I bit down hard on my lip before we all shuffled into the courtroom.

Gray touched my arm and whispered, "By the way, your dad agreed to the media interview. Hoping for a not-guilty verdict, and we can do it right after."

"Great." I pasted a smile on my face. "Thanks."

Before we got down to the atrium, I needed to give my friends a heads-up because after the big TV reveal, I *was* going to need their support. Especially at the dorm. I had no idea what people's reactions were going to be like.

The room was packed, hardly a seat to be had. Many of the people were journalists with their notepads and pens.

Eric, Mom, and I sat in the first row, like usual. Priya and Emma filed in a couple rows behind us.

The procedure to read the verdict started first with the foreman giving a piece of paper with the decision to the bailiff, who handed it to the judge for review. Next, the judge gave it back and said, "Mr. Bianchini, please stand."

The foreman cleared his throat. "In the matter of the United States versus David Joseph Bianchini, we the jury find the defendant, David Joseph Bianchini, not guilty—"

My heart threatened to jump right out of my chest.

"Of the crimes of solicitation of bribes, honest services fraud conspiracy, honest services fraud, and conspiracy to commit wire fraud…"

Mom grabbed on to the guardrail and whimpered like she'd been holding her breath for the entire week.

Dad looked back at us, his mouth open, smiling, while Gray patted him on the shoulder.

My gaze was locked on Dad, my wet eyes making him appear blurry. *Thank God. Thank God.* I'd been hopeful but not confident.

"Of the crime of bribery conspiracy, we have found the defendant, David Joseph Bianchini, guilty."

My heart dropped, crashing straight to the ground. Guilty? Was that what the man just said?

"Ladies and gentlemen of the jury, is this your verdict, so say you one, so say you all?"

In unison they stared at us with blank expressions and said, "It is."

The jury filed out, and Gray and my dad started hugging everyone. Being found guilty of only one of the crimes must not be that bad if we were celebrating, right?

When Dad finally got to me, I hugged him tight.

I glanced behind me at Priya and Emma. They waved and gave me thumbs-ups.

But then the judge started tapping her gavel on the wood block. "Please be seated."

Everyone returned to their seats, and the noises quieted.

"With one guilty verdict returned, written arguments of the Blakely factors and factual findings need to be completed in one week," said Judge Thomas. "An order for presentencing investigation will be returned immediately and sentencing scheduled for two weeks from now. Is there a motion on behalf of the United States?"

"Prosecution moves to have the court revoke the defendant's bail and remand him into custody pending sentencing."

"Bail is revoked, bond is discharged, and the defendant is remanded into custody. Court is adjourned." The judge stood and walked out.

What?

Gray got up and started conversing with the court administrator, but I needed to talk to him. I needed to make sense of the verdict. Of what the judge meant by Dad being remanded into custody.

Then suddenly, I saw a flash of metal.

The bailiff told my dad to stand up and put his hands behind his back so that he could handcuff them.

My mom grabbed my thigh and squeezed hard. "What's happening?" she whispered.

"I don't know," I said.

"It looks like they're taking him to jail," Eric said.

The bailiff started leading my dad away, and Gray held out his hand to speak with him, but I couldn't hear a word. Then in seconds, my dad disappeared.

Even though I was shaking, I could feel Mom trembling next to me.

Gray approached us.

"What's going on?" I asked.

"I need to work on a new bail and bond for your dad for between now and the sentencing."

"Why?" Eric asked.

"Pretrial bail is supported by a constitutional right to a presumption of innocence, but post-conviction is not."

"But they said he's guilty on just one count—there are also a bunch of not-guilty verdicts," Eric said.

Gray tilted his head. "The judge can sentence your dad for up to ten years for the count he was found guilty of. Don't worry, I'll work hard to make it less than a year. Even harder to get him probation with no jail time, but that also means we need to ask for bail again."

I swallowed. My dry, scratchy throat wouldn't clear. "When can you get him out?"

"Maybe today. More likely tomorrow. And, Ade, I'm sorry. I'm not going to have the time to do a media interview at this point."

I nodded and kept trying to swallow. With my dad stuck in jail, me whining about my insomnia problem was completely inappropriate.

As I walked to the back of the courtroom where Priya and Emma sat with confused looks on their faces, I numbed. Like when I'd jumped into frozen Lake Nokomis a few weeks ago. But this time, it wasn't only my arms and legs that I couldn't feel. It was my whole body.

I thought after today everything would be resolved—well, everything except for getting Dallas's eligibility reinstated—but things weren't even close. After Gray figured out how to get Dad back home with Mom, then we all had to get through two more weeks until the sentencing.

FORTY-ONE

THE EVIDENCE

paced back and forth in my dorm room, my wireless earbuds in my ears. I could cover the entire space in five steps. *Only five steps.* No wonder I felt like a lioness in a cage.

My phone rang, and I quickly turned it over.

Finally. Eric.

I pressed answer. "What did he say?"

"Whoa, Ade." Eric chuckled. "I literally just got off the phone with him. Give me a second to process."

I sighed. It was already Wednesday, and I'd been patient now for five days. It had taken that long for a telephone meeting between Plunkett and my brother to come together. But now I couldn't wait any longer. I needed to know if the guy would do it. Would he reinstate Dallas's eligibility?

"Okay. So, he said some interesting stuff."

"Like?"

"Apparently, when an athlete is involved in an NCAA rule violation, the school must declare the athlete ineligible. After that, the school usually investigates, gathers facts, and submits a reinstatement request to the NCAA if deemed appropriate. In Dallas's case, however, no one has instituted an investigation because there has not been any pressure to do so. If Dad had not been terminated, it would have been him putting the pressure on. The new coach hasn't done a thing."

"That's absurd."

"I know."

"Anyway, Plunkett says if evidence can be gathered that shows that Dallas is no longer in violation of the rules, then he'd consider requesting the reinstatement."

"What does that mean?"

"Well, if Dallas gave the money back, I suppose he wouldn't be in violation anymore for having taken money."

"During Dallas's testimony, he said that his dad had."

"Well, then I guess Plunkett would need documents to prove that."

"Got it."

"You want me to call Dallas and ask him about it?"

"No. I'll do it. I'll go talk to his dad and get what we need."

"You know his dad?"

"Sort of."

I ended the call and went to dig through the pocket of the coat I wore the night of the ice cross competition. I pulled out Dallas's dad's business card just as Priya came walking in our door. His name, Michael Reynolds. His title, car sales consultant. Below, the dealership's name, address, and phone number.

"Hey," she said, going straight to her desk to dump her coat and backpack. "What's up?"

"Eric talked to Plunkett." I put the card in my back pocket.

"And…"

"I need to get a bank statement, and to do that, I need to borrow a car. Do you know anyone who has one parked on campus?"

"I do."

"Great." I grinned. "Who?"

She opened her eyes wide and raised her eyebrows. "Dallas."

The smile on my face slipped away. "You know I can't ask him."

"Why not?"

"I …I need to fix this whole NCAA ineligibility thing. That's all. As soon as I can do that, then maybe I'll feel better about talking to him again."

She shrugged. "So you're avoiding him?"

"Sort of. But he hasn't texted me or come knocking on my door either. The avoidance is mutual."

"As a reminder"—she narrowed her gaze on me—"you're the one who told him that things were over, and then when he tried to talk to you after that test, you gave him the silent treatment. He's giving you space because that's exactly what you wanted him to do."

I flinched. She was right.

"And the longer it goes on, the harder it will be to ever not avoid him," she added.

I cringed some more. The truth did hurt. "Okay, okay. Just a few more days. That's all I need."

I took out my phone to text my mom.

Mom, I have a favor to ask.

———

The next day, I pulled into the parking lot of the car dealership in my mom's car and let out a deep breath. My stomach was in knots.

I walked through the glass doors. The showroom was large and airy. The interior smelled of rubber and new cars.

"Can I help you?" A lady at the main reception desk with long manicured nails asked me.

I knew that Dallas's dad was working. I'd called beforehand to make sure. "I'd like to meet with Michael Reynolds."

"Do you have an appointment?"

"No."

She typed something into her computer. "He's with someone

right now, so you can sit and wait for him, or I could pair you up with another of our sales consultants."

"That's okay. I'll wait." I sat on a chair against the outer glass wall. Next to me was a brochure. I started to page through it.

Fifteen minutes went by. I kept squirming in the chair to get comfortable.

"Are you sure you don't want me to find another salesperson for you?" the lady asked again.

"No, I'm fine," I said. "I'll wait."

After another fifteen minutes, Dallas's dad approached me.

I took a deep breath and stood up.

He stuck out his hand. "Hi, my name's Mike. Sorry to keep you waiting."

I shook his hand. "No problem. My name is Adriana. Ade for short."

He squinted. "Do I know you?"

"Yes...well...kind of." I glanced away. His gaze had become intense. "We met the night of the ice cross race, in the tent. I live in Dallas's dorm."

"Oh, right. I thought you looked familiar." He nodded, his shoulders relaxing. "Are you interested in buying a car?"

"No, actually...I came about something else. Could we talk in private?"

He hesitated, cocking his head, his eyebrows furrowing. "Sure. We can use my office. Follow me."

In his office, he shut the door and went behind his desk. I sat in the chair across from him. On his desk was a picture of a woman laughing. Dallas's mom.

My heart squeezed. Poor Dallas's dad. Poor Dallas.

"I assume that this is about my son. Is he okay?"

"Yes, he's fine. I mean...I think he's fine. I haven't talked to him lately, but I...well...Did Dallas ever mention anything more about me to you?"

He shook his head, leaning back in his chair and rocking. "Not that I remember."

"I'm David Bianchini's daughter."

He froze. Solid.

Several seconds of silence went by.

He rolled himself up to the desk and laid his elbows on it. "I know Bianchini has a son. I didn't realize he also had a daughter."

"Well, he does, and it's me."

"They never subpoenaed me to testify, only Dallas. Which was probably for the best. I couldn't even get myself to go the day he was called to the stand."

"I don't blame you, and I'm sorry. Sorry about the whole thing."

"You're sorry?" He shook his head. "You had nothing to do with it. I'm the one who is sorry."

"But it's not your fault either."

He slouched. "Sometimes it feels like it was. I definitely wish I could go back in time and do things different."

"Mr. Reynolds…"

"Call me Mike."

"Mike, I'm here because I want to make things right. I want to help get Dallas's NCAA eligibility back."

"You do?" Mike sat straighter.

"My brother, Eric, spoke with the Minnesota University athletic director, and according to him, if we can give him proof that Dallas is no longer in violation of any NCAA rules, then he could make a request for reinstatement."

"Dallas had said that the lawyers were going to help him with that."

"They haven't, and it is unclear if they will. We want to get the reinstatement process rolling before too much time goes by."

"That makes sense." He pushed himself away from the desk. "So what do you need from me? What kind of proof?"

"During his testimony, Dallas said that you gave the money back that you'd received when Dallas signed his letter of intent. I'm thinking if you could log into your bank account and print a copy of the transaction, or if you wrote a check, a copy of the check that cleared, I think that would suffice."

Dallas's dad spun his chair around and rolled up to his computer at the credenza. "Yeah. I think I'd have all of that. I had a casher's check made out to the booster club."

I sat quietly as he used his mouse and his keyboard to get into his bank account.

"Okay, I need to go back in time here. I went to the bank in early summer last year." He kept scrolling. "Here it is. And look at that. I can print the cleared check and the transaction."

"Perfect." My chest was feeling lighter. This was happening. Things were coming together.

The printer on the other side of the office hummed and then printed.

We both stood, and Dallas's dad fetched the pages.

He looked at them and then handed them over to me. "I think this will do it."

"Thanks so much, Mr. Reynolds—I mean, Mike. I have a good feeling about this."

"Me too." We shook hands. "Thank you for doing this for my son. I'm not sure how the two of you met, but I'm sure he's going to appreciate what you're doing."

"It's a story, Mr. Reynolds. A long one."

"I see."

I put the printout in my bag. "Also, if you wouldn't mind, could you keep our meeting to yourself for a little while? Maybe a week or so?"

"You mean not tell Dallas?"

"Right." I fiddled with the strap on my bag. "I just don't want him to get his hopes up, not until the director actually does the work."

"Sure. I can do that."

I left the dealership and checked my phone. Next stop, the university's athletic complex to hand over the documents.

FORTY-TWO
THE TRUTH

t was Thursday. One week since I'd dropped Dallas's dad's bank statements off at Plunkett's office, and one day until the sentencing. My friends had convinced me to take a break from the cave I'd been living in and go out.

They thought I had good reason to celebrate. I'd received my grade on the chemistry test. I'd gotten a B-plus. A freaking *B-plus*.

Jay had given me a high five so hard it had hurt. I was back in the game. Ready to prove that I could do this. By the end of this year, I might have the grades I needed.

But that didn't mean that everything was falling into place. Not even close.

Thirty minutes ago, I had to down an energy drink because, well, I still hadn't shaken my insomnia. Then I'd changed four times. I just couldn't find the right clothes. The Station was an over-eighteen club and near campus, so not quite like other clubs. I settled on jeans and a three-quarter-sleeve shirt.

Priya came back from the bathroom and paused. "I've never seen you try on so many different outfits. What's with you?"

I shrugged. "Nothing."

"It's Plunkett, isn't it?"

No. Yes. Ugh. The energy drink was giving me the jitters, and truth be told, I was worried about the athletic director. Plunkett hadn't been in his office when I dropped off the printout of the bank transaction, and even though his assistant had told me she'd have him contact me straightaway, he hadn't. Eric hadn't heard anything either.

"I'm fine," I said. "Everything's fine."

Priya, Emma, Jay, and I headed out. We didn't bring jackets. Even in the dead of winter, that wasn't the way one went out at night. How would we lug around oversize coats from place to place, and where would we put them while dancing?

We exited the front doors of the dorm to walk to the club, but Jay turned right around. "Sorry, guys, it's way too cold. I'm calling an Uber."

We followed him back inside, dodging the other residents leaving without jackets.

"They're brave." I watched through the window as they disappeared. "Braver than me."

"They might be, but we're smarter." Jay grinned at his cell. "Uber will be here in four minutes."

"Awesome." But I didn't feel awesome. Probably from the overload of caffeine.

Emma leveled her gaze on me. "You okay?"

"I'm fine. Why does everyone keep asking me that?"

Jay looked over his phone at me. "Because you don't seem nearly as excited as you were when you got the results of your test back."

"Of course I am." I stuck my hip out and plastered on a smile.

He shrugged.

Damn it. I needed to do a better job of looking like I was having fun.

I chewed on my bottom lip until a piece of skin came loose. *Stop it, Ade. You're going to have fun. You will.* But it was hard when I wasn't feeling it. The inside of my body was like a cold gothic castle. Creaking and shuddering.

"Have any of you ever been in love?" I asked, but then flicked my gaze to Priya. "I mean, I know that you have, Priya, but what about you, Emma, and you, Jay?"

Jay unburied himself from his phone once again and lifted an eyebrow. "If we're playing Truth, Dare, Double Dare, Promise or Repeat, I'd never have picked truth."

I smiled. "What would you have picked?"

"Dare," Jay said.

"Interesting," I said slowly, and squinted at him. "Very interesting."

Emma grimaced. "I hate that game."

"Not me," Priya said.

"Okay, Jay." I had an idea. "When we get to the Station, I dare you to ask someone to dance."

His forehead creased. "That's the best you can do?"

"Fine, scratch that." I squared my shoulders. "Jay, when we get to the Station, I double dare you to ask someone out on a date."

"Humph."

"Good. Now Priya, your turn. Truth, Dare, Double Dare, Promise or Repeat?"

"I pick truth, and you don't have to ask me a question. I have a confession to make." Priya tapped the toe of her shoe on the floor. "Umm…okay…my truth is…Luke and I broke up."

Emma's jaw fell open.

I coughed, but then covered my mouth to stifle the noise.

Jay didn't move, just stared at Priya. "What did you say?"

"I broke up with Luke."

Emma shut her mouth and took a deep breath. "As in he's no longer your boyfriend?"

"Correct."

Priya's announcement wasn't a surprise to me compared to how Jay and Emma were reacting, but the fact that she'd gone through with the breakup was…well…unexpected.

"When?" Emma asked.

"Yesterday."

"But you and Luke are the real deal," Emma said. "I'm so confused."

"If you three weren't my close friends, I'd probably tell you that it's a trial breakup. That we just need some time apart. But that would be a complete lie. The truth is I don't want to be with him anymore."

"Whoa," Jay said.

"I know. I'm a horrible, cruel person, aren't I?"

"No." I stood straight. "Good for you. If that's the way you feel, then it's best not to drag things out." But I couldn't relate to her situation at all. I'd never had a supportive boyfriend like Luke in my life. I mean, I'd had Dallas for a brief moment, but that had turned into a disaster.

"What about you, Ade?" Priya asked me. "Truth, Dare, Double Dare, Promise or Repeat?"

My body stilled. I supposed I should take the dare, but I didn't want to. I didn't have the spirit for it.

"Truth," I said.

"Why are you acting so weird?" Priya asked. "Like asking whether or not any of us have been in love before?"

I sighed. I was hoping for something more like *Would you rather share a fantasy suite with Justin Bieber or Tom Hiddleston?* That would be easy. Tom Hiddleston as Loki, hands down.

I took a deep breath. "Last week, you two came to the verdict, which was lovely and thoughtful, and I greatly appreciated your presence, but deep down inside, I was hoping Dallas would come."

All three of them paused and stared at me.

"Are you in love with him?" Emma asked.

I shrugged. "I don't know. That's why I was asking if any of you had ever been in love before and what that felt like, so I can figure it out."

There was a long pause.

Priya put an arm around me. "It sounds to me like you're not over him, and that's okay."

"Right, Ade," Emma said. "Look, it took me months to get over Thad from last fall, and in the end, I'm not even sure I really liked him to begin with."

"And as soon as you hear from Plunkett, I'd meet up with Dallas," Priya said. "Then you can see where you two stand."

Jay glanced at his phone. "Uber's here."

He held the front door open for us, and we raced to the car. The interior was just the right temperature. The driver confirmed our destination, we buckled ourselves in, and the car sped away.

Next to me, Jay said, "If you want my opinion, it doesn't matter if you love him, like him, or hate him. Something else happened these past few weeks. You developed courage. I'm proud of you."

"Wow, thanks." My voice softened, and my heart blossomed. "That's really nice of you to say, but can you remind me what exactly I have done to earn your high esteem?"

"You made peace with your dad, you accepted what happened to you and your family, you don't care what people think about who you are, and your grades are improving." He shifted in the seat. "That's a lot."

"Maybe, but then why am I still not sleeping?"

"You will. It's just going to take time for your body to adjust to this new you."

I smiled back at him. He was right. I'd come a long way, and I was ready. Ready to believe in myself.

FORTY-THREE
THE REVEAL

The next morning, I collected my lightweight jacket, left my dorm room, and headed to the lobby. It was sentencing day.

I watched for my family by the front entrance. Snow was still piled up, but now icy puddles dotted the sidewalks. February was over, and we were starting to get some springlike days. Let the March melt begin.

My family met me inside, including Eric, who had flown in last night. His team had given him family emergency leave. I hugged all three of them and then stepped back. They were picking me up to go to the sentencing, but first we had something to take care of.

"Okay," I said. "Let's do this."

At eight o'clock in the morning, the four of us entered Buford Hall's dining service together. It was packed. Dad, Mom, Eric, and I grabbed trays and selected breakfast items. Goodbye, Adriana Blankin because Adriana Bianchini was back.

At first, no one seemed to recognize my dad. Everyone filling their trays appeared to be half asleep. I sucked in a sequence of breaths. I hadn't considered that this coming-out-as-myself plan might not work.

Dad went to check out. "Good morning," he said to the student working the register. I didn't know the guy personally, only recognized him from here and around the dorm.

He glanced up, probably because it was strange to see a man in his mid-fifties in line.

He did a double take. "Are you…are you…?"

Dad stuck out his hand. "Yes, hello. I'm David Bianchini." Then he stepped aside. "This is my wife, my daughter, Ade, who lives and goes to school here, and my son, Eric."

The cashier stared at us as if in a trance. Eventually, he rang us up, and we proceeded to find a table.

Well, if that didn't start tongues wagging, I didn't know what would. I had to hand it to my dad for getting things rolling.

The four of us sat down together.

Within minutes, a buzz grew in the large room. People stared at us. Pointed. I couldn't help but smile. There. Now everyone would know. The constant fear of being found out was over.

Ten minutes later, Emma and Priya sat down with us, Emma conveniently next to Eric, of course.

"Everyone is talking about you and your dad," Priya said. "It's even reached our floor."

"That was fast," I said. "But I'm glad. Things are working out perfectly."

Jay came and sat with us too. I introduced him to my parents and Eric, telling them everything about him—that we'd gone to high school together, had classes together, that he was on the Minnesota University's cross-country team.

Next, we headed up to my room so my dad and Eric could see it for the first time.

The girls on my floor came to me in droves. "Why didn't you say you were Coach Bianchini's daughter? Or Eric Bianchini's sister?"

I shrugged. In hindsight, it seemed foolish, keeping my identity secret, especially around the people I lived with. But at the time, the reasons had felt valid to me.

Sometimes you had to cope with the circumstances you were dealt.

FORTY-FOUR
THE SENTENCE

I f the judge decided to give my dad jail time, the worst part
would be the bailiffs taking him away again. Through the
door and straight down to the jail, but this time permanently.
The thought of it made it hard for me to breathe.

Court was filling up. I sat next to my mom and Eric, behind
Dad and Gray at the defense table. It was strange to see the jury's
chairs empty.

Eric turned and peered behind us. "I was wondering if he
would come."

I glanced back. "Who?"

"Dallas."

There he was, sitting with a court employee, holding a piece of
paper, his arms fidgety. I turned right back around.

"What is he doing here?" I whispered to Eric.

"Didn't he tell you?"

"Tell me what?"

"That he's making a victim-impact statement."

"A what?" I asked.

"Since he was a victim of the conspiracy, he gets to make a
statement to the judge expressing the impact of the crime on him
and how severe he thinks the punishment should be."

I took in a small breath, turned back around, and shielded my eyes with my hand. "And he told you this when?"

"He called me yesterday. And guess what? He's in talks with the NCAA."

My eyebrows squeezed together. "But Plunkett never said anything about having submitted the reinstatement."

"Apparently, he did. Early this week."

"Did you know?"

"No. He must have taken us out of the equation."

I ground my teeth. Did he ever.

The judge entered. We all stood and sat back down again. There was talking, but I didn't pay attention. I was trying to organize the thoughts in my brain.

"Mr. Reynolds." The judge spoke loudly. "You may approach now."

Dallas walked up the aisle to the podium facing the bench and rested his piece of paper on it. I clenched my jaw, wanting to hear what he had to say, but at the same time wishing I couldn't.

When he started to speak, his voice was cool, calm, confident. "Your Honor, when Coach Bianchini first spoke with me about playing hockey for him, I could never have imagined that I would be in front of you like this today."

He stopped and took a gulp of air.

"When I found out about the windfall that would come my way if I signed with Coach Bianchini, it seemed like a miracle, an answer to my family's financial prayers. Without a second thought, I took it. Deep down, I knew that it was wrong, but I did it anyway. It's unfortunate that I lost my NCAA eligibility because of one poor, reckless decision. I believe we must all accept responsibility for our actions, so I accepted my punishment. And it was a big one. Hockey is the thing I know how to do best. So I am happy to say that after almost a year of not playing and because I am no longer in violation, I've been given a second chance, and a request for my reinstatement has been made with the NCAA and is pending acceptance."

Eric nudged me, and I shifted away from him.

"My point is that Coach Bianchini needs to accept responsibility for his actions and serve out his punishment too. But that punishment need not be so severe as to be unreasonably harmful. We are human. We all make mistakes."

The tightness in my chest released, and I exhaled the air I'd been holding in my lungs. I should have known that Dallas would be reasonable and thoughtful.

I paused.

Because he was, wasn't he? Thoughtful. Rational. Logical.

"Through all of this, there is one regret I do have," he continued.

He turned his head and looked at me.

My stomach tightened.

"I wish I had been honest with the people I care about. For hurting them, I am truly sorry." Dallas looked back at his sheet of paper. It fluttered in his hands. "Going through this has shown me that if you're doing something you feel the need to keep secret, or that someone asks you to keep secret, you shouldn't be doing it. Keeping my secrets hurt not only myself, but also the people who are special to me. And while I wish my experience with Coach Bianchini hadn't turned out the way it did, I'm also thankful to have learned something important from it. That doing what you love and loving someone you're with includes being truthful about it. Rather than being locked away, I hope that Coach Bianchini will have the opportunity to atone for his actions in other ways and do better in the future. I know I will. Thank you. That's all I have."

He stepped away from the podium.

"Thank you, Mr. Reynolds, for your well-chosen words." The judge nodded.

Dallas turned, and his gaze sought mine. Connected. Fused. Like that day at the polar plunge, when our gazes had locked for the first time.

My heart throbbed.

Truthfulness. That was what this was about. For my dad. For me. For Dallas.

"Mr. Bianchini, please stand," the judge said.

Dad stood, buttoned up his jacket, and faced her.

Here it was. This was it.

"Mr. Bianchini, your case has been a long and arduous journey." The judge continued, looking at my dad with eagle eyes. "I have spent a great deal of time thinking about your sentencing, and I tend to agree with Mr. Reynolds. You made mistakes. Actions you took that I believe you regret. Mr. Bianchini, you are sentenced to two months in jail, to be served in a low-security federal corrections institution, one hundred thousand dollars in restitution, and one hundred hours of community service. You'll have a month to get your things in order, and then you can begin your sentence."

That was it. The judge was done. Finished. And they weren't going to escort my dad directly to jail. Thank God.

And…and I needed to talk to Dallas. Right now.

Dad bowed his head. "Thank you, Your Honor."

The gavel clacked, and just like that, none of us would ever have to step foot in this room again. I leaned over the guardrail and gave my dad a hug.

I looked for Dallas, but he was gone. I couldn't let him get away. I wouldn't. He needed to know what was in my heart.

So, I hustled to catch up to him. But just like in the movies, as I entered the hallway, the doors of the elevator closed.

I dashed to the stairs. Down and down I sped to the lobby. I burst through the door only to catch sight of Dallas walking out the front doors onto the plaza in front of the building. I chased after him.

Outside, his fleece beanie was pulled low, his hands stuffed in his jacket pockets.

"Dallas," I called as I dodged iced-over puddles to catch up to him.

In the very center of the plaza, he stopped and turned around.

Within seconds, we were face-to-face, the only thing between us the clouds of condensed air we exhaled.

"I need to tell you something."

He nodded.

"Back in January, I had this not-so-brilliant idea inspired by the internet where I believed having sex would cure the issues I was having with insomnia." I paused to swallow and take a breath.

He nodded again. "I know."

"Then on…on the day of the polar plunge, I heard about your reputation and…and…wait. What did you say?"

"I know, Ade. About the sex cures insomnia. About me being the one to cure it. About how it didn't work."

"You do?" I asked.

"Jay told me."

I narrowed my eyes. "When?"

"A couple weeks ago. After that test we took in chemistry. When you wouldn't talk to me."

I shook my head. "And you're not mad."

"No." He shrugged. "You picked me. It was a compliment."

"But I used you."

He cocked his head and looked to the sky. "Well, when you say it that way…"

"I'm so sorry." My chest tightened. "I should have told you."

He flashed a toothy grin at me. "Nope…nothing for you to feel sorry about. I like being used."

I laughed. He laughed, and I loved the way it sounded. He was everything, and I missed him.

I inhaled a deep breath. My voice came out weak, weaker than I wanted it to be. "I don't want us to end. I want us to start over."

"Me too." His eyes were wide, and at the same time, red with pure fatigue.

"Because you're right." I moistened my lips. "I wasn't being truthful about who I was either, and it was not only hurting myself but also hurting everyone around me. Including you."

He encircled my waist and pulled me toward him. Our lips hovered close to each other, the coldness inside me slowly thawing from the heat of his breath. Our lips touched and melted my entire core.

———

We took the train back to school. It was rush hour, so there was only enough room for us to be mashed up against each together tight. But that was okay. I didn't mind.

Elation, like a sun dog, refracted in my heart.

Dallas cupped the back of my head with his hand. "Thanks for getting that bank statement from my dad and giving it to Plunkett."

"You know about that too?"

"Yeah, when I called my dad to give him the good news, he told me about how you showed up at the car dealership."

I put my hand over his. "So when the NCAA reinstates your eligibility, does that mean you'll give up ice cross and I'll officially be dating a university hockey player?"

He smiled. "Hopefully."

"Emma's going to freak out about this for sure."

He laughed and then kissed my cheek.

I put my hands on his chest and felt the hammering of his heart. I laid my head against him. "I have a feeling I'm going to sleep really well tonight."

He whispered in my ear, "I do too."

ALSO BY LEANNE FARELLA

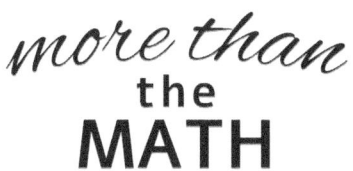

more than
the
MATH

Lacie Cunningham believes love is a problem best solved with logic. As a math PhD student who once had her heart spectacularly broken, she's certain the "optimal stopping theory" is the formula for finding The One. In a few years, when she hits exactly thirty-seven percent of her dating window, she'll pick the next guy who's statistically perfect. Simple. Predictable. Foolproof.

Until Justin Van Meer crashes into her equation.

Five years ago, Justin was her first love—the dreamy musician her parents warned her about. Now he's the lead singer of an up-and-coming band, and seeing him again at a music festival sends all of Lacie's carefully graphed plans straight off the chart.

As old sparks reignite and buried truths resurface, Lacie's perfect formula for love starts to look a lot like chaos. Maybe the heart doesn't need a theory. Maybe it just needs a second chance—and a really good soundtrack.

Smart, funny, and full of heart, *More Than The Math* is a dual-timeline novel about first loves, second chances, and learning that some variables can't—and shouldn't—be controlled.

Release date coming soon...

Subscribe to Leanne Farella's newsletter and receive the first three chapters of More Than The Math

https://leannefarella.com/newsletter

ACKNOWLEDGMENTS

My writing journey has been long and arduous. Roads have opened and closed so many times that finding my way has been like bushwhacking through a jungle with snakes, spiders, and booby traps. At least there were the gorgeous flowers, serene wildlife, and moments of wise reflection that came with it.

I am forever grateful for those who have cheered me on. Thank you to my mom Lavonne and my grandma Gladys (1927-2022) for their many years of encouraging me to keep going and loving my work even when there was little to love. Thank you to my incredible sisters Janele and Elaine for supporting my unlikely endeavors. Thank you to my husband Joe, my son Quentin and daughter Aurelia who are always checking in with me to find out if I'm writing or if I am published yet. They are the reason this story has hockey and figure skates in it. Thank you to the Selby Avenue Ladies for being sounding boards even if you didn't know it.

This book would not be possible without my dear critique group and critique partners. Neroli Lacey—a wordsmith who always listens and gives sound advice. Nan Dixon—the hardest working author there is and with spreadsheets to prove it. Ann Hinnenkamp—a true craftsperson who always knows what a scene needs or doesn't need. Cat Shield—who has a gut instinct for story like no other. Liz Selvig—a traveler at heart whose every exploration brings great insight. Kristina Bak—who brings calm to the storm of book marketing. Kathryn Kohorst—I miss you young lady.

Lastly, thank you to my Editor Natashya Wilson, Proofreader Tiffany Tyler, and Cover Designer Rachel Christley. They are the ones who made this story bloom.

ABOUT THE AUTHOR

Leanne lives in Saint Paul, Minnesota with her extreme do-it-yourselfer husband and two adventurous kids. Even with an engineering degree, she has always been a writer—from entering writing contests as a youth, keeping a diary, to becoming a persuasive writer as an intellectual property lawyer. But fiction writing is her true passion. It allows her to give the heroines in her head the love stories they deserve.

Subscribe to her newsletter and receive information on new releases, giveaways, and much more!

Leanne's Newsletter
https://leannefarella.com/newsletter

facebook.com/leannefarella

x.com/LeanneFarella

instagram.com/leannefarella

tiktok.com/@leannef123